UNBEARABLE
The Woodstone Falls Series
Book 1

ANNA JERR

For the girl who once thought the weight of the world was unbearable.

You are enough. You will not break.

And also to the girls who love a fictional cowboy with a filthy mouth.

This is for you, too.

Content Warnings

While this story is a work of fiction, it addresses some heavy subject matters that you should be aware of before diving in. Some material in this novel may not be suitable for all.

You can find a list of trigger warnings after the acknowledgements section. These are not meant to be spoilers, but rather a precaution in case you find certain content upsetting.

Please skip this page if you do not wish to see these warnings.

ONE

Dotty

MESS IT UP · GRACIE ABRAMS

My mother was the first to introduce me to the concept of death. I understood the idea, but her passing was the moment I truly grasped what it meant.

It had been nearly twenty years since the day my dad sat my brothers and me down to tell us our mom was gone and wasn't coming back. I still remember sitting in the family room of the ranch house, where framed photos lined the walls and the familiar scent of my mother's candles still lingered in the air as he delivered the news. That morning, she'd quizzed me on multiplication tables and teased me for putting syrup on my eggs. Her pancakes were still on the counter.

Then, she was gone.

I cried, while my brothers stayed composed, each of us taking in the harsh new reality in our own way. I don't remember what my dad said after that. I only remember the silence.

My mother was healthy, and I couldn't understand how she was suddenly *gone*. The finality of her death was incomprehensible, and it had continued to remain that way.

While some daughters had years with their mothers, I was one of the unlucky few who had a decade and only a few memories that still felt real.

A voice pulled me from my thoughts as I folded another shirt and tucked it into my suitcase.

"I'm sorry, Dotty." Noah stood in the doorway of my bedroom, sunlight catching the gold in her eyes. "I know this whole situation sucks, but I'm here. Whether you want to talk about it or just complain about your brothers." She smiled faintly, trying to ease the heaviness.

"I'm okay, really," I said, continuing to pack everything I might need for a short stay in Woodstone Falls—plus enough for an extra month, because, well, I'd never figured out how to pack for just one week.

Noah walked over and sat on the edge of my bed. Her brown skin caught the sunlight streaming through the window. "You're allowed to grieve and be sad, you know."

"I have. I did." I paused. "A while ago."

My grandpa's passing wasn't a shock. He hadn't been fully himself since my Gram passed back when I was in high school. The decline was slow and steady. I'd said goodbye to him in small ways for years.

But still, it did hurt.

He and my grandma had stepped up when my mom died. They helped raise us. The thought of both of them being gone left a hollow space I wasn't sure how to fill.

"You sure you're ready to go back?" Noah asked gently.

I didn't answer right away.

I hadn't been back to Woodstone Falls in over a decade. I always had an excuse. Work, deadlines, distance. But the truth was simpler—I didn't want to, and the longer I stayed away, the easier it became to just keep staying gone. At least, until now.

"I want to be there for this," I said finally. "I just didn't think through how hard it would be to go back for a funeral."

Noah nodded. "I know you don't talk about her much," she said. "But if this brings stuff up… I'm here. Always."

She didn't say my mother's name, but I knew who she meant. We'd talked about everything—books, movies, career stuff, periods, bad sex, great sex, but my mother was the one thing she never pushed me on.

"I know," I said. My voice was steady, but something tightened in my chest anyway. "It's just… hard."

"I know, I know, but if you ever want to, you can. You know I'm always here for you."

The truth was, losing my mom hadn't just shattered me —it had a domino effect on my life. Before, I was able to make friends, even if it took effort. After? People didn't know what to say. Some tiptoed. Others stayed silent. The worst ones made jokes. And my friends—who should've stood by me—just faded out.

My brothers tried to step in, but their protectiveness only isolated me even more.

Until Noah.

"Did I lose you?" she asked, pulling me back.

"Sorry, lost in my head," I admitted.

She chuckled. "I'm going to miss you, you know." Her lip pushed out in a half-pout that made me smile. "I'll try to keep your plants alive while you're gone, but no promises."

"If you pull it off, dinner's on me."

"How are you feeling about the trip?" she asked, leaning back and stretching out on the bed.

"I think I'm more nervous about going back for the first time than I am sad about the funeral," I admitted.

"Even if that means I'm just putting off dealing with the emotions."

I tossed a few black outfits into my bag, unsure what to expect. September in southern Oregon was unpredictable. One day could bring clear skies and seventy degrees; the next, freezing rain that'd have me replacing my windshield.

"I'm just a call away if you need to talk," she said.

"Thanks. I left the takeout menus on the fridge."

She scrunched her nose, the way she did when she was worried. "What would I do without you? I don't even know the names of the places we go to. There's *that taco place*, or *the Italian place with the really good cheesecake*. How long are you staying?"

"Taking a month off, but probably just a week there. I don't think I can handle much more than that."

She smirked. "Yeah, can't risk running into a certain hot, grumpy cowboy, huh?"

I shrugged. "I might not even run into him at all."

I was full of shit, and she knew it. Woodstone Falls was a small town with a population barely larger than the number of books I owned. There was no hiding from anyone, especially not the one person I was trying to avoid. The universe liked to make sure of it.

"Keep telling yourself that," she said with a laugh.

My palms itched as I sat on the hard wooden pews, listening to my father deliver the eulogy. Sunlight filtered through the stained glass, painting colorful patterns on the wooden floorboards. And I couldn't sit still for another damn minute.

Quietly, I excused myself and stood, and walked out of the church. The doors creaked as I pushed them open.

Stepping outside felt like a release. I breathed in the fresh mountain air, trying to steady my racing heart and gain some sort of regulation in my body. My tailbone ached from sitting too long, but my breath slowed as my eyes adjusted to the blue sky with a few wispy clouds drifting lazily by.

I'd tried to focus on the eulogy, but running on little sleep, emotions running rampant, and returning to Woodstone Falls after ten years was all just too much. I wanted to be here for my family and loved my grandpa, but I'd be lying if I said I wasn't counting down until I could get back to Seattle and my routine. Stability was what I craved most.

The fall breeze hit against my skin, and I took another breath. Nostalgia crept in as I remembered this small town where I grew up. The mountains were already dusted with snow, and the trees were lit up in reds, oranges, and yellows. Woodstone Falls in autumn looked like something off a postcard.

The church doors creaked open behind me. I turned to see my twin brother, Dorian, approaching with his usual quiet grace. Sunlight filtered through the trees, catching on his dark hair as he stepped closer. When he reached me, he opened his arms. I leaned in without hesitation, and he pulled me close.

"It'll be over soon," he murmured into my hair.

His dark eyes, usually so serious, softened as he looked at me. Despite his reservations with others, he understood me in ways no one else did. He probably knew I was already done with this day, even before the thought of slipping out mid-service crossed my mind.

Growing up as the only girl in the James household,

there was never a dull moment. Our ranch house was large but warm, always filled with laughter and bickering. Amid the chaos, there was a deep, unspoken love that held us together.

Of all my brothers, Dorian and I were the closest. He was protective but never smothering. He always checked in without asking. As kids, we'd spend hours exploring the woods behind our house, building forts, and pretending we were adventurers. It was a stark contrast to the reality we now faced.

I could always count on him. No matter the miles or time between us, he was my rock. He read me without words, understanding when I needed quiet comfort.

"I'm okay," I said, pulling back slightly but keeping his arm around me. "Just needed a minute."

His brown eyes, so much like our father's, held steady. He nodded and squeezed my shoulder.

The doors opened again. My older brothers, Colt and Sawyer, stepped out, their faces solemn.

"It's about over now," Colt said. He was always terse, the stoic one among us. That really wasn't a surprise, considering he'd been forced to grow up overnight when our mother passed, just as he was on the brink of adulthood.

Sawyer gave a small smile. "We'll get through this together."

The ache of loss hadn't gone anywhere, but the weight of it felt easier to carry with my family by my side.

"Just a heads-up—Trent's here," Dorian said.

Of fucking course he is.

Grandpa used to call us the *trouble trio*—Dorian, Trent, and me. Trent had been part of our lives since we were toddlers, when his dad started working on the ranch. His father was a single dad looking for a job and someone to watch Trent while he worked. With my mom already home caring for me and my siblings, adding another kid was a natural fit—especially since it meant added help on the ranch. Trent quickly became an integral part of our family.

My mom used to joke all the time that Trent and I would grow up and get married. She'd laugh, eyes twinkling with mischief, saying it with such certainty it was like she was spinning some damn fairy tale where we were always meant to end up together.

What a joke.

Even as kids, we'd groan and gag at the idea. It was absurd then and even more absurd now.

I'd rather die alone than marry that arrogant man.

Now, standing on the steps of the church in the town I grew up in, it was all pressing in at once. The weight of this place. The memories I'd shoved into corners and tried not to look at. Some of them were still sharp, and some dulled with time, but all of them were proof of why I stayed away for so long.

I hadn't set foot in Woodstone since I left as a heartbroken nineteen-year-old, desperately searching for anything to make me whole. Returning now, years later, was incredibly surreal. There was an overwhelming sense of familiarity, yet at the same time, everything had changed. Or maybe *I* had.

The ranch house was still nestled among sprawling acres dedicated to cattle farming, land that had been in our family for generations. Situated on the outskirts of town, the nearest neighbors were the Reynolds brothers, with no one else living nearby for miles.

The ranch was more than a business. It was a legacy. My father was the engine behind it all, the one who poured everything into making it run—cattle, staff, land, community. The lines between it all blurred out here. I loved it, even if it never quite fit me.

Designing always pulled at me. Creating something from nothing. That itch led me to architecture school and to Seattle, where I'd built a life of my own. Small apartment, steady job, a quiet rhythm that made sense. No big emotions. No surprises. While the city had its downfalls, it offered a sense of anonymity and freedom that the ranch could never provide.

And now here I was, back in the middle of it.

As the funeral concluded, people started ushering out of the church. I sighed and mentally prepared for the socialization that was to come.

Dorian leaned in and smirked. "Talk to a few people, make appearances, and then go hide in my car."

"It's like you know me or something," I replied.

And so, I did as he asked—accepted condolences, listened to people share their stories about Grandpa, how it was a blessing he was with Gram again.

I was scanning for a way to slip away to Dorian's car, hoping to dodge any more conversations, when the church pastor appeared a few feet away.

I swallowed a groan. He was a few years older than me, with some gray starting to show, and a kind face that made it hard to be annoyed. His dad had been the pastor for as long as I could remember, and Jeremy had taken over after he passed. We were never close, but we'd always been friendly.

"Hi, Dotty. I wanted to offer my condolences. Your grandfather was a great man. Please let me know if there is anything we can do to support you." He extended his hand.

"Thanks, Jeremy," I said, shaking it.

He got pulled away a few minutes later, and more people came up to me. Their voices started to blend together, their condolences piling on until everything felt too loud, too close. I continued socializing, giving short answers before deciding I definitely fulfilled my quota. My skin itched. My heart kicked harder in my chest. So, I slipped out and headed straight for Dorian's car.

When I turned the corner to head to the parking lot, I smacked directly into what felt like a brick wall, except it was not brick, nor a wall.

My head hit a chest that I knew immediately. The scent gave him away before my brain could catch up—cedar and spice, unchanged after all these years.

"Dotty James. Looks like you finally made it back to Woodstone," Trent chuckled. He grabbed my arm to steady me so I didn't fall from the sheer force of running into him.

He looked older—different in a thousand ways, and still exactly the same. All broad shoulders and those same piercing green eyes that could see right through me. His presence was a reminder of the past, of all the unresolved emotions that had been left to simmer over the years.

"I really don't have the energy for you right now," I scoffed, pulling away from him.

Once upon a time, we'd been inseparable. Even after Dorian left for college, Trent and I stayed stuck together like always. After high school, Dorian went straight into vet school—he'd had his life mapped out since we were kids. Trent and I took a year off, pretending we were just figuring things out, when really we just didn't want to let go of this town. Or each other.

We spent that whole year together, like we were the last

two people in the world. Then time ran out, and we both left Woodstone.

And now here he was, standing in front of me, looking every bit like the version of him I didn't want to remember. His jaw was sharper. His shoulders, broader. That tousled dark hair that had always driven me crazy—and apparently still did. He exuded a maddening, unmistakably masculine charm that just pissed me off.

Despite the almost unrecognizable man who stood before me, I could still spot glimpses of the boy I once knew. The faint scar on his left eyebrow was from our reckless adventures running around the ranch. The slight crook in his smile he'd developed after being teased for his lopsided dimple. The way his fingers drummed against his thigh—a habit he'd picked up to disguise his impatience.

The intensity of his gaze, the way he carried himself with quiet confidence—it all came rushing back.

Part of me wanted the years to have been harder on him. I wanted something—anything—to take the edge off how easily he still got under my skin. But reality proved crueler than my wishes. If anything, he had only grown more charming with age.

Everything shifted that one day between us, creating a tidal wave of emotions neither of us had the maturity to navigate. So, we simply *didn't*. It was easier to walk away and pretend nothing had happened than to face the tumultuous feelings we'd harbored.

Trent ran a hand through his hair, letting out a slow breath. "I wasn't trying to be a dick, Dot. I'm just… surprised to see you." He rubbed a hand over his jaw, studying me like he didn't quite believe I was real. "You… you look great. It's been a long time." His voice was soft, a familiar melody, stirring memories that I had long since buried.

"Yes, it has," I said, not bothering to hide the bite in my tone. "I'd say we are good for another, what"—I checked my watch for dramatics—"ten years before we are due to talk again, don't you think?" I looked past him, scanning for Dorian's car. "I have to go. I don't have the emotional capacity for this today, *Trent*." The sound of his name leaving my mouth brought a rush of anger to the surface.

He nodded once. "I know it's probably been a hard day for you." His voice softened. "I'd like to see you while you're in town… If you're up for it."

I didn't respond. Neither of us moved.

"Yeah, I'll leave you to it," he said finally. "See you around, Dot."

I kept my expression flat, unwilling to give him anything else. He shoved his hands in his pockets, took a half step back, and gave me a look I couldn't quite read. Then he turned and headed back toward the church.

As I walked away, his voice called after me. "I'm sorry about your grandpa. He was a good man. I know we don't talk anymore, but… I'm still here, if you ever need me."

And just like that, he was gone again.

I made my way toward the car, but my mind stayed behind—caught in the maze of memories that were woven into this small town. Running through fields with Trent. Stealing rides on horses we weren't supposed to take out. Laughing until our stomachs hurt. Those days seemed like a lifetime ago, and yet, here we were, standing on the same soil, but worlds apart.

TWO

Dotty

RIGHT WHERE YOU LEFT ME - TAYLOR SWIFT

"HE LEFT IT TO *ME*?" I ASKED, GRABBING THE PAPER FROM Colt's hands and scanning it.

"Yup," he said, steady as ever.

His long, dark hair was pulled back, making the worry lines on his forehead more pronounced. Colt didn't show much, not unless he meant to, but even now, I could see the loss catching up to him. He was always the levelheaded one—stoic, calm, impenetrable, but I'd learned how to read him anyway.

We were crowded around Dorian's tiny kitchen table, and I let my head fall onto the cold glass surface with a sigh.

He left it to *me*.

Grandpa always was a strange, stubborn man. People said I was his favorite, though I figured it was just because I was the only one who didn't mind his long-winded stories or his bull shit. My brothers were cordial—dutiful even—but I was the one who sat with him. I listened, let him ramble about Gram and the war, about the good old days,

12

and how no one knew how to fix anything anymore. I never minded. I think he knew that.

I pinched the bridge of my nose and stood up, pacing the small space.

This changed everything.

Sawyer ran a hand through his short brown hair and picked up the paper. "It says here: 'I left you all something special. While not equal in financial value, they are all equal in meaning, at least to me. Sawyer gets my old truck. He doesn't need much since he throws a ball around for a living, and I want someone who will take care of it to have it." He paused, dragging his hand down his face. "Dorian gets a college fund for Gracie. I wish I could predict how many great-grandkids I'll get, but he beat y'all to the punch. Colt gets the horses. They have been his, essentially, anyway. Dorothea gets the cabin."

I winced at the use of my full name. Sawyer handed the page over to Colt, who smirked and kept reading.

"'I put a lot of thought into each thing. You can question me all you want, but I'm dead, so you can't argue. Love you all. Smiley face.'" He looked up, eyebrows raised. "He literally drew a fucking smiley face."

"Well, I mean, that does sound like him. You guys okay with this?" I asked, pushing my hair out of my face.

"No," Colt said, flat and unreadable, but not mad. Just Colt.

"I could've done without the shot at my career," Sawyer added with a smile. "But yeah, I'm good. Just glad I was here."

Dorian shrugged. "I'm not complaining. I don't have to stress about saving for the next thirteen years for college for Gracie."

"Oh, shut up, Doctor James," Colt muttered.

"Vet school isn't cheap, and small-town veterinarians don't exactly roll in cash," Dorian said, giving Colt a playful shove.

I tried to smile too, but my stomach twisted. I hadn't planned on any of this, and definitely did not plan on staying longer than a week.

I twisted the charm on my necklace—my mom's necklace—and stared at the paper. Grandpa hadn't even lived in the cabin in years. After Gram passed, he moved into the nursing home. For all I knew, it was falling apart.

"You'll need at least a month," Sawyer said, leaning back in his chair. "Maybe more, depending on how bad it is."

I wasn't eager to fix it up, but I also couldn't stand the thought of leaving it to rot, erasing years of memories in the process.

I sighed. "Looks like I'm renovating a cabin then."

My temples throbbed as the reality set in. Dorian reached over and squeezed my arm.

"How long are you in town?" he asked.

"I was supposed to leave in a week," I said. "But I took a full month off work."

Originally, the plan was to spend a week here, then go back to Seattle and enjoy a blissful, responsibility-free staycation. Binge shows, get a pedicure, maybe finally finish a book. Something easy. Something quiet. Something that didn't involve hauling lumber or worrying about roof leaks.

I'd been climbing my way up the architecture world—school, internship, licensure, all of it. I worked my ass off to be taken seriously in a male-dominated industry, and I was finally up for a promotion I wanted. The timing couldn't have been worse.

But if I didn't deal with the cabin now, I knew I never would.

"I'll check it out tomorrow," I said, glancing around the table. "Might as well see what I'm working with."

They kept talking, but their words faded into the background as my emotions took over. I always thrived on routine, always sticking to what was safe and predictable. Spontaneous decisions—like spending a month in my hometown on a whim—wasn't exactly my thing.

Still, maybe there was something to be gained from all of this. Maybe I could fix the cabin, spend some time with my niece, drink good coffee, sleep in, let my mind rest, and go back home feeling like I did something that mattered.

I yawned and decided it was time for me to call it a day. "I'm beat. I'm heading to Dad's to get some rest," I said.

Dorian and Colt both nodded.

"I'll catch up in the morning," Sawyer said, patting my shoulder. "I've got plans tonight, so don't wait up." Despite his successful career in the NFL, Sawyer always stayed at the ranch when he came home. It grounded him.

We all said our goodbyes and went our separate ways, each of us walking into the night carrying our own version of what Grandpa left behind.

I stepped into my childhood home and was hit by how little had changed. The living room looked exactly as it had the last time I was here, as if time had simply paused.

The ranch house wasn't the modern, classy type, but the nineties, could-probably-use-some-updating kind. However, it had a lot of charm, with scuffed wood floors, matching beams overhead, and original windows. Even the furniture was the same as when I was a kid.

Since Mom died, Dad hadn't touched much. Aside from swapping out the photos on the walls, it was like he was afraid that altering anything would erase what little of her remained.

It had been nearly twenty years since that day. A rainy Friday. She'd gone out for something small—milk or eggs, I think—and didn't come back. She was T-boned in a hit-and-run on the edge of town. The police said the other driver had probably been drunk. There were muddy footprints near the scene, leading from a second car to her door, then back to tire tracks that vanished into the distance. There was no arrest, no follow-up. "Limited resources," they'd said. They figured it was someone passing through town and never investigated further.

That single, senseless moment had split our lives in two. It's what set Colt on the path to becoming a detective.

It still racked my brain how one tiny, fleeting moment could wield such a profound impact that continued to affect the entirety of someone's existence. One late trip to the store. One reckless driver. And just like that, we were four kids and a father trying to hold the pieces together.

Somehow, we did. Gram and Grandpa helped, filling in where they could, being everything we needed when Dad couldn't be. That part, I remembered. But my memories of Mom? They'd faded more than I wanted to admit. I could still feel her warmth, still sense her love, but her voice, her laugh, the details of her face—they'd grown hazy. The photographs scattered around the house helped keep her tethered to my memory. Without them, I wasn't sure I could summon her image at all.

My fingers drifted along the hallway wall until they

landed on a frame. A photo of the six of us taken just months before the accident. She stood beside Dad, a good foot shorter, probably around my height now. Her blue eyes were bright, her blonde waves falling just past her shoulders. I hadn't realized how much we looked alike until now.

People always said I was her twin. The boys were copies of Dad—tall, broad, dark-haired, dark-eyed, but I got Mom's fair coloring, her waves, her curves, her eyes.

A soft sigh from behind pulled me out of the past. Dad stood there, arms crossed, watching me with a tired kind of fondness. His face was more lined, his dark hair streaked with gray, but his brown eyes held the same quiet warmth I remembered.

"She was a beauty, huh?" he said, nodding toward the photo.

Even though I'd made peace with Grandpa's death, Noah was right—it had stirred things I hadn't let myself feel in years.

"Yeah," I said softly, blinking against the burn in my eyes. "She really was."

He stepped forward, wrapping me in a hug that smelled like Old Spice and faint tobacco.

"Oh, sweet girl," he murmured. "What's going on in that head of yours?"

"It's just… a lot lately." I exhaled slowly, grounding myself in the moment. "But it's good to be back in Woodstone for a little while."

The thought of Woodstone no longer being my home weighed on me as the words left my mouth.

"She'd be so proud of you. I hope you know that," he said, straightening the tilted frame. "You look just like her. I don't think it hit me until I saw you standing there."

"And all the boys got you." I smiled faintly, trying to keep things light.

"They pulled the short straw, if you ask me." He chuckled, then his tone shifted. "You still having trouble in Seattle?"

I reached for my necklace and twisted the charm between my fingers. "Not lately. I've been reporting every note as they come, but it's been quiet."

I didn't want to dig into my secret-admirer-turned-stalker situation right now. Not tonight. So I pivoted.

"Did you hear about the cabin?"

If he picked up on the deflection, he didn't mention it.

"That he left it to you? Yeah. I figured he would. Everyone knew how much you loved that place. Way more than the boys ever did."

It still caught me off guard. I'd come back for the funeral, maybe a few lattes at Woodstone Perks, but the cabin? That hadn't been on my radar.

"I've got a month off before I head back to work," I said. "Thought maybe I'd fix it up and maybe rent it out."

"It's rough," he warned gently. "Hasn't been touched since your grandpa moved into the nursing home. Might need more than a fresh coat of paint."

"I figured." I nodded. "I'm going out there tomorrow to take a look."

I moved into the kitchen and pulled two glasses from the cabinet, raising them in silent question. Dad gave a small nod, grabbed the tequila, and poured us each a shot. We sat at the table, clinked our glasses, and threw them back. The fiery warmth quickly subsided, and Dad cleared his throat.

"Let me know if you need help with the cabin."

I narrowed my eyes at him. "What, and you're going to

help in between keeping up on the ranch, helping Dorian with Gracie, and supposedly being *retired*, huh?"

We shared a knowing glance. Even though he'd retired a few years ago, he still worked on the ranch whenever an extra pair of hands was needed, which was often. I knew he understood my hesitation to let him help with the cabin, especially since I had the means to fix it up myself—even if it meant taking a hit to my savings.

"I'm more available than you think, but I bet your brothers and Trent would help out."

I rolled my eyes. "They've got their own lives."

We sank into chairs at the kitchen table—the same table that had hosted years of pancakes, birthday candles, and Sunday dinners. My fingers traced the grooves in the wood.

"Trent, then," he said. "We're heading into the slow season, and he's hired more hands. He might have some time."

He meant well, but he didn't understand. To him, Trent was just Trent. He didn't know what had really happened. Not fully. He assumed we could simply pick up where we left off, but that just wasn't the case.

"Yeah, I don't think so. I want to take care of the cabin because I care about it." I let out a breath. "But my life is in Seattle, and I'm headed back there in a month."

He seemed to catch the edge in my voice and didn't press further. "Well, keep me posted. I'm heading to bed." He stood from the table. "You okay on the couch? Got some pillows and blankets out for you already," he said, putting his glass in the sink.

"The couch?" I raised a brow.

"Well, when you vanish for ten years, I start changing things around." He looked toward the living room. "Never had the heart to change how your mom decorated things down here." He paused, blinking after a moment and turning back to me. "But after you left, I updated the bedrooms. Your old room is my new home gym. Colt and Dorian's room is now set up for Gracie with only a toddler bed in there. Sawyer's room is the same, but I'm assuming he's staying here tonight once he gets back from whatever it is he's doing." The corners of his mouth tugged up. "You could text him and make him take the couch."

I laughed under my breath. "I'll take the couch. Maybe I can move into the cabin soon anyway."

Sleeping on a couch for a month wasn't ideal, but it'd work.

He pulled me into another hug, and kissed the top of my head. "Sounds good. Night, kiddo. Love you."

"Night, Dad. Love you too."

As he disappeared down the hallway, my thoughts traveled to everything he had done for me, for my brothers, even for Trent.

That was the thing about David James—despite the shit card life handed him, losing the love of his life, he never stopped showing up for us, exactly as we needed him to, without a second thought.

THREE

Dotty

COAL - DYLAN GOSSETT

I woke up in a sleepy haze, pulled back to consciousness by the scent of bacon and coffee. Rolling over, I promptly fell straight onto the floor.

All at once, a flood of memories overwhelmed me—the couch, the cabin, the funeral. I involuntarily forfeited those precious, fleeting moments of peace first thing in the morning before reality fully set in.

"Well, that's one way to wake up." Sawyer tried and failed to hide his laugh.

Groaning, I managed to get to my feet. "Good morning to you, too."

"There's breakfast in the kitchen. Dad left early to check on the ranch," he said with a smile.

I squinted at my phone and rubbed my eyes. "It's seven in the morning, and you're already smiling at me? Being all"—I waved a finger at him—"perky? You weren't even home when I passed out. What the hell is wrong with you?"

Sawyer, towering over me with his tall, muscular frame and broad shoulders, broke out in a big smile. "It's really good to have you home, Dotty. I missed your fire." His strong arms enveloped me in a side hug before he ruffled my hair.

"Yeah, yeah, missed you too," I mumbled. "Now don't talk to me again until I've had caffeine."

I shuffled toward the kitchen and poured a full mug of coffee, inhaling like it might save me.

We ate in comfortable silence until Sawyer—being Sawyer—ruined it.

"Any plans today? We're all heading to Outlaw's tonight. Please tell me you'll come." He turned the puppy-dog eyes on full blast.

I had never been to Woodstone Falls' only bar, but it had the reputation as the town's premier hangout spot, no doubt because there was little competition elsewhere.

"I'm gonna check out the cabin, see what it would take to get it rental-ready." I scraped the last bite off my plate and carried it to the dishwasher. "But yes, I will come out. Can't say no to that star-studded face, now can I?"

"Sure can't. They don't pay me the big bucks for nothing." He grinned.

He was six-five and two hundred and sixty pounds of muscle, and the NFL loved him for it, but he loved us the same and never let fame change him one bit—despite being one of the best offensive linemen in the league.

He handed me the keys to Grandpa's old truck—now his—and I set off toward the cabin.

First stop, though—Woodstone Perks. I loved my dad, but his coffee wasn't going to cut it.

The smell of fresh coffee and baked goods wrapped around me the moment I pushed open the door. A soft chime sounded above, and the familiar coziness of Woodstone Perks pulled me in like no time had passed at all. Locally painted art pieces filled the brick walls in a way that felt intentional, not cluttered, and wooden shelves sagged under the weight of well-loved books.

"My eyes must be deceiving, Aiden, because I do believe Dotty James just walked in," Thomas called out theatrically, raising a hand above his brow like he was scouting the horizon.

Aiden turned and smiled, then swatted playfully at his husband's chest. "Oh, hush, you old man." His blue eyes sparkled as he looked at Thomas, before shifting back to me. "Dotty, it's so good to see you. We've missed you around here."

"I've missed you both, *and* your coffee. Can I get a vanilla latte, extra hot, please?"

"Coming right up," Thomas said with a grin as I reached for my wallet.

He waved me off. "On the house today, sweetheart. We were so sorry to hear about your grandfather."

"Thank you," I said, managing a smile. "That means a lot."

This was the peculiar charm of small towns. After years of going to the same café in Seattle, I doubt a single barista ever learned my name, despite writing it on a cup every day, yet here, they had remembered me after over a decade away.

I found an empty table and sank into it, taking in the details that made this place feel like home. The nearby tables were filled with locals, all chatting over steaming cups of coffee as the sunlight streamed through the large windows.

Behind the counter, Aiden expertly moved, pulling shots and frothing milk. The low hum of the espresso machine settled into my brain like white noise.

As I admired a piece of art, I heard the bell jingle above the door as two people walked in. The sound of heeled footsteps echoed through the café. I turned and groaned at the sight of the two people who had entered.

Joanie held a phone to her ear. "I don't care what needs to be done. You work for me. Get it done." She ended the call and marched to the counter, waving a five-dollar bill in the air even though both Aiden and Thomas were clearly busy. She flipped her bleached hair over one shoulder and cleared her throat loudly.

"Uh, hello? Paying customer here?"

"One moment, please," Aiden said without turning.

"We don't have a moment. Two large peppermint teas. Not too hot, or I'll take back my tip."

She slapped the money onto the counter and stepped back, glued once again to her phone. In the span of five seconds, she ran into a table and nearly bulldozed her husband before finally looking up and spotting me.

"Well, well. If it isn't Dorothea James. I didn't know you were in town." She gestured to the man beside her. "This is my husband, Garrett. You guys remember each other, no?"

"Hi, Joanie. Garrett," I said with a nod. "Nice to see you too." Though I could've easily gone my whole visit without it.

Joanie had been one of those girls who made growing up here a nightmare. Her talent for cruelty had been refined. Garrett, on the other hand, had been quiet and mostly kind—proof that opposites really did attract. He smiled politely now, letting her do the talking.

"I'm surprised you came back," Joanie said, smacking her gum. "Thought you were too good for this place."

"Don't worry. I'll be out of your way soon enough," I said, giving her a flat smile as Aiden called out my name.

"Dotty," Aiden called, holding my drink at the counter. "Here you are, sweetheart."

I crossed the café and took the cup with a grateful nod. One sip, and I sighed. "Still the best latte I've had in years."

"Come back soon," Thomas said, giving me a warm smile that creased the corners of his eyes.

"Oh, I will." I lifted my drink in thanks. "See you both soon."

I turned to leave, glancing once more at Joanie and Garrett.

"Have the day you deserve," I said with a polite nod, then pushed open the door and stepped back into the sunshine.

The cabin sat a few miles outside of Woodstone Falls, tucked deep into the arms of the forest. The trees lining the winding road had already begun their shift into autumn, painting the world in colors. It was just chilly enough that I should've rolled the windows up, but the crisp September air felt too good to shut out.

My phone rang, and I glanced at the screen and smiled as I answered. "Hi, Noah."

"Hey, pretty lady. It's been forty-eight hours, and not a single word. I needed proof of life." Her voice was warm and teasing.

We'd met freshman year of college, assigned as random dorm roommates, and had been fused at the hip ever since. Noah, with her dark curly hair, sparkling eyes, and a laugh that could brighten the darkest of days, was everything and more I could ask for in a friend.

Before her, my track record for friends was less than stellar, but she made up for it in spades. We typically never went more than a few hours without talking, but with traveling home and the funeral, I'd been disassociating from reality.

"I'm sorry," I said, exhaling into the speaker. "I've been operating on autopilot since I got here. I think I'm only now starting to breathe again."

"It's okay. I get it. How are you holding up? Any new notes? Or does Mister Creeper not know your new zip code yet?" Her voice was light, but there was a concern behind it.

"No new notes. It's been quiet—longer than usual, actually, but I'll take that as a win." I turned onto the gravel road that led to the cabin.

The *notes* had started my freshman year—anonymous gifts and cards left outside my door. At first, they were almost sweet—white lilies and hand-written compliments. It felt romantic in that fairytale kind of way, but it didn't stay that way. The messages became personal. Too specific. *You looked good in that blue sweater*, or *Do you miss me, too?*

I consistently filed reports with the police, but they never led to any action. They assured me there was no major cause for concern, so they couldn't spare the resources to investigate further. While largely harmless, the notes undeniably made my skin crawl.

"Wait, back up. He left you the cabin? Does this mean

you're staying longer than a week?" she asked as I navigated the winding roads.

"Yes, and sadly, yes." I sighed. "Apparently, it's mine now. I'll probably spend the rest of my vacation here, sorting it out. It's been empty for years, so I'm bracing for whatever disaster I'm about to find."

"Oh, wow. That sounds… fun. I can't say I'm happy you'll be gone longer, but maybe some time there will be good for you. How's everything with your family?"

I loosened my grip on the steering wheel. "Good, well, mostly good. My dad turned my old room into a home gym, so I slept on the couch. If this cabin is even halfway livable, I'm staying here."

"Ugh, I'm sorry," she said. "I'd come visit you sometime before you leave. Maybe see what that small-town life is all about. Honestly, I've been thinking I need a break from the city anyway. Why don't I come the last week you're there? We'll fly back together."

"That sounds perfect. I hate traveling alone."

Even though Seattle to Woodstone Falls was a short flight, I still dreaded every second of it. Driving was an option, but eight hours solo in a car didn't sound any better.

"I can't be without you for long anyway."

It came across as a joke, but we both knew it really wasn't. Noah had been with me through some of my hardest days and had proved herself to be a true friend. The longest we had ever been apart was a week, so spending a whole month away from each other was going to be an adjustment for us both.

"I'll look into flights," she said. "Go conquer your cabin, and please text me photos of any hot cowboys you find."

"Yeah, yeah. Love you. I'm heading out with my brothers tonight, so it might be late before I text."

"Love you too. Have lots of fun! Maybe find *yourself* a hot cowboy."

"Not happening. Talk soon."

I ended the call just as the cabin came into view. At first glance, it was clear it needed some work. The front yard had surrendered itself to waist-high grass and weeds, and half the roof shingles were clinging on for dear life. Still, I could already see the bones beneath the neglect.

As I stepped out, I took it all in. The wraparound porch was beautiful, and the tall, paned windows offered a stunning view of the valley below.

It wasn't just a cabin—it was a two-story beast of a home, built by my grandpa for my gram back when they got engaged. It had been his pride and joy, second only to her.

I'd loved it as a kid. Some of my best memories lived in this house—splashing with my brothers in the creek nearby, swinging on the big white porch swing, curling up on the window seat with Gram's old books. After Grandpa moved, I used to sneak off here sometimes, ride out on horseback, just to feel like myself again.

I stepped onto the porch—and immediately fell through it.

One leg punched straight through the rotting wood.

To-do number one: fix the damn steps.

Shaking my head, I climbed back up, brushing off dirt. I pulled the old metal key from my pocket. The door creaked open, releasing a wave of musty air that hit me like a wall. I batted away cobwebs as I stepped inside, quickly realizing it was far worse off than I'd hoped.

The wallpaper was peeling off everywhere. Furniture was on the verge of falling apart, and there were a bunch of tiny holes along the baseboards that hinted at squatters of the furry, four-legged variety.

Definitely not staying here tonight.

I was already picturing myself back at home curled up in my bed when the sound of tires crunching gravel snapped me to attention. An engine cut off, and my heart raced.

Instinctively, I scanned the room for anything remotely weapon-like. A broomstick. A rusty fireplace poker. Anything.

After years of being stalked and never knowing who was behind the notes or when they'd appear, I no longer shrugged off surprises. I assumed the worst. That was just survival.

But honestly? If someone had followed me here to murder me, it might've been a better fate than attempting to sleep in this place—with the damn mice for company.

I searched for the best hiding spot when I heard an annoyingly familiar voice.

"Is that you, Sawyer?"

I sighed, half relieved that I wasn't about to become the subject of a Dateline episode, and half annoyed to be dealing with Trent. *Again.*

Infuriatingly attractive. Unbearably spontaneous. Not a murderer, technically, but arguably just as bad.

He emerged from his truck and stepped toward the porch like he had every right to be there, taking in the scene.

"Nope, not Sawyer." I stepped out into the entryway.

"Oh," he paused, clearly caught off guard. "Didn't

realize you'd be here this early." He took his stupid cowboy hat off. His dark hair was tousled, giving him a slightly rugged look. "Dorian told me you were coming by today, and I thought I would check it out to see if there was anything I could clean up before you got here. Saw the truck outside and thought maybe Sawyer was doing the same thing."

"He let me borrow it," I said, crossing my arms. "And I don't want or need your help."

Trent looked around and shifted his weight. "Dotty, please. I was just trying to get ahead of it, maybe fix a few things before you even noticed. I didn't come to annoy you."

"Well, congratulations, because you've already done that," I muttered. "If I need help, I've got Dad. I've got my brothers. I can hire someone. I don't need you."

He let out a short laugh and rubbed his jaw. "Sawyer bribed me with game tickets to help. So I'm helping whether you're here or not, but we'd probably make more progress if we worked together."

Of course, Sawyer roped him into this. I should have known returning to Woodstone would have my family back to inserting themselves in my business at every corner.

I exhaled through my nose, annoyed and already exhausted. "Fine, but we're not friends."

Having my heart broken by my brother's best friend, *my* best friend again wasn't in the cards for me. But he was right, I would get a lot more done with his help and be able to return to Seattle sooner because of it.

Trent's smirk tugged at the corner of his mouth, and it took every ounce of self-control not to punch him square in his stupid, stubbled jaw. Maybe a kick to the balls would be more satisfying. After everything that happened between us all those years ago, he'd more than deserve it.

"I can work with that," he said quietly. "I love this place too, you know." His eyes softened as they swept over the porch, the peeling paint, the roof drooping with age. "I want to be part of restoring it."

I scoffed. *Sure you do.* But I needed help, and he had hands and muscles. I was nothing if not pragmatic.

"Fine," I said. "I was planning to start by hauling out the old furniture."

"Good thing I already called in a dumpster," he said, glancing at his watch while I tried not to stare at the veins running along his muscled arm. "Should be here in thirty minutes."

We worked in mostly companionable silence for the next few hours, tossing what couldn't be salvaged and sorting through what little could. We only spoke when necessary. Still, we made real progress.

I was sweeping the thick layer of dust off the floor when his voice broke the silence.

"So… am I allowed to ask what you've been up to all these years?"

I looked up at him and immediately regretted it. His sleeves were pushed up, his forearms dusted with dirt and sweat, and a sheen glistened across his brow. It was unfair how good he still looked. I'd spent ten years trying to forget that face, and in one blink, it was back, carved into my brain all over again.

It'd been only a few hours since he reentered my life, and I was already falling back into his stupid, charming trap.

I focused back on sweeping, and my eyes drifted back to the floor.

"No."

I wasn't ready to talk to him, but I still wanted him to see that I'd built something of myself after I left Woodstone. That I wasn't the same broken girl he once knew.

And I *might* have wanted to know what he was up to.

So I continued, "Fine. I'm an architect. Got licensed a couple of years ago. Working toward a promotion."

His eyebrows rose slightly. "Wow, Dot. That's amazing. Seriously."

I didn't say anything, letting the silence settle between us again. Ten years of not knowing each other at all—of silence, of absence, of distance—now filling the air around us like dust particles we couldn't sweep away.

"What about you?" I finally asked, voice low. "Still on the ranch?"

He nodded. "Yeah. Helping run it. We're hoping to hire a few more hands soon so your dad can finally retire. For real this time." He paused for a moment, then cleared his throat. "Got out of the army about three years ago."

I looked at him again. "Thanks for helping my dad," I said, and I meant it.

Despite everything between us, it mattered. My dad had poured his whole life into that ranch, and knowing someone he trusted was still holding it together meant more than I could say.

Trent didn't just show up one day and start helping— he'd been part of the ranch for years. His dad had worked alongside mine until he passed away our senior year, and with his mom long gone, my father had quietly stepped in, folding Trent into our world like it was the most natural thing. With my brothers scattered in their own lives, Trent had become the obvious successor. And deep down, I knew my dad still saw him as family, no matter how things ended between us.

"Your dad's always been there for me," Trent said. "It's the least I can do."

A moment passed. My broom slipped from my hand, and as I reached down, so did he.

Our fingers brushed the handle at the same time.

And just like that, it was back—the electricity, the pulse-skipping jolt, the sharp inhale I tried to hide. Ten years of distance, and yet the air between us crackled like dry leaves ready to burn.

I had assumed that years apart would dull the effect he had on me, but clearly, I was wrong. Every breath felt loaded, heavy, as if the world was holding its breath along with me.

We stayed there, frozen. My heart pounded loud enough to fill the silence.

Then my phone rang. I jerked my hand back, desperate for something—anything—to break the suffocating tension, and answered the call, my voice shaky.

"Hey, Sawyer," I said, breathless. "What's up?"

"Still at the cabin? Want to grab lunch before I head back tomorrow?"

"You know we are going out tonight, right?" I laughed.

"Yeah, but I don't get to take my sister to lunch every day."

I smiled despite myself. Sawyer, ever the charmer.

"Sure. I'll head home and shower first. Meet you after?"

"Perfect. See you soon."

I hung up and looked back at Trent. He was watching me, expression unreadable.

"I should go," I said.

He nodded slowly. "We made good progress today. I'll

come back later this week. If you need anything, my number's still the same."

I turned toward the door.

"Dot," he called after me. "This place was always yours, too."

I didn't answer. I didn't look back.

Because I wasn't sure what I'd do if I did.

FOUR

Dotty

GOING, GOING, GONE - LUKE COMBS

I SWIPED ON A LITTLE MASCARA AND BLUSH—JUST ENOUGH TO feel human without hiding the faint freckles still hanging on from summer. I twisted my blonde hair into a messy bun more from habit than anything else and headed downstairs.

"I'm ready!" I called, taking the stairs two at a time.

"Finally," Dorian said.

"Oh, please. Half an hour. Spare me the drama." I shot him a look as I reached the bottom step. "Just wait till Gracie starts hogging the bathroom."

My brother had always kept people at arm's length, but he'd been utterly defenseless the moment Gracie arrived five years ago. His whole world shifted overnight. What started as a casual thing with Hallie became anything but when complications during childbirth took her life without warning. Suddenly, Dorian was a single father to a preemie who spent her first month fighting in the NICU, with no time to properly grieve and no roadmap for what came next.

I'd made a point of avoiding Woodstone Falls for years,

but I still saw plenty of my niece. Following Sawyer's NFL career from city to city gave us the perfect excuse to celebrate birthdays and holidays wherever he was playing, and gave me the perfect excuse to stay away from home.

Dorian dragged a hand down his face. "She's already asking for another princess dress and a matching purse. I don't know how many tiny purses one kid needs, but I'm pretty sure we've hit the legal limit."

"A girl needs options," came Gracie's voice, confident and high-pitched, as she strutted in from the kitchen holding a donut like a trophy.

Dorian pinched the bridge of his nose. "And where did you get that?"

"Papa gave it to me. It's Gracie and Papa night!" she squealed, full of sugar and excitement already.

Dorian sighed. "Great. At least he's the one putting you to bed. Have fun with that, Dad!" he shouted over her head.

Our dad walked in, unbothered, sipping his coffee. "We're good. Got movies queued up, popcorn in the microwave. You kids go have fun. Stay out as late as you want—Gracie's room is ready whenever she crashes."

I bent down to hug her, inhaling that faint, syrupy smell she always seemed to carry. I kissed the top of her head, and my Dad gave her a warm pat on the back. Dorian leaned in for a quick hug, too.

And just like that, we were out the door and climbing into the truck, heading toward the bar.

Walking into Outlaw's Bar was exactly what I expected. Faded rodeo posters, rusted license plates, and flickering neon signs cluttered the walls, giving the place a kind of worn-in charm. It smelled like old wood and spilled beer—probably because no one had deep-cleaned it since the '90s. Half cowboy hangout, half unapologetic dive bar. It probably hadn't changed in decades, and somehow, that made it perfect.

"I'll order. Go find a table," Colt said, tipping his head toward the bar. "What do you want?"

"Tequila soda," I said. "Heavy on the soda."

I wasn't a big drinker, but after the week I'd had, it felt well earned.

"Get me a beer. You know the one," Sawyer added, clapping Colt on the shoulder.

"Same," Dorian said, guiding us to an open booth and taking the chair at the end.

Sawyer slid into the seat across from me, taking up more than his share of the bench.

"It's good to have you home, Dotty," he said, and there was no teasing in his voice. "I know being here's not your favorite thing, but I'm glad you came."

His smile was soft and familiar. We were only two years apart and had always been close, especially as adults. Sawyer had this steady loyalty about him. With his kind heart, he always looked out for those around him, sometimes to a fault.

"I didn't expect it, but it's actually been nice." The words slipped out before I could think better of them. "Weird, right?"

Not waking up to the sound of horns outside my apartment and the absence of smoggy air definitely had its perks.

Colt returned and dropped our drinks on the table before sliding in next to Sawyer. "You staying on Dad's couch the whole month?" he asked, his long dark hair hiding under a baseball cap.

"Not if I can help it," I said, already bracing for suggestions I didn't want. "I was hoping to stay at the cabin, but unless I want to share a bed with mice, it's not happening. But I really don't want to live out of a hotel room for four weeks either."

Right then, the front door creaked open, and of course, Trent walked in. Dorian waved him over without asking.

He slid into the booth beside me. Same tall frame, broad shoulders, and that stubborn jawline I hadn't stopped noticing, no matter how mad I was. The air around us shifted. A little heavier. A little warmer.

"You could stay in my room when I'm not there for the season," Sawyer added.

"With you coming home during every spare moment and kick me back to the couch anyway? No thanks."

"What about Trent?" Colt offered casually.

"I'm good," I said at the same time Trent offered, "Guest room's yours if you want it."

I looked at him with a tight smile. "Think I'll take my chances with the mice. The couch was fine last night. I slept great." The squeak in my voice betrayed me.

"You fell off the couch this morning," Sawyer reminded me, grinning like he was enjoying this too much. "Told me not to speak to you before coffee and looked like you hadn't slept at all."

"Snitch," I muttered, then downed the rest of my drink in one go.

"Come stay in my guest room," Trent said again, unbothered. "That couch is older than we are, and you'll just end up sore and cranky."

Dorian chimed in. "Please take him up on it. I can only

handle so much whining about your back before I start looking into retirement homes."

I gave him a look sharp enough to slice glass. "You're an ass."

I didn't immediately shut Trent down, but I didn't say yes either.

I didn't feel ready to be around him every day. Not after everything. Not after ten years of silence and everything that filled the space between us.

Then again, the thought of spending a month on a sagging couch while trying to work on the cabin... wasn't appealing.

"A real room?" I asked, leaning my elbows on the sticky table. "With walls and a door and everything?"

"And a lock," Trent said with a half-smile.

"So I lock you out when you inevitably piss me off?"

Colt, who'd mostly sat quietly observing the conversation, laughed. I dropped my forehead onto the table, not even caring that it probably hadn't been wiped down in too long.

"You'd have your own space," Trent said. "I only keep the room to bribe Dorian into letting Gracie have sleepovers someday."

I lifted my head just enough to look at him. I couldn't believe I was even considering it.

"Are you clean, or are you one of those people who think crumbs don't count if they're small?" I asked.

Sawyer snorted, and Dorian grinned.

Dorian spoke. "After coming back from the military, he's insanely clean. It's almost annoying."

"Like, bordering on OCD," Sawyer added.

Trent scowled. "At least I'm not gross."

What the hell am I doing?

Maybe I should just go back to the city and get ahead on work. My boss was already hinting about the next promotion cycle, and I wasn't exactly in line if I kept disappearing for family time.

Dorian saw the shift in my face immediately. "Don't," he said quietly. "Don't talk yourself out of this. Spend time with Gracie, with Dad. With us. We want you here. Just stay for a while."

I looked at him, and for once, I didn't have a quick comeback. He meant it, and he was right. I'd already come this far, might as well stay a while.

"Okay, *okay*. Fine. I will take your guest room, but only because the idea of sleeping on a couch for a month sounds awful, and none of my brothers were thoughtful enough themselves to plan to have a house with a guest room for their favorite sister."

"In our defense, you never come home," Dorian said.

"What he said," Colt grunted.

Sawyer raised both hands. "Don't blame me. I don't live here."

I leaned back in the booth, staring at the three of them. It had been a long time since we were all in the same place.

And damn, I'd missed it.

I tipped my empty glass toward Trent. "It's your fault, I need another drink."

He stood automatically, offering a hand to help me out. I ignored it. He towered over me, and I was reminded just how tall he really was. He was damn near as tall as Sawyer, which was no small thing considering Sawyer was one of the tallest players in the NFL.

"I can drive you back tonight. The bed's already made up, so you just need to grab your things. We can swing by the ranch house on the way. I'd hate to see you sleep on the couch again."

"Yup, I definitely need another drink to deal with you. Excuse me," I muttered, pushing past him to head for the bar.

Behind me, I heard Colt say, "Good luck. I think you pissed her off."

From a distance, I heard Trent reply, "Don't worry, I can handle Dot."

After a few hours, three tequila sodas, and a buzz that had me feeling equal parts confident and blunt, we decided it was time to call it a night.

Sawyer was the first to haul a tipsy Dorian into his truck. Dorian immediately leaned his head against the window, eyes closing, drool already pooling at the corner of his mouth.

"He doesn't get out much, huh?" I laughed, nodding toward him.

Sawyer grunted. "Nope. You being back makes him happy, so he threw caution to the wind tonight. He'll pay for it tomorrow." He cleared his throat, eyes on me. "You good riding with Trent?"

"Yeah, I'll be fine." I smiled.

Was I fine? Not really. But would I survive? *Hopefully*.

"See ya, sis. Love you." He pulled me into a quick hug before climbing into his truck.

"Love you too." I waved and headed back toward Trent, who was standing by the bar entrance talking to a couple of familiar faces.

I recognized them immediately.

"Well, well. The Reynolds brothers. Been a while," I said, stepping closer.

The last time I saw Henry, we were still in school. We were the same age, navigating those awkward years. Back then, he was a skinny kid with blonde hair. Now, he'd filled out—tall, solid, and undeniably a grown man. When he pulled me into a side hug, his genuine smile made me feel surprisingly welcome.

"Dotty James. You look great," he said.

Chris, Henry's older brother, stepped forward next. He shared the same blonde hair but had a leaner build and had an easy smile that perfectly matched his reputation as the town's jokester.

"Hey, Dotty. Great to see you. I'm sorry to hear about your grandpa," he said quietly.

"Thanks. I'm sorry to hear about your dad, too."

He shrugged, a flicker of hurt in his eyes. "Thanks," he replied.

"I heard you guys closed down your family's ranch a while back?" I asked.

Chris and Henry had inherited their family's ranch after their father passed away, though it no longer served its original purpose, as they now had their careers. Henry was now a police officer and worked with Colt, while Chris worked at the local mechanic shop.

"Yeah, stepped back from the day-to-day," Henry said. "We keep up the property but don't board horses anymore."

"Makes sense. I see you are still friends with this guy?" I said, pointing to Trent.

"We catch a beer now and then. Chris usually tags along," Henry said with a grin.

"Maybe I'll join you guys sometime, especially since I'll be in town for a month fixing up the cabin."

"Well," Henry said, "if you ever want to grab dinner while you're in town, I'd love to take you out."

I blinked, surprised by the forwardness, but smiled politely. Honestly, I didn't really want to go out with Henry. I didn't want to go out with *anyone*. My past relationships were mostly forgettable disasters, and after my last breakup, I was convinced I was better off alone.

Besides, I wanted something real—something that didn't make me second-guess if I even wanted to be there. If I was going to risk my heart and shake up the routine I'd built, I needed to be sure it was worth it.

"Thanks. I'll keep that in mind."

Chris jumped in before I could change the subject. "Your dad was telling me about your job in Seattle. Sounds like you're doing well."

I chuckled. "Yeah, I like it there, but for now, I'm here working on the cabin."

"That's impressive. Not everyone can juggle so much. I can barely manage the auto shop some days," Chris said.

"Well, you're damn good at what you do," I replied. "My dad won't let anyone else touch his car."

Chris smiled, a little pride flickering in his eyes. "Your dad's been great, always sending clients my way. So, if you ever need help with the cabin or anything, just ask. My way of paying the family back."

"I appreciate that."

Being back was oddly comforting. The warmth here was nothing like the cold, impersonal pace of the city. I'd forgotten how easy it was to feel welcome in Woodstone— even if I knew it wasn't home for me anymore.

After a few minutes of catching up, we said goodbye to Henry and Chris and made our way back to the truck.

I was moving slower than usual, still a little off balance from the drinks. I caught the way Trent's jaw. I rolled my eyes after he let out an exasperated sigh.

"Yeah, yeah. I'm a little slow. I think I drank a bit too much," I admitted, trying to ease the tension.

"You're fine, Dot. Take your time."

He offered his hand to help me into the truck, and I took it without thinking. His palm was rough and warm, familiar in a way I wasn't ready for. As soon as I was seated, I let go as if I had been burned, unable to bear another second of contact.

The door shut behind me. Trent circled the front and slid into the driver's seat without a word. He started the truck, and the silence stretched between us—the same quiet that had been there for the last ten years. I stared out the window as my buzz faded. We didn't say anything the entire drive. Just like before, we just existed in the silence once again.

FIVE

Trent

DOWN BAD - TAYLOR SWIFT

I didn't know what the hell I was doing or why I thought offering Dotty James a place to stay was a good idea.

It's as if I laid eyes on her for the first time in years, and all common sense went out the fucking window.

Since the moment I saw her standing on those church steps, she'd taken over every damn thought I had, no matter how hard I tried to push her out. It was embarrassing how one small moment with her could pull everything inside me loose. She'd been gone for a decade, and I thought I'd finally learned how to breathe again.

But then she came back, a storm blowing through and sucking the air right out of my fucking lungs.

After we stopped at the ranch to grab her bags, we headed to my place. Somewhere along the way, she fell asleep, and I couldn't bring myself to wake her. So what did I do? I just watched her like a fucking creep, because for once, she wasn't looking at me like the last ten years were carved into stone between us.

Her head rested against the window, body half-curled

and completely at ease. Her messy blonde hair had escaped its bun, framing those blue eyes that had haunted me for years. Her freckles were barely visible in the dim light as she snored softly. Her unconscious little puffs of air felt like a shot of pure dopamine straight to my bloodstream.

Her presence pulled me in like gravity—inevitable, inescapable, dangerous as hell.

After a few minutes of shameless looking, I shoved down those feelings and reached over to shake her gently awake. "Hey, Dot. Time to wake up. Let's get you to bed."

She let out an adorable little grunt, and her eyes fluttered open. She mumbled what sounded like an apology before reaching for the door handle. I was already outside, rounding the truck to help her out. I put my arm around her shoulder and carried her inside, straight to the guest room. I set her on the bed, and she muttered under her breath.

"What was that?" I chuckled.

"I hate how you can be so infuriating, nice, and handsome all at once. It's annoying," she slurred.

I wanted to beat my chest like some damn gorilla. Any attention from Dotty was a win—even when it came wrapped in insult. I'd take all her jabs just for the chance to be close to the girl I'd dreamed about for years. The girl I thought I might never see again. Yet here she was, in my house.

"Let me grab your bags and some water. Bathroom's through that door on your right if you need it."

She mumbled something again. I went and grabbed her bags from the truck before grabbing a glass of water from the kitchen.

By the time I got back, she was out cold, sprawled across the duvet. Careful not to wake her, I slipped off her boots and gently pulled the blanket from underneath to cover her.

And because I couldn't seem to fucking help myself, I leaned down and pressed a quick kiss to her forehead.

The soft hum of satisfaction she made in response only made me want more.

She always made me want more.

But despite how perfect Dotty James was, I knew better than to get too close to her again.

After a night of shit sleep, I gave up and got out of bed once the clock hit six. I made breakfast on autopilot, then stepped out onto the front porch with a coffee in hand, just in time to catch the sun rising over the mountains.

I'd always been a night owl. Dotty, too. Dorian was the odd one out—he couldn't stay up past eleven if his life depended on it. Growing up, he'd fall asleep on the couch like clockwork while Dotty and I stayed up late, talking for hours in that old ranch house.

Now, watching the sky shift from gray to gold, I let my mind drift back to those nights—when everything felt simple, like nothing would ever change.

"So, Dot," I said, glancing over at her from the opposite end of the couch, "how's high school treating you so far?"

She sat cross-legged across from me, her back pressed against the far armrest. Dorian had passed out over an hour ago, his head tucked against a pillow beside her.

"I mean, I'd be better if I could make friends without them becoming obsessed with you or Dorian, but I guess there's not much I can do about that."

She smiled, but I caught the flicker of something else behind it. Dotty didn't have the easiest time making friends in Woodstone Falls, unless you counted Dorian and me.

I held her gaze. "I'm sorry, sunshine. I can't help being this handsome." I grinned. "Dorian, though? I don't get it. He's kind of an ass."

She snorted and chucked a pillow at me. "Yeah, he can definitely be an ass."

Then she looked at me—chin down, eyes peeking through those thick lashes—and something tightened in my chest. You'd think I'd be used to it by now, but every time she looked at me like that, it knocked the wind out of me.

Somewhere over the last year, Dotty had stopped being just my best friend. She'd become the girl I couldn't stop thinking about. But I would never compromise our friendship by crossing that line, despite how kissable her lips looked.

"You know I'm kidding," I said, trying to keep my tone light. "You'll make friends, Dot. Maybe not here, but one day you'll be out chasing big-city dreams, and you'll find your people. Imagine how many options there are for Ellie Miles-loving, book-obsessed girls outside of Woodstone. And until then…" I winked. "You've got me."

She rolled her eyes. "Seriously, I better find at least one person who actually gets me. Otherwise, I'm stuck with you forever. And if that happens, I'm gonna start oversharing. Like… crushes. Maybe even sex."

I choked on my breath. "Jesus, Dotty. Warn a guy first."

She let out a loud, belly-deep laugh. Dorian grunted and rolled over beside her.

"I just wanted to see your face," she whispered, grinning. "Besides, with an overprotective dad, three older brothers, and you, no guy's ever gonna come near me."

"And that's exactly how we like it."

The thought of anyone getting close to her—anyone who didn't see her the way I did—made my stomach turn.

While most people saw Dotty as cold and reserved, I saw her for what she truly was—light, goodness, and strength.

Knowing Dotty was like experiencing the first warm, sunny day of the year. It was that feeling when you closed your eyes and looked up at the sun to feel the warmth on your face just a little more.

If I could bottle Dotty up into a single feeling, that'd be it.

She embodied the promise of summer, the feeling of hope. To me, Dotty wasn't the cold. She was the warmth that came after it.

And no one deserved her light. Especially not me.

My mom hadn't even stuck around long enough to know who I was. And my dad—though he tried—loved me more out of duty than anything else. It was never like what David James gave his kids. Never that steady, unquestioning kind of love.

Dotty shifted, and suddenly her hand was on my knee. I hadn't even noticed her move closer.

"Where'd you go, cowboy?" she asked softly. Her eyes searched mine.

"Sorry," I said, clearing my throat. "Got lost in my head."

"You know you can talk to me, right?" She gave my knee a gentle squeeze, and for a second, all I wanted was to pull her closer.

Instead, I shook her off and leaned back. "I'm good. Promise. We should probably get some rest."

She pulled away, settling back on her end of the couch. "You're right. Sorry for keeping you up. Better sleep before the sun comes up. Night, Trent."

"Good night, sunshine," I whispered, calling her the name I had since we were kids.

Even if she'd become something more, I wasn't about to risk losing the one person who ever felt like home.

The distant chirping of birds and the soft creak of the front door pulled me out of my thoughts.

Dotty stepped outside, still half-asleep and looking adorably disheveled. Her hair was a mess, blonde strands catching the morning light, haloing her face like she'd wandered straight out of a damn dream. She wore a pale pink pajama set that somehow made her look softer, warmer. The fabric clung in just the right ways, and I had to force myself to keep my eyes above her shoulders.

She cradled a mug of coffee between her hands, the steam curling into the cool air as she walked over. A faint smile tugged at the corners of her mouth.

I rubbed my chest, feeling the ink beneath my shirt that seemed to burn every time she was close.

She settled into one of the big rocking chairs and cleared her throat. "Thanks," she said, raising her cup and nodding.

"No problem. There's food inside if you're hungry," I offered, watching her carefully, still not sure where we stood.

She looked over, expression unreadable. "Thanks for letting me stay here," she said, clearing her throat again. "I know it's kind of weird, and I'm still trying to figure it all out, but since we're technically roommates for the next month... maybe we should set some ground rules."

Dotty and her rules. I guess her need for control and stability hadn't disappeared in the last ten years.

"Sure," I said. "If that makes things easier."

"Do you have anything in mind?"

"Uh… not really. Do you?"

She nodded. "No guests without a heads-up, maybe? Just so it doesn't feel like people are coming in and out."

"Yeah, that's fine. I don't usually have people over. Your brothers drop by sometimes. Is that okay?"

"I don't mind them," she said quickly. "It's just... strangers. I don't want people around I don't know or feel comfortable with, but if that's an issue, I can find somewhere else to stay."

"No," I said, a little too fast. "Dot, I told you. You're welcome here. I don't have people over."

She took a sip of her coffee, then looked back at me. "You probably remember this, but no peanuts."

Dotty had been allergic since we were kids. We never had them at the ranch, and I'd kept the habit. Didn't even think twice about it anymore.

"I don't keep them in the house. You're safe."

"Well, that's all I've got," she said. "I clean up after myself. You do too, or so I've been told." She smiled, but it didn't quite reach her eyes. "I like your place. It's nice here. Very rustic chic."

She glanced around, and her smile tugged a little higher.

My house wasn't the nicest in Woodstone Falls, but it was mine.

"Thanks," I said. "I've put in a lot of work. Colt and Dorian helped with the renovations, and I hired a designer online to help with the rest. I'm useless with paint colors."

I scratched at my beard, mostly to keep my hands busy, and to stop staring at those fucking shorts.

"It's a beautiful home," she said, glancing around. "I love the porch."

"You always said the only thing the ranch house was missing was a wrap-around porch. That and a few extra bedrooms." I paused, unsure if I should have let on how much

I remembered about her even after so much time had passed. "But… uh, at least now you can enjoy the cabin's porch." The only sound was the creaking of the rocking chairs.

"Yeah, it needs a lot of work though."

"What's your plan?" I asked.

She shrugged. "I don't really have one yet. Today I was just going to go back and make a list and figure out what I can tackle and what I'll need to hire out."

"I can help out. I've picked up a lot about renovations from fixing up this place and working on the ranch over the years."

Truth was, I didn't have much free time, but if it meant getting back in Dotty's good graces, I'd make it work.

She looked at me, her expression tight. "Why?"

I blinked. "What do you mean?"

"Why do you want to help?" Her voice was quieter now. "We haven't talked in years. Then I come back to town, and suddenly you're around again—offering help like we didn't ignore each other for a decade."

The words hit harder than I expected.

"I know I can't change what happened," I said. "But it's the past, Dot. Can we start over? As friends?"

There was no hiding the hope in my voice, no matter how hard I tried to keep it casual.

She sighed. "Acquaintances," she said after a beat. "I can do acquaintances."

Yeah, there was little to no difference between friends and acquaintances to me, so I agreed.

"I want to help because I care. About the cabin, your family. Your grandparents. And believe it or not, I care about you, too. That place holds a lot of memories for me. Just because we haven't talked doesn't mean I forgot anything."

Her cheeks flushed, jaw tight as she stared into her coffee. When she finally looked up, her eyes locked on mine—and there was no softness left in them.

"You can't just waltz back into my life and act like nothing happened," she said. "You remember the good stuff. But what about everything else? Did you conveniently forget everything except what was left as a pretty painted memory in your brain? You may be able to move on from that, but I can't. It's not that simple."

I didn't have an answer—only guilt and a growing knot in my chest that told me I deserved every damn word.

"I'm sorry, Dotty," I said, and meant it. "I know I can't undo the past, but I'm here now. I want to fix it. Whatever it takes. Even if we have to start from scratch."

She stood abruptly, pushing her chair back. "Don't expect me to just fall into step with whatever plan you've cooked up. It's going to take more than your pretty words and charming smiles."

"Is this a bad time to point out that you think my smile is charming?" I teased.

She pinned me with a glare that would scare the damn devil himself.

"I'll take that as a yes," I muttered.

"I'm done talking about this," she scoffed. "Just… stay out of my way."

She walked inside, and the screen door slammed behind her.

And just like that, I was alone again—left with the sound of distant birds, the creak of the rocking chair, and a silence that felt far too familiar.

I wanted to do right by Dotty this time. Unlike how I did ten years ago.

SIX

Dotty

———

SILENCE - MARSHMELLO, KHALID

THE DAYS FLEW BY, AND BEFORE I KNEW IT, I HAD ALREADY spent a week in Woodstone Falls. True to his word, Trent kept his distance. We exchanged polite greetings when we crossed paths—just short, clipped little words that sounded more like awkward coworkers than two people who used to know everything about each other.

He never hovered. Never asked how things were going. But somehow, he still managed to be everywhere.

Every time I came back from the cabin, something had changed. A fresh coat of primer on the siding. The front steps were power-washed. A broken light was replaced in the kitchen. He was clearly working on the place when I wasn't around, like we were coordinating via invisible schedules. And I couldn't decide if that made him thoughtful or just infuriatingly evasive.

Still, progress was happening. Contractors were lined up—electrical, plumbing, everything I didn't trust myself not to mess up. I had spreadsheets and estimates and about a thousand flagged emails. But today, I didn't care.

I'd declared the afternoon a responsibility-free zone.

54

Curled up in the oversized armchair in Trent's guest room, I opened a romance novel and let my brain melt. The room was warm and quiet, with soft light spilling through the sheer curtains and pooling across the wood floors. Everything in here smelled faintly of pine and laundry detergent, and for the first time all week, I felt like I could breathe.

I flipped a page just as a knock sounded at the door.

"Come in," I called, not bothering to look up.

"Um, hi. You had a delivery. I wanted to make sure you got it."

I glanced up to see Trent stepping inside, holding a bouquet of lilies. A small white card dangled from the vase.

The blood drained from my face the second I read the message.

I can't wait to see you soon.

Trent's brow furrowed as he clocked my reaction. "Everything okay?"

I took a deep breath. "I don't know," I said, my voice shaky.

He glanced at the card, then back at me, his voice quieter now. "Do you know who sent it?"

"I have no idea," I replied, my mind already spinning through every possibility I'd ruled out a dozen times before.

His jaw clenched. "Are you seeing someone?"

I gave him a flat look. "Not that it's any of your business, but no." I rubbed at my temples, like that could somehow massage the anxiety out of my system.

"What is this, then?"

I hesitated. "I have... a secret admirer?" It sounded flimsy out loud.

"A secret admirer?" he repeated, incredulously. "You mean a stalker?" His fists curled at his sides, veins pushing against his forearms. The tension radiating off him made it hard to think straight—and not just because he looked unfairly good like that.

The last thing I wanted was to walk through this again. Especially with him.

"And before you ask, yes—I've reported every note. Every single fucking time. I get flowers—lilies, always damn lilies. You'd think he could pick a flower that doesn't smell like shit."

I stood and crossed the room toward him. "The cops don't see it as a threat. It's never escalated beyond notes and flowers, so they're not wasting their time. They say it's harmless. So, I just let it go."

The lie came out smooth, practiced.

But in reality, it didn't feel harmless. Not anymore. This note was different than the others. It was a promise, a warning.

Trent didn't move. "Do your brothers know?"

I scoffed, arms crossing over my chest. "What do you think?"

"I don't know, Dotty," he said sharply. "I really don't know you anymore." He rubbed at the left side of his chest like his words physically hurt him.

My voice dropped. "I've never been the kind of person to hide things from my family. They all know. Fuck, I mean, Colt was the first one I told. It's never escalated, and I figured being away from Seattle would make it stop. I guess I was wrong." I shrugged, trying not to let it show

how close that shrug was to falling apart. "I'll report it. I'll move on. Just like I always do."

"Why didn't I know about this?" His voice stayed even, but his emerald eyes told a different story.

I stared up at him. "Because we haven't spoken in ten years, Trent. What, you think I was gonna do? Call you out of the blue? Hey, just thinking of you. Also, I have a stalker who sends me stinky fucking flowers."

My voice cracked. I hadn't meant for it to.

I pulled the claw clip from my hair and tossed it on the dresser. The pressure on my scalp was too much. All of it was too fucking much.

He took half a step toward me, hand lifting like he might reach out, but moved back.

"How long has this been going on?"

"A long time." My voice was flat. Dull. The way it gets when I've already had the conversation too many times.

Trent rolled his shoulders, his jacket shifting with the movement. "What did Colt say?"

"That I'm doing everything right. It's out of his jurisdiction, so all he can do is tell me to keep reporting it. I don't go anywhere alone unless I have to. I carry pepper spray. I check my surroundings. I tell people where I'm going. I've got it handled."

"Good." His jaw ticked.

I stared at him. "I'm sorry, what? Good? You go full angry caveman and now we're just—good?"

"Yes. *Good*," he said again, measured this time. "You're taking precautions. I wish I could do something about it, but you've done everything you can. So... yeah. *Good*." He dragged in a breath.

"Uh... Thanks?" The word came out like a question. I

grabbed my bag off the bed. "Well, I'm heading to Dorian and Gracie's for the night."

"Text me when you get there."

I turned, eyebrows lifting. "Why?"

"God, Dotty, do you have to be so fucking defiant. Just do it." He sighed, voice softening. "Please. For me."

And just like that, he was back to the Trent I remembered. Calm. Dry. Slightly annoying.

"Fine," I muttered, and walked out the door.

Five minutes later, my phone buzzed with a text from Trent.

TRENT

Did you make it?

Calm your tits. Just got here.

Calm my tits? What are you 12?

You're clearly the child here. One in need of a lesson in patience at that.

Patience, huh? Maybe you could teach me sometime.

In your dreams, cowboy. I'm going to see my niece now. Goodbye.

I'm always here if you change your mind.

Keep dreaming.

I tucked my phone in my pocket and headed up the porch steps. The screen door hadn't even clicked shut behind me before Gracie jumped at me.

"Auntie Dotty!" She barreled into my leg and clung on

like a koala. "I missed you! What's your favorite animal?" she asked in her sweet-as-sin little voice.

I crouched and pulled her into a big hug, then leaned back to take her in—messy blonde curls, wild eyes, a spark of mischief I fully supported. "Oh, that's a tough one, but I'm gonna go with an elephant. They're cute, they've got those cool trunks, and they can spray water like a built-in water gun. What about you?"

It was always easier with Gracie. No performance, no second-guessing. Just her tiny chaos and my full permission to lean into it.

"Mine is a unicorn. They're magical." She said it like it was the most obvious thing in the world.

Dorian walked in, laughing. "Unicorns aren't real, baby girl."

Gracie whirled on him. "Daddy, you can't say that. Just because you haven't seen one doesn't mean they don't exist. Like Santa or the tooth fairy. Right, Auntie Dotty?"

She turned to me with big eyes, her entire argument hanging on my response. Oh, how I missed the sweet innocence of childhood.

"I believe you are absolutely correct, Gracie girl." I didn't even try to hide my smile.

"*See*, Daddy?" she said, triumphant. "I told you. Auntie Dotty went to college. She knows things."

I bit back a laugh as Dorian scrubbed a hand over his face.

"Yeah, yeah. What do I know? I'm only a doctor." He looked dead on his feet. "Time for homework. Go start, and call out if you need help."

Gracie dashed off, and I watched Dorian rub at his temples like the weight of dad life was catching up to him.

He'd been running on fumes for a while now. Between

the vet clinic and single parenting, I didn't know how he kept it together most days. He'd gone to school about thirty minutes from Woodstone, planning to head somewhere bigger after undergrad, but then Gracie happened. He stayed. Built something steady. Took over Dr. Smith's practice three years ago and never looked back.

Classic Dorian. Always showing up when it mattered. Even if it meant giving up everything else.

Gracie gave me one last dramatic squeeze before skipping down the hall like she hadn't just won a full debate. Dorian dropped onto the couch. I followed, sinking into the cushion beside him, and sighed.

He leaned his head back and studied the ceiling like it might offer answers. "Okay. What happened? I can see your brain ticking."

"Was gonna ask you the same thing. Sometimes this twin bond thing is annoying," I muttered.

We didn't actually have a twin bond—no psychic signals or spooky energy, but we'd been faking it since we were kids. But really, Dorian could just read me like an instruction manual. All it took was a pause too long, and he was already putting the pieces together.

"I got another note today," I said quietly. My voice barely cracked, but I still hated how it sounded.

"Fuck. Again? Here?" He sat up straighter, hand dragging down his face.

"Yep." I popped the p, trying to inject a little levity that neither of us bought. "Apparently, being out of Seattle doesn't do much for my anonymous fan club."

"You report it?"

"Already called Colt on the way here." I ran a hand through my hair. "Trent answered the door, so now he knows too."

Dorian let out a long breath and shook his head.

"You know, I don't know what happened between you two, but I do know Trent. He cares about you, even if he's got his own… unique way of showing it." His dark eyes searched mine. "What made you hate him so much?"

I shrugged. "Nothing. I went to college in Seattle. He joined the army. We went our separate ways. He's always annoyed me. Can we not talk about Trent?"

"All I'm saying is, you both left and never came back the same," he said, glancing at me with concern etched on his face. "You were always fire, Dotty. Since we were kids, you had this unique spark, but somewhere along the way, that fire turned to stone. At some point, your reservations turned into restraint. Your need for stability became an unwillingness to change your routine. You're still you, but I see the real part of you that you hide, trying to avoid whatever it is you're afraid of."

"Damn, tell me how you really feel." I stood up, needing to move, to shake off the heaviness his words brought on. "I came here to see my niece, not get a therapy session on how I'm a shell of a person."

He grinned. "Well, whenever you're ready to talk about it, I've got tequila just for the occasion."

I snorted. "You have trauma dumping tequila ready for me? How sweet."

He smirked. "You still deflect with humor, so at least some things never change," he teased.

Gracie strolled in right on cue, saving me from further introspection. "Ta-da! Homework's done. Can Aunt Dotty come play?"

I smiled and took her hand. "I would love to, G."

The next few hours disappeared in a blur of books, dolls, and endless chatter about Ellie Miles—Gracie's favorite singer. Being here, with her, was the best part of coming back. Watching her grow up in person beats any video call. My heart ached thinking about all the moments I'd missed with her, trapped by fear and distance.

Gracie's small hand cupped my face. "I love you, Aunt Dotty. You're the best auntie ever."

"Well, I'm your only auntie, but thank you. You're my favorite niece."

She beamed.

Dorian appeared at the doorway. "Hey, Gracie, it's almost bedtime. Can you get your pajamas on and brush your teeth?"

"Okay, Daddy." I kissed her forehead as she skipped toward the bathroom.

Dorian and I walked to the kitchen, where he poured himself a drink and raised the bottle. "Want one?"

"No, thanks. I'm driving back soon."

He sat at the table, taking a sip. "So, you sticking around for a while?"

"Yeah, I'm on vacation for a few weeks. Might extend it if the cabin needs more work. What's up?"

"I was hoping you could watch Gracie for a weekend. I've got a conference in Seattle coming up in a couple weeks, and I don't want to ask Dad. He's done enough lately."

"Sure, I'd love to." And a break from Trent's place wouldn't hurt. I smiled. "You can crash at my apartment if you want."

"Oh, thanks. That'd be great." His smile flickered into something warm and familiar that reminded me of Dad.

After Gracie went to bed, Dorian and I stayed up talking—everything from work to how much he loathed Gracie's Ellie Miles phase. I teased him to chill, considering there were way worse role models out there. He agreed and even admitted that her music was *tolerable*, which, for him, meant he secretly liked it but would never confess.

"I should get going," I said, standing. Dorian opened his arms.

"It's good to have you home. I missed you." His grin was rare and real, but I caught the shadow behind it—the weight of everything he carried.

I looked up at my brother and smiled in return. "It surprisingly feels good to be back." As the words left my mouth, I realized I wasn't lying, not even a little.

It really *was* good to be back in Woodstone Falls.

SEVEN

Dotty

HOME · MATTHEW HALL

RENOVATING THE CABIN HAD QUICKLY BECOME A FULL-TIME job. Instead of enjoying my vacation hours, I was knee-deep in repairs, barely finding time to catch my breath. But despite the exhaustion, seeing the space transform before my eyes made it all worthwhile.

The hours I spent working in silence weren't just physically demanding—they gave me time to reflect. Why was it so important to fix this place instead of letting it sit and gather dust?

The cabin wasn't just an old building; it was a symbol of something bigger. It represented a fresh start—a chance to prove to myself that I could create something beautiful not only on paper but also in real life.

What Dorian said kept replaying in my mind, and deep down, I knew he was right. Spending the time, money, and energy fixing up the cabin wasn't just a project—it was a challenge I needed. It pushed me out of my comfort zone, out of my routine.

Even if the place was full of goddamn mice.

It was no longer filled with trash, and I'd called an

exterminator, who was scheduled to come next week. I spent hours plastering holes in the walls, cleaning out years of accumulated dust, grime, and dirt. It wasn't quite livable yet, especially since it needed furniture, but it was finally starting to come together.

Realizing I was in over my head, I decided to hire a home inspector to get a clear picture of the major repairs. Designing homes was my forte, but assessing structural damage? Definitely not.

The inspector, Austin, arrived that morning and got to work. While he went through the ins and outs of the house, I stayed upstairs, pulling up the last of the old carpet. Just as I yanked free the final stubborn piece, I heard him call out that he was finishing up.

"One sec," I yelled, dusting off my hands before hurrying downstairs.

Resting my hand against the kitchen counter, I huffed out a breath. "So, how bad is it?" I braced myself.

"It could be worse—much worse. No foundation issues. Your roof needs to be replaced, along with an outdated electrical system. The plumbing could use some updates, but nothing major. An updated HVAC system wouldn't be a bad idea, but overall, you're looking pretty good. I'll send you a full report in the next couple of days."

Austin's neatly trimmed dark, wavy hair and sharp brown eyes gave him an air of quiet confidence. A hint of stubble lined his strong jaw, and his fitted flannel shirt accentuated broad shoulders that showed the kind of strength earned from hard work. His easy smile and relaxed demeanor put me at ease, even as I mentally tallied the laundry list of repairs.

"Great, thanks. I wasn't sure what to expect."

In truth, it sounded expensive—more than I had anticipated spending before coming to Woodstone. Luckily, I'd saved a considerable amount over the past few years, giving me the disposable funds to tackle a project like this. It was an investment, sure, but one I believed would pay off in more ways than just financially.

"It has really good bones. With some TLC, it'll be a great home," he said with a small smile.

Austin was a few years older than Trent, Dorian, and me, but I didn't know him well growing up. We only really crossed paths later, when we ended up at the same university in Seattle. It had been nice to have a familiar face from Woodstone in the city, even if he was a few years ahead of me. He had earned his MBA before returning to Woodstone to help his dad take over the family business. After he moved back, we lost touch, but he'd always be a happy, familiar face whenever I ran into him.

"Yeah, I think so too. How's business going?" I said, wiping the sweat from my forehead with the back of my arm as I walked to the kitchen sink to wash the dust from my hands.

Austin swayed on his feet. "It's been great. My dad's been able to step back, and my brother and I handle most of the day-to-day operations now. How have you been? I haven't seen you in years."

"I'm good. Just visiting and trying to fix this place up before heading back to Seattle."

"I didn't realize you stayed there after college," he said.

"Yeah, it's great. I love it there, but it's nice to be back in Woodstone for a bit, too."

"For sure." He smiled, his lips twitching like he wanted to say more but decided against it.

There was no denying that Austin was attractive.

Thinking back to college, he'd always been friendly and kind —qualities that hadn't changed. If Noah were here, she'd probably kick me for not asking him out. She was always nudging me to get back out there, but dating wasn't my priority. My life was comfortable the way it was, and I wasn't interested in introducing another unpredictable factor into it.

"Thanks for everything. I'll walk you out."

"No problem at all. It's great to see you. Good luck." He slid his business card across the kitchen counter.

"Thanks, Austin. Take care."

As I walked him out, I spotted Trent's truck in the distance, pulling up the driveway. They acknowledged each other with a wave before Austin drove away. Trent jumped out of his truck, looking annoyingly attractive in his hat and boots. His whole image screamed rugged cowboy, which did things to my insides that I really didn't want to analyze too deeply.

"You checking me out, Dot?" he teased, his grin widening as he strolled up.

"Once again, keep dreaming." I crossed my arms, trying to ignore the heat creeping up my cheeks.

"Yeah, sure." He cocked a brow.

"What do you want me to say?" My voice rose an octave. "Oh, Trent. I just can't help it. These small-town boys are built different."

"That's more like it," he said, just as I added, "You know, the small-town type—cocky, arrogant, and annoying as hell."

"Yeah, right. I know you missed me," he shot back.

"You're delusional."

"Ouch." He clutched his chest dramatically. "You wound me."

"You'll survive." I patted his shoulder, resisting the urge to let my hand linger.

His grin widened, dimples cutting into his cheeks, and for a second, I forgot how to breathe. Trent always had that effect—annoying as it was. He chuckled, narrowing his eyes like he knew exactly what I was thinking.

As I climbed the front porch steps, he sighed and said, "It's been a few days since I've been here. Busy with the ranch. Thought I'd stop by to check out the progress. Maybe we can head into town and grab whatever supplies you need?"

I folded my arms, glancing at the cabin. "There's still some prep work to do before I paint, but I've been meaning to grab sample cans to see what works best in the space. I also need to pick up supplies for the roof."

"What else did Austin say?" Trent asked, frowning as he tilted his head to study the cabin.

"The roof, electrical, plumbing," I said with a sigh. "And probably a new HVAC."

"I can help with the roof," he offered casually. "Did mine a couple years back. I'll help you pick out what you need."

"Oh, thanks. That's a huge help, but it seems like a lot. I can just hire someone."

"Nah, I can rope Colt and Dorian into it. Maybe Sawyer, too, if his season hasn't started. Between us, it'd take a weekend, tops. I can call Henry and Chris if we're short-handed."

"That would be amazing." I grinned. "I'll feed you guys and maybe even take you out for beers after."

Trent's expression shifted, and he smiled.

"What?" I asked.

"Did we just have a normal conversation?" His dimples made a reappearance.

"Don't ruin it." I rolled my eyes and headed for his truck, ready to make the drive to Harmony Hardware.

"Admit it, Dot. You like having me around."

"I like the silence when you're not talking," I shot back.

"So you do like me. Just in very small, quiet doses."

"Don't push your luck." Tossing a smirk over my shoulder, I climbed into his truck.

"Too late," he said, low and amused, and damn it if I didn't feel that somewhere deep inside.

Our trip to Harmony Hardware was a success. Miraculously, we found everything we needed for the roof and even picked up a few extra things.

Walking the aisles with him felt weirdly…normal. Familiar in a way I hadn't let myself feel in a long time. We even laughed. Like, actual laughter. No sarcasm required.

Eventually, we split—he had cattle to check on, and I needed caffeine like my life depended on it. It didn't matter that it was late afternoon. Desperation doesn't check the clock.

Woodstone Perks was buzzing with quiet chatter when I stepped inside. Aiden stood behind the counter, wiping down the espresso machine, his usual easy smile already directed at me.

"Told you I'd be back," I said, returning his smile.

"Hi, Dotty. Good to see you. Same as last time?" he asked, wiping his hands on his navy-blue apron.

"Yes, please. I'm paying this time, don't argue with me."

I handed him my card and gave him the full force of my don't-even-try-it glare.

He held his hands up in mock surrender. "Yes, ma'am. Anything to avoid being on the receiving end of that face again."

"Smart man," I muttered as he swiped the card.

After signing off on a tip large enough to cover my last visit, I moved to the other side of the bar to wait for my drink.

"It'll be right out for you," he called over his shoulder, already busy working his magic at the espresso machine.

I let my eyes wander to the artwork on the walls, losing myself in the abstract swirls and muted tones, until a familiar voice brought me back.

"Dotty, hey. It's good to see you. How're you holding up?"

I turned to find Pastor Jeremy standing nearby, coffee in hand, smile kind and familiar.

"Hi, Jeremy. I'm good. I'll be in town longer than expected, working on the cabin, but it's been a good distraction."

Though grief still tugged at me, I'd made peace with the loss. Working on the cabin felt like honoring my grandpa in a way I hadn't expected.

"That's wonderful to hear. We'd love to see you on Sunday. The doors are always open for you."

I felt a little uneasy at his comment but brushed it off. "Thanks, I appreciate that."

Jeremy's order was called, and he gave me a quick nod before grabbing his drink. "Well, it was good to see you, Dotty. I'm sure I'll see you around."

"You too," I said. "Take care." The bell above the door jingled as it closed behind him.

As I stood there, coffee cup in hand, I realized how much the little things—the warm greetings, the familiar faces, the rhythm of a small-town afternoon—were starting to settle something inside me. I'd dreaded coming back to Woodstone, but maybe this place had more to offer me than just memories.

Aiden called my order, and I grabbed my cup, ready to take on the rest of the afternoon.

EIGHT

Trent

SHAKE THE FROST - TYLER CHILDERS

I barely had the truck door open before Gracie came flying at me like a pint-sized rocket. I stepped out just in time to catch her mid-air, staggering back a step as she threw her arms around me and squealed into my ear.

"Uncle Trent!"

I laughed, holding her tight. "Whoa there. You trying to take me out?"

She was heavier than I remembered—still all limbs and elbows, but longer, leaner, and definitely not the tiny nugget I'd hugged when I first got back to Woodstone. It hadn't been that long, a couple of years maybe, but somehow she'd gone from toddler to little human with opinions.

"I missed you!" she said, grinning up at me with a proud little gap where her front tooth used to be.

"Missed you too, sweets," I said, ruffling her hair. "You lose that tooth in a bar fight, or what?"

"No!" She giggled. "I put it under my pillow, and the tooth fairy gave me money!"

"Well, clearly I'm in the wrong business. Let's go see

what kind of treasure that fairy left behind." I let her grab my hand, and we headed inside.

Dorian's place was nice. Sleek and modern, but warm too. You could tell he'd made it a home, not just a house. It still messed with my head sometimes, seeing my best friend as a full-blown dad. He'd stepped up in ways most people wouldn't, especially after everything with Gracie's mom. He deserved more credit than he ever took.

And me? I was just the guy who showed up with a hammer and bad jokes.

Dorian was the closest thing I had to a brother—besides Dotty, if I could still count her as part of the equation. The three of us had been glued together as kids. Even now, he was the one person who saw through all the bullshit. He could read me like a book, even when I was trying my best to play it cool.

I'd had a good childhood, mostly, but not having my mom around left a hole I didn't know how to name until I was older. And when my dad died... everything just changed. Dotty was getting ready to leave for Seattle. Dorian was in college. I felt stuck in place, like I'd missed the turn everyone else had taken.

So I joined the military. Just like that. One late-night impulsive decision, one long drive, one signed form. I was usually more of a go-with-the-flow kind of guy, but back then, I needed structure, something solid to grab onto. And the army gave me that.

It knocked the cocky fucker right out of me, at least for a little while. Taught me how to show up, how to lead, how to lose. I made friends I'd take a bullet for. I also lost one I still think about when the nights get too quiet. That grief reshaped something in me.

Eight years later, I came back different. Not totally changed, but steadier. Less reckless. More grateful.

Through it all, Dorian never let me drift too far. Even when we were halfway across the world from each other, he'd check in. Just that steady presence I always knew I could count on.

Some people are anchors like that. He's mine.

And maybe—if I stopped screwing things up—Dotty could be too again.

"Hey, man. Good to see you," I said, stepping into the kitchen where Dorian was leaning against the counter. Gracie's small hand still clung to mine. "This one nearly knocked me flat on my back. She's getting huge."

I let go of her hand, and she skipped off to the dining table like it was her throne.

Dorian chuckled. "She told me she was gonna tackle you. I just didn't think she meant it literally."

"Daddy, what does literally mean?" Gracie asked, tilting her head.

"It means… literally. Like, when something is literal," he stammered, scratching his neck.

She squinted at him. "That doesn't make sense. I thought you were a doctor."

I laughed. "She's got you there. You used the word in the definition. Rookie move."

"That's enough out of you," Dorian muttered, trying to hide a smile. "Gracie, go wash up. Dinner's almost ready."

"Okay, Daddy. Can I play until it's ready?"

"Sure thing."

She gave my leg a quick hug before darting down the hall, leaving behind the scent of shampoo and whatever glittery bath product kids used these days.

Dorian dropped into a chair, folding his arms. "So what's up? Didn't expect your text."

I brushed some dried mud off my jeans, then sat down. "Been running myself ragged, honestly. That bug's still working its way through the herd, and two of the ranch hands called out sick, so I've been doing everything short of milking the damn cows myself."

He snorted. "I'd pay good money to see you try."

"Add it to the town fundraiser," I smirked. "On top of that, I've been helping Dotty with the cabin."

He raised a brow. "She's letting you help?"

"She's not thrilled about it," I admitted. "But I think I'm slowly wearing her down. I mostly work on stuff when she's not there, so she can pretend I didn't."

Dorian gave me a long, knowing look. "Are one of you ever gonna tell me what actually happened?"

I sighed and leaned back in the chair. "Nothing happened. We just… went our separate ways."

"Funny. She said the same thing." He paused. "But you don't go from being best friends to strangers over nothing."

I rubbed the back of my neck and groaned. He'd asked me that a dozen times over the years, and I didn't have a better answer now than I did then.

The oven beeped, saving me. Thank God.

He stood and grabbed the food from inside. "So how's the cabin coming along?"

"It's getting there. Needs a new roof. That's kinda why I stopped by. Wanted to see if you'd be up for helping. We've already picked up the materials, just need more hands."

"I'm in," he said without hesitation. "I'm out of town this weekend, but I'll drag Colt over next. Should knock it out easy."

"Appreciate it. Where are you headed?"

"Seattle. Vet conference."

I raised a brow. Dorian leaving town was a rare sight. "Gracie going with you?"

"Nah. Dotty's watching her, so she will be out of your hair for the weekend."

He shot me a look that was way too smug for my liking.

"Don't," I said.

"I didn't say anything."

"You looked something."

He smirked, but thankfully let it drop as he called Gracie for dinner. She bolted into the room like she hadn't seen me in years, then climbed into her chair and launched into a full rundown of her day—including tooth fairy economics, playground drama, and a passionate plea for Ellie Miles tickets.

As I listened to her ramble, smiling like an idiot, I felt it settle in my chest again—that quiet reminder of why I came back.

After everything—the military, the noise, the grief—I needed something that felt steady. Woodstone was that steady. This house, this table, the laughter floating between bites of dinner… it was all the kind of peace I didn't know I needed until I came home.

Dorian and I caught up between bites, slipping back into our rhythm like no time had passed. He talked about the clinic being slammed, and I told him about the ranch—how there was always something to fix or fence to mend, but I wouldn't trade it. Not for anything.

After Gracie went to bed, we migrated to the couch and watched reruns of old nineties sitcoms. We didn't talk much, didn't need to. Silence had never been weird with Dorian. It was the good kind.

It was well past ten when I finally decided to head back,

hoping Dotty would already be tucked away in her room for the night.

Thinking about her stirred a knot in my chest—I wanted to be near her, but knew I needed to keep my distance.

"I think I'm gonna head out," I said, pulling my boots on.

Dorian cleared his throat. "You know…" He paused for a moment. "You really can talk to me about Dotty. You *should* talk to me. Lord knows you don't talk to anyone else."

I shrugged, trying to keep it casual, but hell, I knew he was onto something. "Nothing is going on," I replied.

Because really, nothing was going on between us, at least right now.

He gave me that knowing look. "It just seems off. You dodge her for years, then suddenly you offer her a place to stay? After all that distance? And now she's crashing with you? Doesn't add up."

His words hit hard. I couldn't explain why I let her stay. Part of me wanted to be close, but another part told me to keep my distance. Made zero sense, and I hated that.

"I care about you both, but Dotty hasn't been back here in ten years. I'd hate for things to go wrong and for her to disappear for another decade." His words seemed to carry an unspoken message: I know she left because of *you.*

I shook my head, forcing a grin that didn't reach my eyes. "Nah, man. It's nothing like that. I offered her a place because we're friends." Well, acquaintances—if we're being technical—but I wasn't about to admit that. "You know I care about her. Always have. She's like a sister to me."

Lying sucked, and the words felt sour in my mouth, but I needed to give him something to hold onto.

The truth was, Dotty was definitely not a sister to me.

My thoughts about her, especially late at night when she slept only a few feet away, were anything *but* brotherly.

That knot in my chest tightened. Like always, I wondered if I'd ever be enough for her. Even Dorian's concern felt like proof that I wasn't.

My tattoo burned suddenly like the ink had just been pressed into my skin instead of settled there for years.

I pulled up into the driveway, and already a familiar ache was creeping behind my eyes. With a resigned sigh, I headed inside, bracing myself to face Dotty.

My usual easygoing streak had vanished somewhere between that talk with Dorian and the nonstop grind of ranch work, fixing up the cabin, and doing my best to avoid Dotty. It felt like I was being pulled in every direction, my brain stuck in a fight it wouldn't quit.

I wanted to be near her—to see her, talk to her—but I just couldn't. Being close to her was like stepping into a storm that never passed, dragging up every damn thing I wished I could forget. And honestly, I understood why she barely tolerated me. Hell, if I were her, I'd probably feel the same.

But fuck, I wanted her.

I tossed my keys on the counter and dropped onto the bench to kick off my boots. Her scent was still in the air— sweet, maddening, and *her*.

Did she have to smell so fucking good?

I kept my eyes on the floor, not wanting to meet hers as she sat on the couch. After a day like today, my walls were down, and I wasn't sure I could hold it together if I looked at her.

"Hey," she said quietly. "I'll get out of your way. Was just about to crash for the night." She grabbed her laptop and water bottle—the one with all the stupid stickers all over it.

I grunted, offering nothing more.

"Alright then." She tucked a strand of hair behind her ear, pausing just long enough to chip at my resolve. "Did you talk to Dorian and Colt about the roof? I want to make sure before I plan anything else."

"Next weekend," I said, voice tight and closed off.

"Okay. Sorry to bug you. Good night."

"Mhm." I kept my reply short and headed for my room before she could say more.

The door closed behind me, and I let out a sharp breath. I hated myself for it, yet I couldn't bring myself to regret it. I had to learn to keep my distance because, despite everything, I would always be fucking greedy for more of Dotty James.

And wanting her was a battle I was destined to lose.

NINE

Dotty

WHO'S AFRAID OF LITTLE OLD ME? - TAYLOR SWIFT

OVER THE PAST WEEK, TRENT HAD NEARLY PERFECTED THE FINE art of avoidance; communicating with me through little more than grunts and nods. Not that I particularly cared. I didn't exactly have the time or energy to unravel why my very existence suddenly seemed to offend him.

This hot-and-cold routine was completely new for him, at least where I was concerned. Trent had always been the happy-go-lucky type, the guy who cracked jokes and lightened every room he walked into. He was not the kind of man who brooded like one of my grumpy brothers. Yet here he was, leaving extra coffee in the pot for me every morning, stocking the freezer with my favorite ice cream and snacks, while simultaneously acting like I was the last person in the universe he wanted to see. Kindness in action, total cold shoulder in attitude.

I'd long accepted that understanding the male psyche was beyond me—and frankly, I had no desire to decode Trent Akers.

I zipped up my bag, double-checking I'd packed

enough activities to keep Gracie busy for the weekend. Just as I opened the door to leave, I nearly ran straight into Trent.

Of course.

Every time I saw him, it still took a second to reconcile the man in front of me with the boy I grew up with. The Trent I remembered had been all limbs and too-long hair, with a tragic excuse for a mustache and a grin that got him out of trouble. But the man standing before me was tall, broad-shouldered, and all too grown-up. His dimple, the one that only appeared when he smiled, was still there.

He raised a brow at me, catching my lingering gaze.

I cleared my throat and looked away, adjusting the strap on my bag. "I'm heading to Dorian's for the weekend," I said, forcing my voice to sound casual. "I'll be watching Gracie while he's at the conference. I should be back Sunday night or Monday morning."

"He told me," he said. "Any updates on the cabin?"

"The electrician's coming out next week to take a look. That's it for now." I shrugged.

"You leave in two weeks?"

"Yup," I replied.

"We'll get it done," he said. "Don't worry. Have fun with G, and tell her I said hi."

"Are you coming to dinner on Sunday?" I asked, already bracing for the answer.

"Not this week," he replied.

I nodded and stepped to the side to pass him, but he didn't move right away. His eyes met mine—all soft, unsure, and so damn green. Everything else about him had changed. But those eyes? They hadn't at all. For a beat, we just stood there, stuck in that strange middle ground between past and present, unsure who we were to each other now, or what to do with it.

Eventually, I cleared my throat and slipped past him, heading for the door.

"Hey, Dot?" His voice stopped me in the doorway.

I turned back, my grip tightening on the strap of my bag. "Yeah?"

"Text me when you get there safely, yeah?"

He winked. He really fucking winked.

This man, who had spent the entire week pretending I was air, had the audacity to wink like we were still on good terms. Like we were still us.

I rolled my eyes and walked out before he could say anything else.

I climbed into Sawyer's truck. With him back in San Francisco for the season, it worked out well for me to borrow it while I was here. I tossed my bag in the passenger seat and started the engine.

As I backed out of the driveway, I could still feel Trent's eyes on me, and worse, the flutter in my stomach from that damn wink.

This man was going to be the end of me.

I pulled up to Dorian's house, grateful for the break from Trent's home.

Before I could knock, the door flew open, and Dorian pulled me into a hug.

"Hey, I missed you," he said, in that voice he reserved only for a very short list of people.

"Don't go soft on me," I teased, hugging him back. "I saw you, like, two days ago."

"I know." He didn't let go right away. "Still good to have you home."

Dorian had always been quietly affectionate, at least with me and Gracie. He didn't wear his heart on his sleeve the way Sawyer did, who practically announced how much he loved people with a bullhorn. Dorian's loyalty ran just as deep, but he kept it closer to his chest. You had to earn it, and once you did, he never let you forget it. Colt and I were the quieter ones in the family—reserved to a fault, but steady in our own way.

"The longer I'm here, the harder it is to leave," I admitted as we stepped inside. "Seattle has its perks, but this…" I motioned around his warm, lived-in house. "This feels more like home than anything else."

He nodded, shutting the door behind us. "You could always stay."

"My life's in Seattle."

"Yeah, yeah. Keep making excuses."

Before I could answer, a flash of pink tulle rounded the corner.

"Auntie Dotty!" Gracie squealed, twirling in what could only be described as a princess explosion. "Look at me! I'm a real princess!"

"You absolutely are," I said, picking her up and planting a kiss on her cheek. "The most beautiful princess I've ever seen. Is this for Halloween?"

She nodded, her curls bouncing. "I have to practice saying *trick or treat* so I get the good candy!"

"With that smile? Girl, you're gonna clean the whole neighborhood out." I set her down and crouched to her level, lowering my voice. "Guess what I brought? Nail polish. Face masks. And… Lip gloss!"

She gasped. "Really?"

"Shh," I whispered, glancing toward the kitchen. "Don't tell your dad."

"I heard that," Dorian called, pretending to scowl as he packed something on the counter.

Gracie crossed her arms with a huff. "Daddy never does the fun stuff with me. Ugh, boys just don't get it."

We both laughed, but when I glanced at Dorian, I caught it—that flicker of something in his eyes. A quiet kind of guilt, one I knew too well. He was doing everything he could, but even the best dads couldn't be everything.

"Well, lucky for you, I'm in town," I said, brushing a curl off her forehead. "We're doing all the girly stuff."

While Gracie ran off to her room, Dorian went over her routine like it was a military operation. He handed me a neatly written list of emergency contacts, double-checking it before he finally let himself relax.

"Take a deep breath," I said, giving his arm a squeeze. "We've got it covered. Enjoy your trip. Don't worry about us."

"Love you, Dotty. Thanks for this," he said, pulling me into one more hug.

"Love you too. Drive safe. Send updates."

As the door shut behind him, I pulled out my phone to text Trent—realizing I hadn't told him I made it.

Sorry, forgot to text earlier. I'm at Dorian's.

TRENT

Forgot about me already?

I guess you are easily forgettable.

Brutal. Guess I'll have to try harder.

Good luck with that.

You know, you're still mean as hell. Even in your old age. Guess some things never change.

Hey, I've been told I age like fine wine.

I don't like whoever told you that.

But they're not wrong.

Relax, it was my best friend.

Anyway, I'm being summoned by the tiny princess. Talk later.

Counting down the minutes

Smiling to myself, I slipped my phone into my pocket—still half-annoyed and half-amused—then turned to find Gracie standing there with her hands on her hips.

"Ready for the best girly weekend ever?" I asked, reaching for her hand.

"Duh," she said, already tugging me down the hall toward her room.

And just like that, I let myself be dragged into a weekend full of glitter, princesses, and the exact kind of chaos I needed to keep my mind off everything else.

After two at-home mani-pedis, a glitter explosion, and a full-blown princess movie marathon, I finally got Gracie tucked into bed. She'd fallen asleep mid-sentence, still wearing her tiara. I tiptoed out of her room, grabbed my phone off the counter, and realized I hadn't checked it in hours.

NOAH

> Hey, call me when you get a sec. Miss your
> face.

I tapped her contact to video call and propped the phone up on the bathroom shelf while I pulled my hair into a bun.

She picked up on the second ring, her skin glowing under soft bedroom lighting and her signature oversized sleep tee slipping off one shoulder.

"Hey!" she beamed. "I miss you. How's everything going?"

"It's actually been... good. The cabin's coming along. I'm not totally in over my head yet." I glanced at the time. "Did Dorian get there already?"

"No, not yet. That's not why I called, though." Her smile faltered just a touch. "I've got bad news."

"Okay... what's up?"

"You know how I was supposed to come visit next week? Spend some time before flying back?"

"Yeah?"

"Well, I'm stuck here instead." She winced, guilt written all over her face.

"That's okay," I said automatically, but I could already tell there was more.

"No, it's not. Work's been a mess with back-to-school, and I forgot I promised John I'd go with him to some ridiculous fundraiser dinner. I double-booked myself and totally dropped the ball."

I nodded, trying to keep my face neutral. "You've got a lot going on. It's okay. Seriously."

"You're being way too nice about this," she sighed. "But... I was thinking, maybe we could plan a trip this summer? If you decide to come back. Which, by the way, you should."

I smiled. "Yeah. That sounds perfect."

Noah was a kindergarten teacher with a savior complex and a to-do list longer than mine. Her boyfriend, John, worked in tech and always felt a little... curated. Like he was trying to be charming, but only because he'd read that it worked well in studies. Still, he made her happy, or at least, she said he did, and that was what mattered.

We caught each other up on everything we'd missed—school chaos on her end, construction chaos on mine. I told her about Gracie's princess outfits and the face masks we'd used that smelled like strawberries. She told me about a kid in her class who tried to sneak a lizard in his lunchbox.

After a while, I let out a yawn, and Noah leaned toward the screen, squinting. "Okay, you're fading. You look half-asleep."

"I'm fine," I said, rubbing at my eyes.

"Liar."

"You're right," I admitted with a groan. "The renovations are a good distraction, but I'm exhausted."

"Speaking of distractions... how's your grumpy cowboy roommate?"

I groaned. "Confusing. One minute he's teasing me like we're still fifteen, and the next, he won't even look at me."

She gave me a look. "Is he being a jerk, or is he being weird?"

"Weird mostly. It's like... I don't know, like he's mad I'm here, but also maybe not? I feel like I'm in a room with a landmine and no fucking map."

Noah snorted. "Men. Emotional toddlers with facial hair."

"Tell me about it. You'd think with three brothers, I'd have a better handle on this."

"Maybe he's just thrown off. I mean, you kinda dropped in out of nowhere. You don't just slip back into people's lives without kicking up a little dust."

I leaned against the sink, already feeling the crash coming. "Yeah, it will be okay. I'll figure it out."

"I know you will," she said gently. "Okay, now go get some sleep. You've got a niece to keep up with tomorrow."

"Alright, alright. Love you."

"Love you more. Night, Dotty."

"Night."

Sunday evening rolled around, and Gracie insisted on wearing her princess costume to family dinner. Honestly, I didn't even bother arguing. If it made her happy to live out her little fairy tale for one more night, who was I to stop it?

It felt strange to be back after so long, attending Sunday dinner at the ranch house again. Sunday dinners had been a constant growing up, a tradition that held steady no matter what the rest of the world threw at us. After everything that had happened, returning to this familiar place felt like stepping into something safe. Something that still existed, even when so much of the rest of my life had fallen apart.

When Mom died, those dinners took on a whole new meaning. Dad stepped up in ways I never expected. Even carrying his own grief, he balanced work and home like it was second nature, never letting the cracks show. Looking back, I knew it wasn't easy. He just made it look that way.

I could still remember that first Sunday after the accident. None of us expected to have a proper dinner with all that grief hanging between us. But Dad made a pot of his famous chili anyway. We sat around the table, and somehow the fact that we were still there made it a little easier. That tradition stuck, even as life pulled us apart—Dorian and me going to college, Sawyer's NFL career taking him away from Woodstone, Colt often traveling into Shadow Ridge for work. Still, no matter where we were, we found ways to keep the thread connected—whether it was an hour-long call or a quick text just to say, "I'm here."

Pulling up in front of the ranch house now, I almost heard Mom's voice in my head—calling us in for dinner or waving us off from the porch as the school bus rolled up. The house looked just like it always had, frozen in time. But my chest ached with all the memories tucked inside those walls.

Gracie was out of the car before I could even unbuckle her booster seat, sprinting up the porch steps like she was on a mission. "Hi, Papa!" she yelled, running into Dad's arms.

"Well, hey there, sweet girl!" Dad scooped her up. "How's your weekend with Aunt Dotty?"

"It's been amazing!" Gracie's face lit up as she rattled off the highlights. "She helped me ride my bike without training wheels!"

Dad laughed, then kissed the top of my head as he gave me his usual warm welcome. "Sounds like a good time."

"Hi, Dad," I said with a small smile, feeling the grounding sense of home that wrapped around me the moment I stepped inside.

The scent of chili drifted in from the kitchen as we

settled into the living room, making me smile. Dad had already set the table—neat placemats, mismatched dishes, the whole deal.

The front door creaked open, and Colt strolled in, still in his uniform. Gracie launched herself across the room.

"Uncle Colt!" she squealed, arms flung wide.

Colt grinned, picking her up. "Hey, how's my favorite girl?"

"I'm so good! Auntie and I had the best weekend," she announced, her little face glowing. "How's my uncle?"

"Oh, I see how it is. Not your favorite uncle anymore?"

Gracie giggled. "I have lots of uncles, and Uncle Sawyer gets me lots of presents, but I think you both tie for first place."

Dad, walking past with a stack of bowls, chimed in without missing a beat. "Don't tell Trent. Poor guy's fragile."

"I'll take the tie," Colt said, holding Gracie close and letting out a soft laugh.

Gracie beamed and gave his cheek a dramatic kiss before wriggling out of his arms and disappearing down the hall to 'check on her dress.'

Colt turned to me with that steady presence he always carried, his expression softening. "Hey, Dot. How's the cabin coming?"

While Dorian and I shared a deep, unspoken connection as twins, Colt and I shared a different kind of bond. We didn't need to fill space with words. He was more reserved than me, always had been, but somehow we understood each other anyway. He didn't push, didn't pry—just showed up, steady and solid.

"We're making progress. Slow but steady," I said,

bumping his arm with mine. "Roof's next. You free next weekend? I pay in pizza and beer."

He nodded. "I'm off shift. Count me in."

"Perfect. We could use the help." I smiled.

The oven timer beeped just as a knock sounded at the front door, and Dad walked over.

"I think it's for you," my dad called, his voice suddenly clipped and serious.

Something cold settled in my chest.

Before I could even process it, Colt was already on his feet, his body going rigid like he'd shifted into cop mode.

I glanced at Gracie. "Hey, sweet girl, want to work on your puzzle for a bit? Or maybe find a movie?" I handed her the remote with a smile I didn't feel, then followed the tension straight to the front of the house.

A teenage girl stood on the porch, awkward and wide-eyed, holding a bouquet of white lilies.

My stomach dropped.

Colt stepped forward. "What do you know about this delivery?" His tone was sharp enough to make the poor girl flinch.

"I—I don't know much," she stammered, shifting her weight. "I just deliver them. I can ask Mrs. Sterling when I get back to the shop. She handles the orders."

Colt handed her his card. "Have her call. Tonight."

She looked from him to me, eyes wide. "Is something… wrong with the flowers?"

Before Colt could make it worse, I stepped in. "No, not at all. You didn't do anything wrong. It's just—" I let out a breath. "I've been getting flowers from someone anonymously, and we're trying to figure out who. That's all."

The girl visibly relaxed. "Oh. Okay. Thanks…" She

offered a nervous smile, gave the lilies one last glance, then hurried back to the van.

I watched her pull away before looking down at the bouquet in my hands—another set of white lilies. Same as the last ones. And the ones before that.

Colt didn't wait. He grabbed the note tucked between the stems, his jaw clenching as he read it.

"What the hell is this, Dotty? Since when does he say shit like this?" he growled, running a hand over his stubbled face.

I took the card and read it.

Soon, Dotty James, you'll be mine. I promise.

I went clammy all over. My palms, my spine, the back of my neck—like my body had sounded the alarm before my brain caught up. My tongue felt too big in my mouth, and I couldn't think past the scratch of panic at the back of my throat.

I swallowed hard. "This is the first one that's felt… like this. The others were weird, yeah, but they were vague. This is different. This feels personal."

My dad's expression darkened as he looked to Colt. "That's a problem."

Colt was already pacing into the next room, phone to his ear, barking orders into the line before I'd even registered what was happening.

"Who are you calling?" I asked, my voice hoarse.

"The station. You need to file this. Tonight. And I want the contact you worked with in Seattle."

I texted it over, fingers shaking so badly I had to retype

it twice. Colt didn't slow down—already rattling off badge numbers and case notes while my brain spun in place.

Until now, I could convince myself it was all just… annoying. Creepy, sure, but not serious. But this? This changed everything. Whoever he was, he'd gone from sending cryptic lines to making a promise. A claim.

I'd been trying to ignore it for months—brushing off the unease, rationalizing every note or bouquet that showed up at my door. But deep down, I'd always known I was being watched. Like someone was just a few steps behind me. Close enough to track my patterns. Close enough to find me here.

And now, I couldn't lie to myself anymore.

"This isn't just creepy. This is escalating," I said quietly, almost to myself. "He's getting bolder."

My dad wrapped an arm around my shoulders and pulled me close. "We'll keep you safe. If he's slipping up, that makes him easier to catch."

I leaned into him, the weight of it all pressing down. "Thanks, Dad."

He gave my arm a firm squeeze and led me into the living room. "I think you should stay. Don't rush back to Seattle. We've got more eyes on you here."

"He already knows I'm here," I said, sitting down on the couch.

"Yeah, but it's a small town," Dad said. "Someone new doesn't go unnoticed."

"I'll talk to work. See if I can stretch my time a little." I didn't want to stay longer than planned, but pretending everything was fine felt like a luxury I couldn't afford anymore.

"I just want you safe, sweetheart."

"I know," I said, my voice softer now. "I love you."

"Love you too, Dotty."

Colt came back in, dropping into the seat beside me. His jaw was tight. "The order was placed online under a fake name. They're tracing the IP now. Seattle PD's sending everything over." He rubbed a hand down his face. "Just keep your guard up."

Before I could respond, Gracie peeked around the corner. "Papa? I finished my puzzle. Can we eat now?"

Her sweet voice brought a sense of calm, and for a moment, it almost felt like everything was normal again.

Dinner was quiet. We went through the motions, tried to make conversation, but it all felt like background noise. Afterward, Gracie picked another princess movie, and Colt settled in beside her with a resigned sigh, throwing me a look that said I better get a medal for this.

Halfway through the movie, my phone buzzed with a call from Dorian.

I answered quickly and put it on speaker. "Hey. You on your way?"

"No, I'm staying another night. I wanted to let you know and say hi to Gracie."

Gracie immediately popped up like a damn jack-in-the-box. "Daddy! I miss you so much! I can't wait until you come home because you give the best hugs!"

Dorian chuckled. "I miss you too, G. Want me to pick you up from school tomorrow?"

Gracie squealed, already bouncing. "Yes! Yes! Yes!"

I barely got a word in before Colt plucked the phone right out of my hand.

"Hey!" I said, glaring.

He waved me off. "One sec, Gracie. I need to talk to your dad." He took it off speaker phone and held it to his ear. "Did you see my text?" he asked Dorian.

Dorian's sigh came through the phone. "Yeah. I won't be home tonight. Can you stay with the girls?"

Of course. Overprotective fucking brothers.

"Yeah, I'll stay with them." Colt shot me a look, his brow raised.

Gracie squealed again. "Sleepover!"

TEN

Dotty

JULY - NOAH CYRUS

Despite being a full-grown adult, I didn't argue when Colt insisted on staying with us. With Gracie involved, I wasn't about to put up a fight. He took Dorian's room, which left me with the couch—a win, honestly, considering it wasn't decades old like my dad's.

After brushing our teeth and getting ready for bed, Gracie and I curled up for a couple of stories. I kissed her goodnight, tucked her in, and waited until her breathing evened out before I slipped back to the living room. I sank into the cushions and stared up at the ceiling. The fan spun lazily overhead, its steady rhythm doing its best to calm the mess in my chest as I fell asleep.

I jolted awake to the sound of crying. Groggy and half-panicked, I shot up and followed the noise down the hall. Gracie was curled on the bathroom floor, her eyes glossy with tears.

"I got sick," she whimpered.

"Oh, sweet girl." I knelt beside her, touching her forehead.

Warm. Too warm.

"I think you've caught a bug, G—" But she leaned forward and threw up again before I could finish.

For the next hour, she stayed on the bathroom floor, her little body shaking with each wave of nausea. When she wasn't sick, she lay with her head in my lap, cheeks flushed and forehead damp with sweat. I stroked her hair, helpless to do anything but stay close and hold her.

Eventually, she quieted. I slid a folded towel under her head and asked gently, "Do you think you're okay for a sec? I want to grab you some medicine and a thermometer."

She gave the faintest shake of her head. "I think I'm okay."

I kissed her clammy forehead and quickly padded to the kitchen, the wood floors cold under my bare feet. The clock on the microwave glowed 2:13 a.m. as I grabbed the medicine and a thermometer, sending Dorian a quick text to let him know what was going on.

When I returned, Gracie hadn't moved. She was softly snoring now, her small body exhausted. I gently ran the thermometer across her forehead. It beeped—102.1.

Not good.

"Hey, Gracie, can you take this medicine for me?" I nudged her shoulder lightly.

She let out a groggy grunt but opened her mouth, swallowing the purple syrup with a faint grimace.

"Come on, let's get you back to bed."

I scooped her up and brought her to her room, setting towels, blankets, and a trash can nearby just in case. She curled into the sheets without a word.

Too drained to head back to the couch, I settled on the floor next to her, propping myself up with an extra pillow, and managed to doze off.

The soft hum of voices pulled me out of sleep. Groggy and stiff, I blinked up at the ceiling, momentarily disoriented until Gracie's giggle carried down the hall, mingled with Colt's deeper voice.

Every joint in my body protested as I sat up. Sleeping on the floor was a young person's game—and I was apparently no longer a contender.

I shuffled into the kitchen, and there she was. Wide awake and beaming like she hadn't spent the night curled around a toilet.

"Hi, Auntie!" Gracie said. "I feel much, much, much better. Thank you for helping me."

I dropped to my knees and pulled her into a hug, pressing a kiss to her forehead—cool now, thank God.

"I'm so glad, sweet girl." I held her a second longer than necessary, mostly to make sure she was real and breathing normally.

When I stood, I glanced at Colt. "How?"

"I called Dorian," he said, arms crossed. "He had anti-nausea meds in the cabinet. Gave her a dose. Worked like a charm. She even asked about school."

"Of course she did," I muttered, shaking my head. "She had Tylenol around two, so she's probably due for another dose soon."

"I've got it," Colt said, already moving toward the medicine. "You look like you're about ten minutes from passing out. Go sleep."

"I can stay with her until Dorian gets back," I argued, even though my limbs felt like wet spaghetti.

He gave me a look—head tilted, brows lifted, all no-nonsense big brother energy. "She's fine. Ate toast. Kept it down. You, on the other hand, look like you got hit by a truck."

I sighed, too tired to argue, and held up my hands in surrender. "Fine. But text me if anything changes."

He nodded. "I will."

Gracie waved at me. "Bye, Auntie! Love you!"

"Love you too, G."

I rolled the window down as I drove, letting the sharp fall air slap some life back into me. Downtown Woodstone Falls came into view, all charming storefronts and postcard-worthy stillness. Weathered cafés with chipped paint and warm light spilling through the windows. Hand-stitched leather goods in one display, a crocheted pumpkin garland in another.

It was everything Seattle wasn't—slow, familiar, unapologetically itself. A reminder of why I'd always loved this place, even when its charm used to feel more like a cage than a comfort.

After the drive through town, I pulled up to Trent's house and climbed out of the truck. The second I stepped inside, I was hit with that familiar scent—cedar and spice. Warm, woodsy. Pure Trent. It wrapped around me before I even saw him.

"Hey," he called from the living room. His eyes landed on me, and his whole expression shifted—brows pinched, face softening. "I thought Dorian wasn't back yet. Everything okay?"

"Gracie's sick," I said, barely recognizing the rasp in my voice. "She was throwing up all night. Colt stayed over. Just sent me home to sleep."

Trent straightened. "Colt stayed with you guys?"

"Yeah… there was another note. He didn't want to leave us alone."

His concern lingered, but something in his shoulders eased. "I'm sorry, Dot. You look wiped. Go rest. Sounds like you had a night."

I expected him to leave it at that.

Instead, he crossed the room and pulled me into a hug.

It caught me off guard—not just the contact, but how natural it felt. Like muscle memory. Like we hadn't spent years avoiding things we didn't know how to say. I didn't pull back. Couldn't, really. My body leaned in before my brain caught up.

When he finally let go, his hand lingered for a beat too long on my shoulder. "I've gotta head out to the ranch. Fence blew over. Text me if you need anything, alright?"

"Okay," I said quietly, watching him go.

The door clicked shut behind him, and the house settled into stillness. Just the faint scent of cedar, and the sudden, hollow ache of being left alone.

I woke up in a panic, drenched in sweat and gasping like I'd surfaced from underwater. My head pounded. My limbs ached, and the sour twist in my stomach confirmed what I already knew.

I was sick.

I'd known it was coming—staying up all night with a

feverish six-year-old didn't exactly scream immunity—but I'd still held out hope. Stupid, misplaced hope.

I reached for my phone. Nothing. No new texts. No missed calls. The screen glowed too bright against the dark room. With a sigh, I let it fall to the mattress and rolled onto my side, the sheets damp and twisted around me. The nausea rolled in again, low and steady, and I closed my eyes, willing it to pass.

Sleep pulled me back under before I could decide if it would.

The nausea hit hard and fast, no warning, straight from the dead of sleep. A twist in my stomach, and the bitter burn climbed up my throat before I could think. I barely made it to the bathroom before I was on my knees, heaving into the toilet.

Cold sweat beaded across my forehead as I reached blindly for a towel, clutching it against my chest like it might settle me. It didn't.

The chills came next—violent, full-body tremors that left me shaking and breathless. Whatever was in my stomach didn't stand a chance. It all came up in miserable, gasping waves.

By the time it stopped, I was slumped on the tile floor, too drained to move, too queasy to care. The towel was still clutched in my hands. My skin was clammy. Everything ached.

I didn't try to get up. I just lay there, waiting for it to pass.

Strong arms lifted me off the cold tile, and for a second, I wasn't sure if I was dreaming. My body barely registered the shift.

"Let's get you to bed," Trent muttered..

The scent of cedar hit me first. Then the warmth of his chest. Then the soft give of the mattress beneath me as he set me down. Everything felt familiar, wrong, and kind all at once.

When I cracked my eyes open, he was still there, leaning over me. Close. Too close. Light cut across his face, catching the lines of his jaw and the faint scruff dusting his skin. He looked impossibly handsome, unfairly steady, and entirely unreadable.

A cool press touched my forehead.

"101," he muttered. His brow pinched, and without a word, he handed me two pills and a glass of water.

Our eyes met as I took them without a word. I swallowed hard, the dryness in my throat catching. I wasn't sure if the shiver that followed was from the fever or the way he was looking at me.

"Thanks," I said quietly, voice scratchy, and my heart doing things I didn't have the bandwidth to unpack.

"You must've caught what Gracie had." His tone was gentle, but there was something beneath it—strain, worry, something too familiar. "You've been out for a while. Try to sleep. You need it."

He said it like a command, but not an unkind one. I wanted to argue. I didn't.

My eyes fluttered shut before I could think of a response, the weight of exhaustion was dragging me under.

I thought I imagined it—his voice, barely above a whisper, just before I slipped under again.

"Sweet dreams, sunshine."

A soft nudge pulled me out of whatever half-sleep I'd been stuck in. I blinked up to find Trent sitting on the edge of the bed, his hand resting near mine on the duvet.

"It's time for more meds," he said gently. "How're you feeling?"

"Like hell," I rasped. My voice was hoarse, barely there.

He hesitated. "Want some tea? Peppermint's supposed to help with nausea. Or I can run you a bath? What do you need?"

There was a crack in his voice he didn't quite manage to hide, and it hit me harder than the question itself. All that concern sitting right there on the surface, with no attempt to bury it.

"I'm fine," I mumbled. "I can take care of myself."

"I know you can, Dotty," he said softly. "Doesn't mean you have to."

I didn't have it in me to argue. I took the pills from his hand and reached for the water. I managed a sip, but the second I tried to swallow, it all got stuck. I tried to wash them down with another drink, but it was no use. The lump in my throat forced me to rush to the bathroom, where I emptied my stomach once again.

"Go away," I snapped, voice strained between dry heaves. "Let me throw up in peace."

He didn't.

Instead, I felt him kneel beside me, one hand gathering my hair, the other resting gently on my back.

"No," he said, calm and solid. "Not happening."

He didn't say anything else. Just stayed there while my body tried to turn itself inside out. When it finally stopped, I slumped against the wall, too wiped to speak. He didn't push. Didn't fill the silence. Just stayed close, quiet, and stupidly patient.

The rest of the day blurred. Fever dreams and cold sweats. Sleep that never quite stuck. I drifted in and out, half-aware of the world, half-lost to it.

But I always knew when he was near.

ELEVEN

Trent

SLUT! - TAYLOR SWIFT

THE LAST THING I EXPECTED AFTER A TEN-HOUR DAY ON THE ranch was to find Dotty passed out on the bathroom floor, covered in a towel.

It took some effort, but I eventually got her settled. Once she was lying down, I sat beside her, listening to the soft rhythm of her breathing. She was beautiful—always had been—and having her so close stirred a constant battle of emotions within me. The need to be close to her, to touch her, to be the one she smiled at was almost too much to take.

But then I'd remember how we left things all those years ago.

Dotty had built an incredible life for herself in Seattle, while I had nothing to show for the years that passed. Eight years in the military hadn't left me with a future I wanted. It gave me discipline, but it didn't give me peace. The ranch did. I needed the solitude, the quiet.

Still, I couldn't shake the feeling that my life would never measure up to hers. She had spent years proving herself in a badass career. And me? I was just a guy who had come home to work the land, hoping it was enough. I had been stationed in Tacoma during my enlistment, so close to her, and yet I was a world away.

I missed the camaraderie, the structure, the never-ending missions that kept me busy. It helped keep me from thinking about everything I was leaving behind. But I knew it wasn't a forever thing. The stress of constant change and looming responsibilities wasn't what I wanted for the rest of my life.

When David James offered me a chance to help run the ranch, I took it. My military contract was ending, and his offer was the final push I needed. I think my frontal lobe finally matured or some shit, I finally decided to stop running and returned home.

But sometimes I sat and wondered what would have happened if I hadn't joined the army.

If I would still be in Woodstone or if the situation between Dotty and me would have been any different. The unanswered questions haunted me, but I knew enlisting was the right decision, even if I didn't go about it the right away.

After my dad passed away in high school, I felt adrift. Dorian and Dotty were living their lives, and I was just existing. I had no ambitions and no plans. So, when an army recruiter approached me, I took it as a way to find some purpose.

Ten years ago, I rode off on the bus across the country, leaving my entire life behind. My body went with me, but my heart and soul stayed here in Woodstone with her.

It didn't matter the years that had passed, she would always be imprinted on my soul.

Dotty stirred in her sleep, a soft groan slipping from her lips, pulling me from my thoughts. Her eyes fluttered open, looking around as if unsure where she was. I handed her a glass of water.

"Here, take a sip. You've been out for a while. You must be thirsty."

"Thank you," she whispered, her voice rough. As she drank, I couldn't help but watch the delicate movement of her throat. Everything she did affected me, even the smallest of things.

"How are you feeling?" I asked, brushing a strand of hair behind her ear, seizing the moment while her animosity toward me seemed to be at bay.

"Better. What time is it?"

"Just after midnight. You've been asleep all day." Her hair was piled high in a messy bun, no makeup, and a flush still lingering on her cheeks. But even like this—disheveled and sick—there was something about her that made her more beautiful than ever.

"Oh, God. You really didn't have to look after me. I'm okay. Go get some sleep."

"I want to help," I said before I could stop myself. It felt vulnerable. "You've always been a big baby when you're sick. Can't leave you to fend for yourself. What do you need? I picked up some tea."

"Oh, shut it. You are the one who would always get the man-flu." She sat up and rubbed her eyes. "But yeah, tea sounds nice. Maybe if I can keep it down, I could try some toast."

I stood, offering her my hand. She looked up at me through long lashes, and for a moment, everything else disappeared. The warmth of her hand in mine triggered a domino effect of chills through my body.

After our first hug in a decade, I remembered exactly why I was trying to keep my distance. All it took was one single touch, and all I could think of was the feel of her waist under my calloused hand. How it might feel to drag my hand down her bare legs.

We walked into the kitchen, and I busied myself with the tea kettle. Dotty sat at the dining table, her tired eyes watching me.

"Thank you." Her voice was light and airy and fucking *everything*. "For everything—letting me stay here and invade your space, for taking care of me… I guess what I am trying to say is I appreciate it." Her voice grew strained, and I knew she was slightly uncomfortable giving me her gratitude.

"Anytime. I'd do anything for you," I said before I could think better of it.

Her gaze softened, and I could see the hesitation, the strain in her voice when she asked, "You would?"

"Of course. Always," I answered.

The kettle whistled, and I poured the hot water into our mugs. The smell of peppermint filled the air.

"Careful, it's hot," I said, smelling the peppermint as it steeped.

She smiled, looking down at her tea. "Do you remember Joanie Rivers? Well, I guess she would be Joanie Allen now, since she is married."

"You mean the Joanie Rivers whose brother I punched because she told everyone you peed your pants in sixth grade?"

"Yes, that one." She laughed, and the sound echoed in my head. I wanted to stop everything just to listen to it again and again.

"Yeah, but where the hell did that come from?"

"I ran into her when I first got into town. She was at Woodstone Perks with Garrett, who apparently is her husband now. He didn't say a single word to me, but she sure had a lot to say." She paused, taking a sip of her tea. "She ordered a peppermint tea and always smelled like peppermint growing up."

"I think she religiously popped breath mints and drank peppermint tea, thinking it would increase her chances of someone kissing her," I said, and she laughed again.

And God, that fucking laugh was intoxicating.

"Well, I couldn't exactly punch her, and her brother was just as bad, so it worked out. Who goes around spreading stupid rumors like that anyway?" I asked.

"Middle school girls. That's who. She was one of the lovely ones that decided to make fun of the fact that I didn't have a mom." Her eyes lowered to her tea as she swirled the tea bag.

"Her loss. You turned out better than all of them," I said, my voice firm. I wanted to tell her how much I respected her, but I didn't know how to make those words sound right. "Did you make any good friends in Seattle?"

She nodded. "Yeah, my roommate, Noah. She's like my sister. We met right when I moved, and we've been inseparable ever since. I'd go through those lonely years again just to have her in my life."

"Sounds like you've found your place," I said, my chest swelling a little. I was glad she wasn't alone anymore. She deserved that.

She let out a hum in response.

"Hey, I know this is kind of out of the blue..." I said, and cleared my throat. "But I have a wedding to go to in a few weeks for one of my military buddies. I RSVP'd for a plus one a few months ago when I was dating Sandra. I don't really want to go alone and look like a loser. Think you could put up with me for it? I'll feed you."

I did RSVP for two, although I didn't tell anyone who it was for but could easily go by myself. I should go by myself, but I just couldn't fucking stay away.

"Wait a second. You dated Sandra Barker? The girl who was mean to us our entire childhood? Best friends with Joanie Rivers?" she asked, her jaw dropping.

"Don't remind me." My hand brushed through my hair. "Not one of my finer moments."

Dating wasn't a big priority for me, especially since coming back home after years away, but when Sandra asked me out, I figured, why not? I had been dating her for two months when the invite came in the mail, and she convinced me to put her down as my plus one. We ended breaking up soon after that because she really was mean as shit.

"I don't know if I will still be in town. I need to call my manager and see if I can take more time off or possibly work remotely for a while, since the cabin isn't anywhere near ready yet. But if I'm here, I will put you out of your bachelor life misery for one evening," she teased, and it felt good to gain some traction with her.

"Perfect."

The hours slipped away as we caught up on everything that had happened over the past ten years. We reminisced about my time in the military and her journey through architecture school, discussing all the challenges and triumphs she faced in getting licensed. Glancing at the clock, I realized it was after three in the morning. A yawn escaped me.

"I should let you sleep. You probably have to work in the morning," she said, stifling her own yawn.

"I texted your dad saying you were sick, and he told me he has everything covered for the morning. I figured I'd be here if you needed me. I don't take a ton of time off work, so it might be good for me to have a lazy day anyway."

She gave me a soft smile. "Well, I'm going to take a shower and then head to bed. I'm sure once I start reading, I'll probably pass out right away, even after all that sleep today."

We parted ways, and I walked to my bedroom, closing the door behind me. I leaned against it and slowly sank to the floor, my mind going haywire with conflicting emotions. Talking to Dotty had always been effortless, and tonight felt like we had seamlessly returned to where we left off before everything fell apart.

Yet, I couldn't shake the sense that I was in over my head. Taking care of her, talking to her for hours, finding out what she's been up to, and learning about her friends— it all highlighted a painful truth.

I was no longer part of her life.

And that was going to make watching her walk away ten times harder. I didn't have the ability to watch her walk away before, and I knew I couldn't do it now.

I had to figure out how to keep my distance from Dotty if I had any chance of surviving when she leaves.

I threw my shirt over my head and glanced down at the tattoo on my chest.

The small outline of a sun had faded with time, but was still there, reminding me of everything good in the world, even if it was out of reach.

My sunshine.

TWELVE

Dotty

EVEN IF IT BREAKS YOUR HEART - ELI YOUNG BAND

THE WEEK FLEW BY IN A BLUR OF EMAILS, SAWDUST, AND LATE-night takeout, but at least it was productive. My manager approved an extra two weeks of vacation and gave me the green light to work remotely for the next three months.

I wasn't ready to leave Woodstone Falls—not yet. I missed the rhythm of the city, my job, and Noah's voice echoing through the apartment, but being here settled something in me. There was a quiet to this town I hadn't realized I needed.

Noah had been understanding, maybe even a little bummed when I told her. She promised to visit once things slowed down on her end. My manager, surprisingly kind despite our team drowning in deadlines, told me to take care of myself.

The cabin, however, was dragging. Contractors were knee-deep in structural repairs, which meant I was sidelined for now. Once they were done, the rest—flooring, paint, fixtures—I could handle myself. It was bleeding my savings dry, but it felt like the right kind of investment. Something rooted. Mine.

Today, Dorian, Colt, and Trent were on their way to help with the roof. I'd bribed them with snacks and beer. I wasn't above tactical hospitality.

The cooler was packed and waiting by the door when Trent emerged from his room. His hair was still damp from the shower, and his jeans casually hung on his hips.

"Ready?" I asked, adjusting the strap on the cooler.

"Yup," he grunted.

Conversations between us had taken a nosedive back into the monosyllabic. After talking for hours while I was sick—real, vulnerable talking—he'd gone quiet again. Not cold exactly, just… restrained.

His keys jingled as he grabbed them. "I'll drive. Supplies are in the truck," he said.

"Can we swing by Woodstone Perks? I called in coffee for everyone."

"Sure."

And that was that.

The ride to the cabin was filled with the sound of tires crunching gravel and the low hum of the radio. Every time I tried to start a conversation, I got short answers in return. Eventually, I gave up, settling into the silence.

After the quick coffee trip, we pulled up to the cabin to find Dorian and Colt already making themselves at home on the porch swing.

"I wouldn't trust that swing if I were you. Especially with the two of you," I called out, setting the cooler down. "But I brought coffee!"

Colt grinned, hopping up and pulling me into a hug. "Swing's solid. Just needs a little paint."

"I should get one for Gracie," Dorian added, testing the chain.

"She'd love it," I said, hugging him next. "Glad you're back. How was the trip?"

"Good. Thanks again for watching G. Sorry she got you sick. She's like a walking petri dish this time of year."

"We had fun before that. She's tougher than she looks."

"She doesn't get that from you. You and Dorian are the worst when you're sick," Colt said, slapping Dorian's back.

"Shut up," I said, punching his arm.

"He's not wrong," Trent added, finally jumping in. "You were a nightmare."

I shot him a look. "Oh, please. I was not."

"Alright," I said, clapping my hands, redirecting. "Let's get to work. Trent's got the supplies. We've got a roof to fix."

"Yes, ma'am," Colt said, tipping an imaginary hat.

We split into pairs, tearing off the old shingles. Dorian tried to argue that I shouldn't help, but I waved him off. This was my cabin. I wasn't about to sit on the sidelines while the guys did all the work.

The crisp air was tinged with the first hints of winter as each of us worked on our respective sections. The physical labor provided a welcome break for my mind. At one point, I noticed Trent and Colt had completed their sections while Dorian and I lagged, and Colt and Trent had both started helping remove shingles from our section.

By the time the old shingles were piled into trash bags and the tarp rolled up, we were filthy, sore, and halfway to delirious. Colt wiped the sweat from his brow and looked around.

"Not bad for a bunch of amateurs," I said.

Trent and Dorian laughed about something on the far side of the roof. Colt gave them a side-eye. "What are you two giggling about?"

"Garrett Allen," Trent said, barely suppressing a grin. "Dorian ran into him the other day. Asked if you were still around. Looked like he'd seen a ghost."

"Ah, the second-grade gum incident," Colt supplied. "He teased Dorian, and you went feral putting gum in his hair on the school bus."

"He called you both stupid dorks. I had to defend your honor." I shook my head. "It's a terrible insult. Contradictory, even."

"Thank fuck for contacts. I'll never have to get insulted in my dorky glasses ever again. The only person who sees me in them now is G." He chuckled.

"You're welcome, by the way," I said. "I had to lie to the principal, remember? Dad only found out a few years ago that it was on purpose."

We were all laughing now—loud, genuine, full-body laughter.

After a few hours, we laid the new tarp and started securing fresh shingles. Trent took the lead. Halfway through the job, he flipped his hat backward like he didn't already look unfairly good.

As we shoveled the last of the discarded shingles, Dorian broke the silence. "Looks like you and Trent are getting along better. Not at each other's throats anymore."

"I don't know about that," I said, trying to brush it off.

"I'm serious. You're getting along," Dorian insisted.

"Yeah, well, I'll be glad to have my own space back in Seattle," I said, though the words felt bitter.

"I wouldn't call that your own space. Noah seems to be a homebody," Dorian pointed out.

"She doesn't count. She's practically an extension of myself." I stopped and narrowed my eyes at him. "I didn't realize you two had talked while you were there."

Noah hadn't said anything to me about Dorian except that he showed up and seemed nice. Which was odd in itself, since Dorian typically was talkative to anyone outside of our family or Trent.

"What? You want me to just show up and not speak to her at all? She's nice. I can see why you're friends."

I eyed him suspiciously. "Don't get any ideas. She has a boyfriend," I warned.

"That guy's a dick," he scoffed.

"John? He seems nice to me," I said, continuing to clean up.

"Yeah, well, it's none of my business anyway," he shrugged, tying off a trash bag and tossing it into the bin.

"You're right. It's none of your business," I teased, slapping his shoulder playfully.

After everything was completed and cleaned up, I cleared my throat. "Well, gentlemen," I said, tossing out beers. "Job well done. Outlaw's later? Drinks on me."

"Don't have to ask me twice," Colt said.

"I'll check with Dad. If he's good with Gracie, I'm in," Dorian said, already texting.

"I don't know," Trent muttered, rubbing the back of his neck. "I'm beat."

"Oh, come on," Dorian replied, elbowing him. "Live a little."

"Yeah," Colt added. "You can't bail now."

Trent sighed and finally gave in, tossing me the keys. "Fine, but you're driving."

I caught them midair and rolled my eyes. "Fine, but you're buying the first round."

THIRTEEN

Dotty

TEQUILA - DAN + SHAY

Outlaws was alive with energy as we stepped inside. Neon lights bathed the room in a kaleidoscope of colors, casting a warm glow over the rustic decor. A vintage jukebox in the corner hummed classic country tunes, setting a lively rhythm to the buzz of conversations.

The bar was crowded with patrons nursing their drinks, bartenders expertly mixing cocktails and pouring beers. As we navigated through the crowd, the scent of whiskey filled the air. Almost every table was occupied, the hum of laughter and chatter growing louder with each step.

We exchanged waves and nods with familiar faces—neighbors and friends from around Woodstone. The atmosphere was contagious, even making Trent's usual cheer shine through. In the corner, an unoccupied pool table seemed to call to us, its green felt pristine, cues neatly lined up.

"Want to play while we wait for a table?" I asked, pointing to it with a raised brow.

"Let's do it. You're on my team, though," Dorian said,

already heading over. He grabbed a few cues and passed them around.

Trent's trademark smile grew as he and Colt took their spots. "Looks like it's you and me," he said. Colt responded with a noncommittal grunt.

Trent racked the balls. "Ladies first," he said.

I gave him a fake smile and lined up my shot. I pulled back and sent the balls scattering in one fluid motion. "Stripes," I declared as one sank. I pocketed two more before passing the turn to Trent and Colt.

Colt gestured to Trent with a smirk. "Ladies first."

Trent rolled his eyes and then aimed, sinking a solid with ease. Dorian groaned in response.

"What can I say? I'm a natural," Trent teased, grinning as he lined up another shot.

As we continued to play, Trent's effortless shots complemented my own calculated approach, while Dorian and Colt were mediocre at best and heavily relied on us to carry our respective teams.

Colt missed his shot yet again. "Fuck, I need a drink for this."

"Same," Dorian muttered, scratching his head. They made their way to the bar, leaving me to line up my next shot.

Trent came up beside me, with that infuriating smirk tugging at the corner of his mouth. "Need pointers, Dot?"

I gave him a sidelong glance. "I think I've got it covered. Thanks," I said, calculating internally how my next shot would play out.

He chuckled softly, his gaze lingering on me. "Just offering my expertise." He shrugged. "But it seems like you're already a pro."

I set the cue down and stuck my tongue out at him,

expecting a smart-ass comment or maybe a sarcastic bow. Typical Trent. But instead, he stepped in close—too close— and before I could register what was happening, he fucking grabbed my tongue between his fingers.

"What the hell?" I jerked back, swatting at his chest as heat flared across my face. "Are you insane?"

"You stuck it out like you're asking for trouble." His voice was low, playful, but the look in his eyes was anything but.

Then, he slowly brought his fingers to his mouth and sucked on them—just once, just enough to make my stomach do a damn cartwheel.

I stood there frozen, with the cue limp in my hand, trying to remember how my basic motor functions worked. My brain had exited the building.

"You're something else, Trenton Akers," I muttered, breath catching halfway through his name.

He grinned like he knew exactly what he was doing. That fucking bastard.

Still rattled, I forced myself to refocus. I bent over the table and lined up the shot. My hands weren't as steady as I would have liked, but muscle memory took over. Click. Thunk. One ball down. Then another. Clean, efficient, like I wasn't seconds away from combusting.

Behind me, he gave a low whistle. "Remind me never to bet against you when you're trying to prove a point."

"I've had practice," I said. "And being an architect doesn't hurt."

Spatial reasoning and angles? That was my jam. Half of my college bar tabs had been paid for in pool games. Math and a competitive streak—it was a dangerous combo.

Dorian returned with a tequila soda I hadn't asked for but definitely needed. I took it with a grateful nod.

"No drink for me?" Trent asked, taking his turn and missing.

"You didn't ask," Dorian said with a shrug.

"Neither did Dotty."

"Twin telepathy," I replied, clinking my glass to Dorian's.

The game carried on, and despite Dorian's... minimal contributions, we won.

As I racked the cues, I saw Henry approaching, Chris trailing behind.

"Hey," Henry greeted, eyes flicking to Trent before landing on me. "Didn't know you were out tonight." He directed his question to Trent, but it rubbed me the wrong way. I brushed off the feeling.

"Last-minute plan," Trent answered. "We finished the roof at Dotty's cabin and figured we earned a drink."

Henry nodded before turning to me. "How's the settling in going?"

"Good. I'll be sticking around through the end of the year," I replied with a weak smile.

His face lit up. "That's great. Any chance you've thought about my offer to take you out?"

Over the past several years, I kept my distance from anything resembling commitment, preferring the security of solitude over the unpredictable world of dating. Noah always insisted on finding *the one,* while I kept a more skeptical view, shaped by past disappointments, especially with my most recent ex-boyfriend. She had always been a hopeless romantic, while I was a pessimistic realist. We balanced each other out well.

Despite my wariness, I couldn't shake the feeling that maybe this was something worth exploring. Maybe *someone* worth exploring. Noah wasn't wrong—eventually, I had to stop standing still. I didn't want to end up alone forever, watching everyone else build something while I stayed safely on the sidelines. At some point, I had to take the first step. Maybe this was it.

Trent nudged me gently, a quiet reminder that Henry was still waiting for my answer.

I glanced at him—his eyes steady and expectant—and something shifted inside me. It was the same look he'd always had when pushing me, pulling me just beyond the edge.

"Yeah... sure, that sounds nice," I finally replied.

"How about Friday? The Cove? I'll pick you up at seven?"

"I'll meet you there," I said, aware of Trent beside me, silent but tense.

"Perfect. See you then." Henry smiled and turned to leave.

"See you guys around," Chris said, giving a mock salute before walking off with his brother.

I sipped my drink, watching the swirl of ice in the glass, and trying to quiet the sudden noise in my head. I couldn't tell if it was relief, guilt, or the subtle shift in Trent's jaw that made me uneasy.

And then, without warning, the past rose vivid and uninvited—summer days from years ago, when things were simpler but the stakes felt just as high.

"Slow down, Trent!" I called out, struggling to keep pace with him. The summer sun spilled gold over the fields, painting everything in that soft, late-afternoon light.

But Trent didn't slow. He just glanced back with that ridiculous grin, wild and carefree. Up ahead, Dorian jogged at a steady pace, calm as ever—always the quiet anchor to Trent's chaos.

By the time we reached the edge of the fields, I stopped, bent at the waist, trying to catch my breath. Trent didn't even notice. He just kept going, already halfway down the hill.

"Come on, Dotty!" he shouted over his shoulder. "We're almost there!"

He meant the creek. The one that ran just beyond the fence line, shallow and cold and always just out of reach for me. He'd been trying to get me to cross it all summer. Dorian had done it last week for the first time, but I'd stayed back—feet planted firmly on familiar ground where it felt safe.

Now I stood at the edge again, caught between the comfort of what I knew and the pull of Trent's voice.

Dorian must've seen it in my face, because he slowed beside me, voice quiet.

"You don't have to rush. Just go when you're ready. We'll be right here."

That was how it had always been—Trent pulling, Dorian steadying, me resisting. Somehow, it worked.

"You've got this, Dot," Trent called again. "I believe in you."

And maybe that was all I needed. Not a guarantee. Just someone who believed I could.

So I took a deep breath, and then I leaped.

Because Trent made me brave.

FOURTEEN

Dotty

SOMETHING IN THE ORANGE - ZACH BRYAN

MY FINGERS TRACED THE SOFT FABRIC OF MY SWEATER DRESS again and again—a simple, elegant choice I'd agonized over far too long. It was supposed to strike the perfect balance between casual and chic—at least, that's what I kept telling myself. But as I stared at my reflection, a hollow ache settled deep in my chest.

Tonight wasn't just any date. It was a date with Henry. And no matter how many times I adjusted the neckline or smoothed out a nonexistent wrinkle, I couldn't tell if the fluttering in my stomach was because of him—or simply because I'd agreed to a date at all.

I was lost in my spiraling thoughts when a shadow shifted behind me. I barely had time to turn before Trent appeared in the doorway, arms draped lazily over the frame. His stance was casual, but the sharp lines of his muscles pulled at the fabric of his shirt.

"Hey," he said. "Heading out?"

"Yeah," I said, smoothing my dress one last time, then glanced back at the mirror. "Date with Henry."

His reflection caught mine. His expression was unreadable, but his jaw ticked, barely perceptible.

"Don't forget the roommate rules," he said after a pause, his voice sharp.

A flicker of irritation sparked inside me. "I know," I snapped, grabbing my purse. Like I'd ever bring someone back here—especially one of his friends.

I brushed past him, desperate to escape whatever this was, but his hand closed around my elbow, stopping me dead in my tracks.

"What?" I scoffed, spinning to face him.

His green eyes locked on mine, searching. His thumb brushed lightly against my arm, and that small contact sent a jolt straight through me.

He didn't say anything at first, lips parting then closing as if weighing the risk. Finally, he exhaled—a flicker of vulnerability breaking through that stoic mask.

We stood frozen, the silence between us crackling with everything left unsaid. Then, just as suddenly as he'd stopped me, he released my arm and stepped back.

"Just... have a good time tonight," he said, voice low and rough. "Henry's a good guy."

What the hell?

My friendship with Trent, once a sanctuary, now felt like a web of conflicting emotions threatening to consume me whole. With one last glance over my shoulder, I stepped out into the hallway, my mind still reeling.

The soft glow of candlelight bathed the elegant interior of The Cove, Woodstone Falls' finest restaurant. Warm flickers of light danced across the room, creating a serene ambiance. Across the table, Henry's eyes sparkled as he recounted his latest arrest at the station.

"We were sitting on Main Street when Mrs. Williams sped through town at over sixty miles per hour in a thirty. I had to jump into the car so fast, I spilled my coffee!"

"Wow, can't say I'm surprised. Mrs. Williams has always had a lead foot." My smile faded as he continued his story.

I wanted to listen. I really did. It should have been refreshing—talking to someone who wasn't family, Trent, or Noah. After being away from the office for a while, I'd missed that kind of easy, casual conversation. But as Henry took a slow sip of his wine and the silence stretched, I realized I definitely didn't want to be here.

"What about you, Dotty? Any fun escapades of your own?"

"Just fixing up the cabin. It's been a lot of work, but honestly, kind of fun too. Nothing too crazy—definitely nothing as wild as your story. We did replace the roof last week, though, and convincing my brothers that drinking thirty feet up wasn't exactly smart was its own challenge." Henry grinned, but there was something off about it I couldn't quite place.

"Sounds like the James brothers, that's for sure. Always a wild bunch."

"That we are." My smile was genuine, but a small, nagging feeling of discomfort began to creep in. As the evening wore on, our conversation flowed, but I found myself growing increasingly restless. We talked about everything from my job in Seattle to his complaints about trying to keep up with mowing the grass at their family's ranch that now sat unused. We even discussed his brother Chris, who was busy working at the local auto shop.

The conversation was never strained, but it felt like nothing more than a friendly chat. Yet, there were moments when Henry's gaze lingered a bit too long, or his laugh seemed a touch too forced.

He excused himself to go to the restroom, and I was grateful for the break in conversation.

Henry was a good man—kind and attentive in all the ways that mattered. He had a good career, a good head on his shoulders, and there was no denying he was attractive.

But something was missing.

I couldn't see him in my life as anything more than a friend. My phone buzzed inside my purse, and I reached in to check it. The anxiety of the evening hadn't subsided, and I needed the distraction.

UNKNOWN NUMBER

Stop ignoring my notes.

Confusion settled over me as I stared at the screen. Texts from blocked numbers were nothing new—usually scams, nine times out of ten. But this one felt different, like a shadow brushing the edge of something I wasn't ready to face.

I shook my head, trying to shove down the rising unease. Probably a wrong number. Definitely just over-thinking it.

"Everything okay, Dotty? You look a little pale," Henry's voice pulled me back as he slid back into his chair.

I shoved my phone into my purse and forced a smile. "Yeah, just some spam text. Nothing serious."

"Ugh, those are the worst. I get them all the time. So annoying," he said with a chuckle, but his smile didn't quite reach his eyes.

We finished our meals, the conversation light but

lacking the ease from before that text came in. When the check came, Henry insisted on paying, though he finally let me cover the tip.

Outside, the night air was cool. Standing by his car, the weight of the evening pressed down on me—an inevitable moment I'd been quietly bracing for.

"I had a great time tonight," he said.

He leaned in, steady and expectant, but my body acted before my mind. I stepped back, feeling a sinking feeling in my chest.

"Thank you for dinner. It was a lovely evening," I said, voice soft but sure.

Henry shifted on his feet. "Why do I feel like there's a but coming?"

I winced. "But… I think we're better off as friends."

His eyes flickered—anger, frustration, maybe—but he swallowed it down, folding it into a tight smile. "Can't say I'm not disappointed. Thought we had something, but friends, it is."

"Thanks again, Henry."

"Yeah, any time. I'll let you go. Have a good night."

"Night," I said.

I watched him walk away, the click of his car door loud in the quiet parking lot.

Sliding into the driver's seat of Grandpa's old truck, the echoes of the evening lingered. My unease from that message hadn't eased—it clung to me, curling around my chest like an invisible weight. I took a few deep breaths, trying to steady myself.

After a moment, I turned the key. The engine sputtered, coughed, and fell silent. I tried again. Nothing.

A frustrated groan escaped me. *Just my luck.*

The parking lot was nearly empty, with only a few cars

scattered under the dim streetlights. None of them looked familiar. Pulling out my phone, I opened the family group chat and fired off a text.

ME

Anyone free right now to pick me up from The Cove? The truck won't start.

DORIAN

Sorry, just got Gracie to sleep. If you can't find a ride, give me a call, and I'll wake her.

SAWYER

Sorry, sis. Wish I was in town. I'll call someone to tow it to the shop tomorrow.

COLT

On a case right now. Can Trent pick you up?

My dad hadn't replied, but knowing him, he was probably already in bed for the night. I let out another groan before shooting off another text.

Any chance you're not doing anything right now?

Trent didn't bother texting back—he called. My head thunked against the steering wheel with a groan as I answered.

"Hello?"

"What's wrong?"

"Nothing. Well... not nothing," I sighed, resting my forehead on the wheel. "The truck won't start. Dorian already put Gracie down, Colt's tied up at the station, and I didn't want to bother my dad this late. Any chance you could come get me?"

"Where's Henry?" he snapped.

"He left," I said, voice tight. "I didn't realize the truck wouldn't start when I said goodbye."

"He should've made sure you were okay before driving off," Trent bit out.

"Yeah, well, he didn't. Ugh, never mind. I'll call my dad."

"I'll be there in ten," he interrupted, voice firm, no room for argument.

"Trent, you don't have to—"

The line went dead.

Great. Just great.

I blinked hard, willing away the sting behind my eyes, but the tears came anyway. I wasn't even sure who they were for.

For the stupid truck.

For Henry.

For Trent.

Maybe for all of it.

FIFTEEN

Trent

I AM NOT WHO I WAS - CHASE PEÑA

As I turned onto the quiet streets of Woodstone Falls, the headlights cut through the dark like a slow exhale. I wasn't shocked her grandpa's truck had broken down—the thing was older than both of us combined. What did surprise me was how fast I'd dropped everything the second she called.

Not that I *should* be surprised. It was Dotty.

My fingers tightened on the wheel as my thoughts spiraled. We'd grown up side by side—two stubborn kids tangled in the same small town, same backyard, same everything. And then somewhere along the way, things blurred. One look, one late night, and it stopped being just friendship. We never called it anything. Probably because naming it would've made it real, and neither of us was ready for real.

And now?

Now she'd gone on a date with Henry.

My Dotty. God, I hated how fast that possessive thought came. Henry was a good guy. A friend. Which only made it worse. I had no right to feel this way, but that didn't stop the knot in my chest from cinching tighter with every damn mile.

Since she left earlier, I had done way too much trying to distract myself. I'd tried to read, put on a game, and even attempted a workout to burn it out of my system. But nothing touched it. I kept picturing her laughing with someone else. Letting someone else see that soft, guarded part of her, she barely let me near anymore.

Maybe she'd already let him in.

The thought made my stomach turn.

The truth was, I never really got over Dotty. Hell, I don't think I ever even tried. Every girl since her was just temporary, safe, and fucking easy to walk away from. Because they weren't her, and I couldn't pretend otherwise. I didn't want to build a life knowing the one person who ever really saw me was still out there, just out of reach.

I hated that I'd made it this way. That I let everything we could've been slip through my fingers.

When she called, I left mid-workout—sweaty, shirt damp, hat on to hide the mess of my hair. I didn't care how I looked. The only thing that mattered was getting to her. Fast.

Because she was alone, and someone had been watching her. The thought made my blood run cold.

As I pulled into the parking lot, I spotted the old truck in the distance. Dotty sat on the truck bed, her hands resting in her lap, feet swinging back and forth.

Even from a distance, she looked like a dream. *My fucking dream.*

I sat there for a second, just watching her. My breath stalled, and I realized in that moment, I couldn't stay away. I could try for the rest of my damn life and fail every single fucking time. The pull to Dotty was too much to resist, especially when she was so damn close.

As I approached, I saw her eyes were tear-streaked, and her chin wobbled in that way it always did right before she tried to pretend she was fine.

My heart dropped.

I shoved everything else—my jealousy, the aching pull, the guilt—down where it couldn't touch her and climbed out of the truck. She didn't look up. I crossed the distance anyway.

"What's wrong?" I asked, opening my arms.

She leaned into me instantly. "Nothing. I'm fine," she hiccuped, against my chest. "Just exhausted."

She melted against me, but she was still trembling. I held her tight, gave her a second to breathe, then pulled back just enough to lift her chin with my fingers.

The little gasp she let out nearly undid me.

"Talk to me," I said. "Is this about Henry?"

She wiped her eyes with her sleeve. "What? No. Henry was... great." My jaw clenched, and she saw it. "I told him we should just be friends," she added quickly.

Some of the tension coiled tight in my chest let go, but I couldn't tell if it was relief or just the fact that I wouldn't have to go hunt the guy down.

"So what is it, then? If it's the truck, don't worry— Sawyer can fix anything short of the apocalypse."

"It's not the truck," she whispered, and her voice cracked.

She reached into her pocket and handed me her phone. My stomach dropped as I read the text.

"Dotty," I muttered.

"I know." Her voice was small as she leaned back into me. I wrapped my arms around her again, this time tighter, like I could physically keep the rest of the world out if I just held on tight enough.

And damn, it felt too right. Like this—her in my arms, mine to protect—was exactly where she belonged. Like my whole damn life had been waiting to snap into place and finally had.

"Come on," I said, softer this time. "Let's get you home. I'll talk to Colt first thing. But tonight? You just need sleep."

She nodded. Then, before I could think twice, I scooped her up in my arms.

"What the hell are you doing?" she asked, voice somewhere between a squeak and a growl.

"Taking care of you," I grunted, walking toward the truck.

She didn't fight me on it. Whether it was because she was too tired or because she didn't want to—I didn't know. Either way, I wasn't about to complain.

I opened the passenger door, lifted her in, and leaned over to buckle her seatbelt. Our faces were close—too close—and I swear time slowed. Her eyes were still glassy, her lips parted just slightly. My gaze dipped to them. Full. Pink. Barely a breath away.

I wanted to kiss her.

I almost did.

But before I could act on anything, I stepped back and rounded the truck. Rational thought was the only thing stopping me. If I was going to have a shot with Dotty James, I was going to do it right.

The drive was quiet and comfortable, but charged. Dotty had mostly composed herself, her usual guarded expression back in place like armor she'd slipped into on instinct.

"I'm sorry for losing it earlier," she said eventually. "It's been a long couple of weeks. That text… It's probably nothing. Spam, maybe."

"It could be," I said carefully. "But we both know your gut is telling you that isn't the case. I'll talk to Colt first thing tomorrow. We'll figure it out."

I gripped the steering wheel tighter than necessary, then loosened it with a sigh. "You hungry? I know you just ate, but… dessert? Scoops is still open, I think. Like old times?"

Her head turned just slightly, lips twitching like she was trying not to smile. "Is it even open this late?"

"Friday night football. You're in luck." I shot her a quick grin. "They always stay open late for game nights. Gotta fuel the high school heartbreak."

She let out a soft laugh. "Lucky indeed. Let's do it."

That tiny smile nearly knocked the air out of my lungs. The way her freckles still dotted her cheeks like they had when we were kids—faded but still there, like they were creating a constellation that was uniquely Dotty James.

I forced my eyes back to the road. We pulled into the parking lot, the old neon sign buzzing faintly overhead.

"Don't move," I said, already hopping out of the truck and circling to her side.

She rolled her eyes but didn't stop me. I opened her door and held out my hand. She hesitated—just long enough for me to notice—then slipped her hand into mine and stepped down.

"Look at you," she said dryly. "Still capable of being a gentleman."

I grinned. "Shocking, I know."

We stood there for a beat longer than we should've.

"I'm sorry," I said, but it came out rough. "For being such an ass lately. I didn't know how to handle… all of this. Seeing you again. I missed you. I missed us, and Dorian, and the way things used to be. I hate what I did, and that I never said sorry for it. So… I'm sorry. For everything."

Her eyes softened. Just for a second.

"I forgave you a long time ago, cowboy," she said, voice quieter now. "Doesn't mean it stopped hurting. I just never had the guts to bring it up."

"You're not the only one." A smile tugged at my mouth. "Cowboy, huh?"

"Shut up," she muttered, bumping her shoulder into mine.

I pulled her into a side hug, her head resting briefly against my chest before we turned and walked toward the glowing Scoops sign.

And just like that, Dotty James managed to hold a power over me by simply existing.

We sat on the front porch, legs stretched out, ice cream melting slowly in the crisp autumn air. The kind of night that made everything feel nostalgic. Dotty's laugh floated beside me, light and familiar, like it had been waiting years to come back.

While Dorian and I were always switching things up—rocky road, pistachio, coffee crunch—Dotty stayed loyal to mint chocolate chip.

"Why mess with a good thing?" she said, taking a bite. "Imagine the betrayal if I risked a new flavor and hated it."

I turned my hat backward and leaned into the creak of

the rocking chair. "Next time, you try something new, and I'll order mint chocolate chip. If it's terrible, we trade."

She shot me a look over the rim of her cone, a little amused, a little skeptical. "You don't even like mint chocolate chip."

"I don't hate it," I said with a shrug.

"You said it tasted like toothpaste once."

I grinned. "Still does." I scooped a bite of rocky road into my mouth, watching her smile with a soft warmth that made my heart beat a little faster.

"No, it doesn't."

She laughed, head tilting back just slightly, and for a second, I forgot how to breathe. I watched as she licked a drip from the corner of her mouth, and before I could stop myself, I reached over, thumb swiping the spot gently.

Her lips parted. My fingers lingered.

And then I was tracing the freckles along her cheek with my middle finger, like the past and present had collapsed into this one quiet moment under the porch light. Every brush of skin felt magnetic.

I wanted so badly to close the distance, to lean in and capture her lips with mine, but we both hesitated, caught in the dance of what could be.

I started to lean in.

And then her phone rang.

She blinked, and I dropped my hand.

"It's Dorian," she said, moving back as she answered. "Hey. You get home okay?"

His voice came through the speaker. "Yeah. Just checking you made it back alright."

"Trent picked me up," she said softly. "Thanks for checking in."

"Good. Just wanted to make sure before I crashed."

"Love you," she said.

"Love you too, sis."

She hung up and turned back to me, her expression already changing, retreating into something closed off.

"I should probably go to bed," she said quickly. "It's been a long day."

I nodded, even though every part of me wanted to stop her. She disappeared inside before I could say anything.

I stood there for a second, staring at the empty spot where she'd just been. Then I turned and headed for my room, closing the door behind me as I pulled out my phone.

Dorian picked up on the first ring. "Hey. Everything alright?"

"Kind of," I said, rubbing the back of my neck. "Dotty got an unknown number text today telling her to stop ignoring the notes."

There was a beat of silence. "Shit. She didn't tell me."

"I'm calling Colt next, but I wanted to talk to you first." I hesitated. "I need to say something."

"Okay…" he said slowly. "Say it."

"You remember what you asked me a few weeks ago? About Dotty?"

"Oh, hell. It's happening, isn't it?"

"What?" I asked.

"You're finally admitting you like my sister."

I blew out a breath. "Yeah. Yeah, I am, and I'm not calling to ask your permission, because I'm not gonna treat her like something I need clearance for, but I respect you. I respect her. And I don't want to screw up what any of us still have."

"You don't have to ask for my blessing," Dorian said, voice softer now. "You've had it. Always."

"You sure? 'Cause last time it felt like you were warning me off."

"I was poking around. Trying to figure out if you'd admit it, or if something was going on. I've known for a while, Trent."

"How?"

"It's the way you look at her," he said simply. "And how you both avoid talking about each other, like if you say the name out loud, the whole damn thing might unravel. When she came back… the way you looked at her? You're gone, man."

I smiled, just barely. "Maybe."

"No, maybe about it," he said. "But good luck breaking through. She's different now. Closed off. I love her, and I love you, and whatever happens—just don't screw it up."

"I'm trying not to," I said quietly. "I want to get it right."

"You've got your work cut out for you."

"Yeah," I murmured. "I know."

But I wasn't scared of the climb. I'd spent too long pretending I didn't care.

I finally was done running from my feelings for Dotty and was ready to start fighting for her.

SIXTEEN

Dotty

WHITE HORSE - TAYLOR SWIFT

I TRIED EVERYTHING TO STOP THINKING ABOUT THAT MOMENT on the porch with Trent.

And failed.

Miserably.

How did I go from avoiding him like the plague to almost kissing him in the span of a few weeks? Because he picked me up once and wasn't a total jackass for five minutes?

I didn't know what the hell was wrong with me, but if I let myself spiral any further, I was going to end up banging my head against the wall, and not in the metaphorical way.

Clearly, I needed to talk this out. With someone who wasn't related to me or emotionally stunted.

Which ruled out all my brothers on both accounts.

I grabbed my phone and hit Noah's name before I could second-guess it.

She answered on the first ring, her face filling the screen, all bright-eyed and smiling like I hadn't just called her mid-crisis.

"Hey! I've missed you. Our daily texts aren't cutting it.

I'm coming to see you soon," she whined, her bronze-skinned face filling the screen.

"I miss you too. Girls' night in sounds perfect. Being surrounded by men all the time is slowly killing me," I replied.

"No kidding. Too much testosterone in one family," she laughed. "And all your family actually likes each other? That's… kind of suspicious."

I shook my head. "Nope. Totally normal. Your family's the weird one."

"Ain't that the truth. Oh, and before I forget—prepare yourself—I officially killed all your plants. Despite my best efforts." She giggled, scrunching up her nose.

Not surprised. Noah couldn't keep a cactus alive if her life depended on it. "Perfect excuse to buy more," I said with a smile.

"So, what's going on? You've got that look—the one when you're overthinking something."

I groaned, dropping my head into my hands. "Sometimes, I hate how well you know me."

"Spit it out."

"I almost kissed Trent."

She practically dropped the phone. "You did what?! What about your date?"

"Uh…" I bit my lip, looking away, wincing.

"Oh my God. Spill *everything*."

I told her about the whole mess—my mediocre date, the truck breakdown, and Trent playing knight in shining jeans by rescuing me and taking me for ice cream.

"Swoon. Dorothea Mae James. You're literally living my dream. Childhood best friend turned swoony cowboy who's low-key pining? Jesus, does he have a brother?"

"No, but I have three," I laughed. "But we're not a

thing. He's got his life here, I've got mine in Seattle. Plus, there's too much history."

"Babe, he offered you a place to crash so you wouldn't have to sleep on your dad's couch. Took care of you when you were sick. Rescued you when your date bailed. Then ice cream? Dotty, you better go get that damn cowboy before I do."

I groaned, half-defensive. "Yup. Definitely not one-sided. But seriously, why not, Dotty? You never do anything for yourself. Maybe you have the occasional hookup when I drag you out, but it never goes anywhere. If you don't want to be an old cat lady, you need to put your-self out there. You haven't dated anyone since Jared cheated on you forever ago."

"Ugh, I don't even like cats," I muttered.

She narrowed her eyes.

"I know, I know," I muttered. "But seriously, there's just too much history between us. I promise, when I get back to Seattle, I'll try to go on a few dates. Can't be your third wheel forever."

Noah glanced away from the camera.

"Uh oh. What's going on with you?"

"No, no, I'm fine. We're talking about you," she said quickly.

"Noah." My voice was serious.

"It's nothing. John's been distant lately—acting weird. I don't know what's going on."

"I'm sorry. If you need a break, come here for winter break. We'll hang out, I'll show you the ranch, get you the best latte you've ever had, and take you to all the local shops."

"Aw, small towns are so cute," she smiled. "I might just

take you up on that. Feels like forever since I've seen you. I'm going through withdrawals."

After more than an hour catching up on everything from work drama to our favorite shows, we finally said goodbye.

But even after the cheerful chat, thoughts of Trent gnawed at me. I sighed and buried my face in my pillow, desperate to shove the memory of that almost-kiss far, far away.

The smell of Dad's famous pizza hit me the second I stepped into the ranch house.

Dad pulled me into a hug, warm and familiar. "Hi, sweet girl."

"Hi, Dad."

Colt, Sawyer, Dorian, and Gracie were already camped out in the living room for Sunday dinner. We'd had a few dinners since I got back, but this was the first one Sawyer made it home for in weeks.

Sawyer spotted me from across the room and came barreling toward me, sweeping me off my feet and giving me a big bear hug.

"I missed you, too, big man," I laughed as he gave me a noogie and set me down.

"It's my bye week. Figured I'd come home for a few days. Missed you, kid."

"Uncle Sawyer might've missed you," Gracie piped up, "but not as much as I did!"

I kissed her cheek. "I missed you, too, sweet girl."

"It's good to have you home," I said to Sawyer, just as the front door opened.

"Hey, guys," Trent said, stepping inside. He was barefoot, already having taken off his muddy boots. He took his cowboy hat off and set it on the coat rack before removing his jacket.

I forced myself not to stare. His hair was messy and damp, sticking up in all directions like he'd run a hand through it a hundred times. His stubble was longer, and his jaw looked annoyingly sharp. The worst part? My stomach fluttered like I was sixteen again, and I hated that he could still do that to me.

"Looks like you got the brunt of the rain," Dad called.

"Sure did. All good though." Trent looked over at me and winked. Just a little one. Just enough to piss me off.

We all sat around the big dining table, and I couldn't stop smiling. Everyone in one place, food on the table, banter bouncing across the room—it felt like home in the best and worst way.

"That was a hell of a catch last week," Dorian said to Sawyer. "One-handed, huh?"

"Don't inflate his ego," Colt muttered.

"You really caught it with one hand?" Gracie gasped, holding up her tiny fingers. "Like this?"

We all laughed as she tried to reenact it.

"That's right," Sawyer said, flexing dramatically. "Uncle Sawyer's still got it."

Trent leaned back in his chair across from me, arms folded, that same easy smile playing on his lips. I tried to avoid looking at him. Failed miserably once again.

Fucking cowboys.

"You know, Dotty," Sawyer said, "I could use your help with a new touchdown dance. Something dramatic. Flashy. Maybe a little hip action."

He stood and did a ridiculous shimmy, earning a squeal of laughter from Gracie.

"I think you've got the choreography down," I said. "I'm more of a blueprint girl than a dance coach."

"I'm out," Colt said flatly. "I don't dance."

"I got it!" Gracie stood and started dancing in place. "Do this!"

Sawyer scooped her up and grinned. "Knew I should've asked you first, G."

After dinner, Dad and I caught up—ranch stuff, work stuff, my plan to start working remotely next week. Once he joined Gracie for a board game, I was left with the dishes, the hum of the quiet house settling around me.

Trent's footsteps were soft, but I felt him coming before I saw him.

"Need a hand?" he offered, his voice gentle as he reached for a towel.

I swatted him away. "I've got it."

He didn't flinch. Just stepped closer and gently took the towel from my hand like I hadn't said a word. "I know you do."

Our eyes met, and something heavy passed between us. I looked away first.

Fighting with Trent when he was like this—steady, quiet, stubborn—was a waste of time. He'd already decided he was helping, and that was that.

We washed and dried in silence. The tension slowly melted into something quieter, easier. Still charged, but softer around the edges.

"About the other night…" I started, turning toward the sink.

He bumped against me as he reached to put a plate

away. "You don't have to thank me again. I was glad to come get you."

That wasn't what I meant, and we both knew it. But maybe he was giving me an out.

"Well… I appreciate it anyway."

"That's just a fancier way of saying thank you." He let out a low, husky laugh.

"Shut up." I shoved his shoulder lightly.

Before I could blink, his hands were on my waist, spinning me to face him. My breath caught. He was right there —too close—and suddenly I was hyper-aware of every inch between us.

"You really don't make things easy, do you?" he murmured, a smirk tugging at his mouth.

Then his fingers slid up my throat, unhurried but sure, and stopped at the base of my neck. He pressed gently, right over my pulse. He felt it. The way my heart gave me away.

I tilted my head back to meet his eyes, and the second our gazes locked, the rest of the world disappeared.

"God, the things I could do to that bratty mouth of yours."

He shook his head just as a throat cleared behind us, causing me to jump back. I looked over to see Dorian, his brown eyes wide.

Of course.

"Uh, hey…" He scratched the back of his neck, clearly trying not to laugh. "Gracie's out cold on the couch. I tried to wake her, and she said she'll only go to the car if Aunt Dotty carries her."

"On it," I said, my voice a touch too high as I slipped away.

I walked into the living room and scooped up Gracie, her little arms curling around my neck.

She smacked her lips, never opening her eyes. "I love you, Aunt Dotty."

"I love you too, G."

"Do you think you'll stay here forever?" she asked.

My heart clenched. "I don't know, Gracie girl. I have to go back to Seattle soon. But I'll spend as much time with you as I can before then, okay?"

"Okay," she whispered. I kissed her forehead and closed the door.

Dorian leaned against his truck, arms crossed, eyebrow raised. "So…"

"Nope, not having this conversation with you." I turned around.

"There's nothing going on, huh?" he called out.

"Not now. Not ever. Goodnight, brother."

"Sure," he drawled. "Keep telling yourself that. Love you."

"Mhm."

SEVENTEEN

Dotty

OUTSKIRTS - SAM HUNT

THE TRUCK WAS QUIET AS WE CRUISED THE BACK ROADS. TRENT let out a sigh. He had one hand on the wheel, and the other resting casually on his thigh like he hadn't just wrecked my peace of mind tonight. And of course, he had to look all irritatingly charming too.

"That wedding's coming up soon," he said, breaking the silence. "You still good to be my plus-one?"

Shit.

I'd completely forgotten I said yes. At the time, it felt harmless. I figured I'd be long gone before it rolled around. I also hadn't planned on… almost kissing him.

"Uh, yeah. Sure." I cleared my throat. "Where is it again?"

"Mount Leston. Couple hours east of here."

I rolled my eyes and crossed my arms, leaning against the window. "I know where Mount Leston is, Trent. I grew up here, remember?"

He didn't even look at me, just smirked like he was waiting for that exact reaction. "Roll your eyes at me again, sunshine. See what happens."

It took me a beat to find my voice. "You did not just say that to me."

"Pretty sure I just did." He chuckled under his breath, all smug and satisfied.

I didn't know when he became so demanding, and I really didn't know why I found it so hot.

"But seriously," he continued, like he hadn't just turned me inside out, "you sure you can make it? I already told the guys I'm bringing you. They're looking forward to meeting the girl I've been talking about for years."

My head whipped toward him. "Hold up. How do they even know who I am?"

"I've spent almost a decade with those guys. You think I never mentioned you?" He shrugged like it was obvious. "They know all about you."

I blinked. "We didn't even talk for ten years."

His knuckles tightened on the wheel, but his voice stayed steady. "Didn't mean you weren't on my mind. I mean, you're always on my mind. Especially while you were gone."

A month ago, if someone told me I would be going to a wedding with Trent, I would say they were insane. But I wasn't one to go back on my word.

He met my gaze, his eyes speaking volumes. We lingered in that moment before he turned back to the road, and my thoughts wandered to the past.

Trent and I wandered down Main Street, ice cream cones in hand, the last of the sunlight dipping behind the mountains and turning the sky a watercolor of orange and pink. The town was quiet, save for the occasional bark of a dog or the hum of tires on pavement in the distance.

"You always know how to cheer me up," I said, nudging his elbow.

It had been a shit day. My rejection letter from my top-choice university was still folded up in my jacket pocket like a bruise I couldn't stop poking. Apparently, a 3.8 GPA wasn't impressive enough. Luckily, Seattle had said yes. Rain and coffee and a fresh start—there were worse outcomes.

"You're easy to cheer up," he said with a lopsided grin, bumping my shoulder. "Just takes sugar and a little company."

I took a slow lick of my ice cream. "Still... I'm surprised you remembered mint-chip was my favorite."

He scoffed. "How could I forget? You've ordered it every single time since we were nine."

"Why mess with perfection?"

"Because it's boring," he said, mock-serious. "You've gotta live a little. Try something new. What would you even do if Scoops ran out of mint chip?"

"Cry," I said flatly. "And then settle for vani—"

"Vanilla," he finished, smirking. "With rainbow sprinkles. And whipped cream if you're in a mood."

I stopped walking and looked at him. "Trenton Akers. Who gave you permission to know me that well?"

"We've known each other since diapers, Dot. We've spent more time together than apart. I basically have a PhD in you."

"Okay then, genius." I raised an eyebrow. "Prove it. What else do you think you know?"

He tilted his head, like the challenge was too easy. "Ellie Miles is your favorite singer. Your favorite book is that vampire one where the guy sparkles—don't try to deny it."

"I wasn't going to," I muttered.

"You sketch buildings in every notebook you own, which is what got you into architecture in the first place. You act tough, but when you care about someone, you're all in—like, zero chill, headfirst into the fire."

I blinked.

He wasn't done.

"Your favorite color changes depending on your mood—right now it's purple, but last month it was yellow. And you pretend like you don't believe in soulmates, but deep down, you do."

My mouth parted slightly, the ice cream forgotten in my hand.

"I..." I shook my head, staring at the sidewalk. "I didn't realize you thought about me that much."

He looked at me for a beat too long. Long enough to feel it in my chest.

"You're always on my mind, Dot."

The rest of the drive was quiet, Trent's hand resting on the center console, palm turned up as if waiting for me to take it. Part of me wanted to stop overthinking and just grab it, but I couldn't let myself go there with him.

Cabin renovations had taken a backseat since I started working remotely, but being back in the groove felt surprisingly good. I wasn't in the Seattle office, and I didn't miss it. What I did miss was this—working on projects that made my brain light up. Sitting cross-legged on the guest bed, a stack of sketch pads beside me and my laptop balanced on a throw pillow, I felt more like myself than I had in weeks.

Architecture had always been the thing. Even when I tried to talk myself out of it—too competitive, too long of a road, too many people in my ear telling me to choose something "more practical"—it never really left me. I took a gap year to figure things out, but all that did was make me more certain. I liked building things. I liked that my brain never really turned off, always tinkering with new layouts and better angles and how to make a space work.

My pen moved absently over the corner of my notepad while the Zoom meeting droned on in the background.

"Next, let's touch base on the Jones project. Any updates, Dotty?" Jordan's voice cut in.

I straightened. "Yeah, I've been coordinating with the structural engineer, and we finalized the foundation plans. We're still on track to break ground next month."

"Perfect. I've updated the interior layout based on the last round of client notes. I'll send that over to you today."

The rest of the team chimed in with project updates, but I stayed locked in. The day flew by in a haze of meetings, revisions, and emails. I barely registered the knock at my door until it came again, louder this time.

"Come in," I called, still mid-email.

Trent's head poked in. "Hey. It's almost eight. You eat yet?"

I glanced at the clock, surprised by how late it was. "Shit. No. Sorry. I got caught up—just trying to catch up from being offline for a bit."

He stepped inside, giving the room a once-over. His brow ticked up. "You've been working like that all day?"

I glanced down at the sad pile of pillows I'd been using as back support. "It's fine."

"It's not fine. You don't need to hunch over in bed like that all day. Use the dining table."

"I don't mind," I said, too quickly.

He gave me a look that said liar, but didn't push. Probably picked up on the fact that the dining table felt like neutral territory that wouldn't stay neutral for long. Being around him too much was dangerous—I was already toeing the line.

"I'll reheat the leftovers," he said, still watching me like he was trying to solve a puzzle. "Come out when you're ready."

"Thanks," I mumbled, eyes dropping back to my screen, but I felt the heat of his gaze for a beat longer before the door clicked shut behind him.

A pleased hum slipped out as I took a bite of Trent's tacos. "When did you get so good at cooking?"

He watched me, expression unreadable even with my mouth full.

"Uh…" He cleared his throat. "Military life—had to learn quick if I didn't want to survive on cafeteria slop. Ended up being the cook because no one else wanted to bother. Got tired of the same old crap, so I started hunting down recipes."

He rubbed the back of his neck, dark hair falling over his brow.

"Well, you've definitely figured it out," I teased. "I remember when you could barely manage a peanut butter and jelly sandwich. Those friends of yours—are they the ones getting married?"

"One of them, yeah. Mark's tying the knot with his longtime girlfriend. Daniel and Nick will be there too."

"You met them all through the military?"

"Mark and I met in boot camp. Daniel and Nick came along when we got stationed in Tacoma. Mark's been with Daisy since forever."

"Tacoma, huh? Like Washington?" I nearly choked on my bite.

"Yeah. Six of my eight years were there. The other two I was training or deployed."

I looked up, caught by how closely he was watching me.

He ran a hand down his face and exhaled. "I wanted to reach out when you were in Seattle, but it never felt like the right time. Or maybe I just didn't have the guts. I'm sorry, Dotty."

I looked down, avoiding his eyes. "We don't have to dig into that. It's all good."

"It's not," he said quietly.

I met his gaze, steadying myself. "Okay. But it is now. Let's start fresh and leave the past where it belongs."

A slow smile broke across his face. "I can do that."

The next day, I stepped into the dim, dusty cabin, coughing as the stale air hit me. The only time I had to work on the place was after a full day at work. No time for leisurely renovations. First order of business: tear out the outdated bathroom vanities and those ridiculous nipple-shaped light fixtures before the new ones arrived.

With headphones on, I mapped out a plan. I'd watched a handful of DIY videos to prep. I designed buildings for a living—how hard could ripping out some old fixtures be?

A sudden tap on my shoulder made me jump, fists shooting up. I spun around to find Trent grinning at me. Pulling off my headphones, I rested a hand on my chest.

"Jesus, Trent. Could you maybe announce yourself next time?"

"I did. You just didn't hear me," he said, nodding toward my headphones.

"Oh, right. Sorry. What're you doing here?"

"Well, you've been avoiding me, and I figured since you weren't at the house, you'd be here. Thought you might want some help."

"I'm not avoiding you," I said, but even I knew that wasn't entirely true.

"Uh-huh. Sure." He smiled.

"I've been busy, okay? Working and trying to fix this place up." I wiped a bead of sweat off my forehead with the back of my hand.

"I know. So I'm here to help. What's the plan for tonight?"

I crossed my arms and pointed to the bathroom. "Start by ripping out this vanity. The new ones arrive in a few days. Got another for the other bathroom, plus new light fixtures to swap out."

"Sounds like a plan. Let's get to work. Then we'll order takeout. My treat." His dimple flashed.

"Think food's gonna earn you brownie points?" I raised an eyebrow.

"Always has," he said with a laugh that sent an unexpected shiver down my spine.

"You're impossible sometimes."

As we wrestled the first vanity loose, Trent couldn't resist teasing me while I struggled to lift my side, and he effortlessly hoisted his.

"You got that? Don't want you flooding the place by accident." He cocked his head.

"I know what I'm doing," I shot back, shaking my head.

"Fair. Just like to rile you up." His green eyes sparkled.

Hours slipped by, The sun was long gone by the time we finally quit.

"Not bad. We've made a dent. I'll make sure the old

stuff's out before the new deliveries show up," Trent said, wiping dirt from his forehead.

I smiled, the corners of my mouth tugging up despite the grime. "Yeah. Starting to look less like a dump and more like a home."

Looking around at the mess—dust, debris, and all—I felt something electric. This cabin was changing, and so was I. There was still a mountain of work ahead, but for the first time in a while, I was ready for it.

Gravel crunched under my tires as Trent's house came into view. It had been a long day, and all I could think about was a hot shower and slipping into my favorite pajamas.

Trent's truck followed mine, and before I even had a chance to turn off the engine, he was slamming his door and striding straight towards the front porch.

That's when I saw it—a large bouquet of lilies sitting on the steps.

Trent had his phone pressed to his ear. "Dotty got another bouquet. Waiting for us when we got back from the cabin." He sighed, glancing at me. "Alright, see you in a sec." He hung up, shaking his head. "Colt's on his way."

My fingers twisted around my necklace, and I nodded at him, swallowing hard. "Thanks."

Walking over to the flowers, I picked up the note, ignoring the bitter taste in my mouth.

I've been admiring you from afar for years. But now it is time for you to see me. Soon you'll notice me.

The escalating tone of the notes, the frequency of the lilies, even the possibility of texts had started to unnerve me. This wasn't feeling like a secret admirer anymore. It was becoming downright unsettling.

My life wasn't perfect. But I loved my career, my family, and Noah. I had learned to love my comfortable, predictable routine, and this had thrown a big wrench in that.

Trent looked at the note from over my shoulder. "Dotty, this is not good." He dragged his hand across his face.

"I know."

Trent

IN CASE YOU DIDN'T KNOW - BRETT YOUNG

COLT'S POLICE CAR CAME INTO VIEW IN THE DISTANCE. THE nauseating smell of fucking lilies hung in the air, pissing me off. I tried to keep it in check, knowing the last thing Dotty needed was me losing my shit.

But this was getting worse. Way worse.

Colt stepped out. "Hey." He opened his arms, and Dotty stepped into them. He kissed the top of her head, then pulled back with a grim expression.

"You shouldn't have received anything," he said. "I spoke with the owner of Falls Florals myself. She promised nothing would go out without notifying me."

"How the hell did this slip through?" I snapped. "This should've stopped."

Dotty folded her arms, her voice quiet but steady. "Could it have come from another shop? Outside of town?"

"Possible," Colt said with a nod, "but delivery this far out isn't cheap. Which means whoever's doing this is willing to spend."

"Which is... great," I muttered, jaw clenched.

"Any leads?" I could see the worry etched into every line of her pretty face under the glow of the porch light.

Colt shook his head. "Fake name. Untraceable VPN. We don't have the tech Seattle does, and they've backed off now that it's out of their jurisdiction."

Dotty let out a shaky sigh and dragged a hand through her hair. "I just don't get it. Why would someone do this?"

I reached out and rested a hand on her shoulder, pushing past the anger boiling inside. "We'll figure it out," I said. "You're not in this alone."

She looked up at me, eyes wide and glassy, trying like hell not to show just how scared she was. But I saw it. I felt it.

Whatever doubts I still had about Dotty, whatever hesitation I'd been holding onto, it was gone. Completely. Replaced by one thing—the fierce need to protect her. No matter what.

Colt nodded. "He's right. You're not alone in this." He motioned toward the bouquet. "What's the note say?"

I handed it over. "You're not gonna like it."

Colt read it, his jaw tightening. "You can say that again. I'll try tracing the order, but this one's longer than the last few. He's getting bolder. Maybe careless."

"Great," Dotty muttered. "Just fucking great."

"You need someone with you at all times now. No exceptions," Colt said firmly. "We can't take chances."

"Yeah, of course. Whatever you need me to do." She hesitated. "Wait—Trent and I are supposed to go to Mount Leston next week for a wedding. Is that okay? Or should I stay in town?"

Colt considered it. "Going out of town's probably better. Less predictable. As long as someone's with you."

"I'll be with her the entire time," I said.

"Not the entire time," she cut in, giving me a look.

"The. Entire. Time," I repeated, sharper this time.

She muttered something under her breath about over-protective men. I let it go. She could complain all she wanted, but I wasn't about to give an inch on this.

"You're safer with him there," Colt said, backing me up. "He hasn't approached you yet, but if he's escalating, that could change." He looked to me. "Don't let her out of your sight."

"I won't."

Dotty exhaled. "Fine, I won't go anywhere alone. If I go to the cabin, I'll bring someone."

"If I'm not out working, I'll come with you," I said.

She rolled her eyes. "Fine."

But she didn't argue again, which told me everything I needed to know.

She was scared.

And so was I.

The week blurred by in a slow-motion haze.

With things winding down at the ranch for the season, most of my time went into keeping an eye on Dotty—not that she needed it. But after everything, I wasn't taking chances. She was still a homebody at heart, thank God. She worked during the day, and in the evenings, we chipped away at the cabin together.

The new fixtures and vanities had come in, and we spent a few nights installing them. The place was finally starting to take shape. Next up was the hardwood flooring —what I figured would be the real turning point. Once those old planks were sanded and sealed, it'd feel less like a forgotten shack and more like a home.

One night, she stepped into the guest room and froze mid-step at the disaster I'd made.

"What's this?" she asked.

"It's your new desk," I said, wiping dust off my hands.

Her brows shot up. "My new desk? What do you mean, my new desk?"

I shrugged, trying to play it cool. "I couldn't let you keep working from the bed. And I've been meaning to fill that corner with something anyway."

That was only half true. I'd wanted to put something there. I just hadn't known what until I saw her sitting cross-legged on the mattress with her laptop overheating her thighs and her notes scattered across the bed.

She sat beside me and grabbed a screwdriver without a word.

"What are you doing?"

She gave me a look. "You bought me a desk. The least I can do is help build it."

We worked side by side, wrestling the disaster of a desk into something functional, despite the god-awful instructions.

"You ready for the wedding?" she asked.

"Yeah. Been a minute since I've seen some of the guys. It'll be good to catch up." I paused, smirking. "They're way too excited to meet you, by the way. Every time we talk, they ask about you."

She let out a short laugh. "I'm curious to see what kind of friends you've collected over the last ten years. I mean, aside from my brothers."

"They're solid. You'll like them. Especially once they see you give me shit—they live for that."

"Oh, so I'm being used for entertainment."

"Absolutely."

We kept working, settling into the same quiet that had carried us through most nights at the cabin. She didn't try to fill the silence. Neither did I. That was part of what I liked about being around her—it didn't matter if we didn't talk for hours. It still felt like something.

And I wasn't sure she realized how rare that was. Or how much I looked forward to it.

To her.

As I slid into the driver's seat, the hum of the engine settled some of the noise in my head. Outside, everything felt still, like the world was holding its breath. It still felt like a long shot that Dotty was actually coming with me to this wedding, but there she was, climbing into the passenger seat, legs tucked up like she owned the place.

We agreed on an audiobook for the drive, something light to fill the silence. I couldn't tell you a single word of it. My mind was a million miles away, stuck on the fact that I'd be seeing my old friends again. Or most of them. Because someone who should've been there... wouldn't be.

When I got to boot camp, I was a wreck—half angry, half lost, all sharp edges. But the comfort came quick when I realized everyone else was running from something too. That's how I met Mark and Steven. We were idiots together, holding each other up when everything else tried to knock us down. They filled the empty space without even knowing it.

We pushed through the worst of it together. Training. Deployment. Shitty coffee. Real fear. Real friendship. War didn't care who you were or where you came from—it came for all of us just the same. But we were solid. Always the three of us.

Until one Tuesday morning, we all woke up.

And that night, only two of us went to bed.

Steven died during a routine patrol gone sideways. One minute, we were giving him hell for snoring too loud, and the next… gone. Just like that. It was fast. It was brutal. It was war.

He fought like hell. But that's not always enough.

That loss did something permanent to me. It left a scar I stopped trying to cover. I didn't want to be someone who coasted or waited around to say the things that mattered. I didn't want to waste time on people who didn't feel like home. It made me loyal to a fault. Protective to a flaw. But it also taught me what real love looks like—even if I'm still trying to figure it out outside of combat boots and blood.

I glanced over at Dotty. She was half-listening to the story, chewing her thumbnail, lost in her own thoughts. She didn't know it, but her presence grounded me—made the weight a little easier to carry. Like her just being there was enough to keep me tethered.

Steven should've been here. He would've loved her.

The audiobook kept playing, but I wasn't hearing any of it. All I could think about was him—and how much I wished I'd had the chance to tell him goodbye.

After more than an hour of silence, I cleared my throat. "We've got about thirty minutes left. Want to stop? There's a rest area coming up."

"I'm good. Unless you need to."

"Nah, just making sure you're comfortable."

"All good." She leaned her head against the window. "Tell me about your friend getting married. Mark, right?"

"Yeah. Met him in boot camp. We bonded fast—both lost our dads around the same time, both trying to outrun the grief. That kind of pain makes for easy ground to stand on." I glanced over at her. She was listening, really listening. "He's the guy who always kept us laughing, even when shit hit the fan."

She smiled, and damn, I wanted to be on the other end of that smile every day.

"Sounds like a good friend to have."

"He is. You'll like him. You'll like all of them—Mark, Daniel, Nick."

She turned slightly, amused. "And what do they know about me? Should I be worried?"

"Oh, they know everything."

"Oh really?" she asked.

"Blame the whiskey. I was a locked box at first, but those two cracked me open. Mark and Steven—they were relentless. Wouldn't let me brood in peace."

"Is Steven going to be there?" she asked.

I hesitated. "Uh… no. Steven passed away during one of our deployments.

Her smile faltered. She reached across the console and rested her hand over mine, light and steady. "I'm sorry, Trent."

I nodded once, jaw tight. "We did everything together, the three of us. Losing him… it changed something in me."

The words sat heavy between us, but she didn't flinch. "Thank you for telling me," she said quietly. "I'm glad you had people like that in your life. Even in the hard parts."

I gave her hand a gentle squeeze, grateful for the calm she carried like it lived in her bones. Dotty had always been the kind of person who made silence feel like a safe place instead of something that needed to be filled. At least to me.

I stole a glance at her from the corner of my eye, watching the way the late afternoon light danced across her freckled cheeks. The golden hour cast shadows on the gentle curve of her jaw and the delicate slope of her nose.

Looking at Dotty, I saw the sun—everything wrapped up into one being. It seemed like a fucking miracle how all of that could be encapsulated into a single person.

And now, as she sat next to me, that same warmth radiated through the truck, a gentle glow that seemed to fill the space whenever she was around. I found myself subconsciously rubbing the spot on my chest, where my tattoo sat inked on my skin below my shirt.

Maybe she was the sun—the light, the hope, and the warmth—of the entire world.

But I had a feeling that it might have just been *my* world.

NINETEEN

Dotty

IMGONNAGETYOUBACK - TAYLOR SWIFT

THE HEAVY OAK DOORS OF THE LESTON LODGE CREAKED AS WE stepped inside. Soft lighting filled the lobby, making everything look cozy against the dark night outside. Fresh flowers spilled from ceramic vases on every surface.

I'd driven through Mount Leston dozens of times over the years, always meaning to stop at this little gem tucked into the mountainside, but somehow never making it happen. Trent had mentioned Mark's family owned the place, that he'd practically grown up running through these halls.

Behind the reception desk, a woman that looked to be in her fifties looked up. Her smile was genuine, the kind that reached her eyes and made you feel like you'd just walked into your favorite aunt's house.

"Good evening. Welcome to the Leston Lodge. How can I help you tonight?"

Trent stepped forward and slid his license across the counter. "I have a reservation under Trenton Akers. Two rooms."

I watched her fingers dance across the keyboard. Her smile flickered for a moment before she masked it.

"Oh." She cleared her throat delicately. "Mr. Akers, I'm terribly sorry. There's been a situation with the wedding block—apparently there was some miscommunication about how many rooms were available, and Mark asked us to change your two rooms to one. You still have two queen beds, but they're in the same room now. I do apologize for any inconvenience."

The silence stretched between us.

One room.

I kept my expression neutral, like that didn't just short-circuit every nerve in my body.

Trent just let out a quiet sigh. "It's fine with me if you're good with it. We share a space at my place anyway."

Right. Totally the same thing. A shared hallway. Two separate doors. A buffer.

I nodded once, careful not to make it weird. "Yeah. No big deal."

Lying. So much lying.

The receptionist smiled, clearly relieved. "There's a complimentary bottle of champagne in the room—our way of saying sorry for the mix-up. If you need absolutely anything else, day or night, just call down."

"Thank you," Trent said, slipping the key card into his pocket.

We headed down the hallway in silence. My pulse thudded loud enough in my ears I half-expected Trent to hear it.

One room.

All weekend. Great.

By the time the elevator arrived with a soft ding, I'd mostly managed to collect myself.

And then his hand touched the small of my back—just a brush, probably without thought—and all that composure? Gone.

The room was charmingly rustic—dark wood accents, faded floral wallpaper, and, thank God for small favors, two beds. Sharing a room hadn't been part of the plan, but Woodstone Falls was hours behind us, and there was no graceful exit now.

Trent had offered the bathroom first, so I took him up on it, hoping a hot shower might rinse off the weird tension still clinging to me.

It didn't.

By the time I'd dried off and tugged on my pajamas, my skin felt overheated and my thoughts were no less chaotic. I braced myself, then stepped back into the room.

"All yours," I mumbled, not quite meeting his eyes.

"Thanks," he said, his voice low.

I climbed into the nearest bed—white sheets, too many pillows, the kind of mattress that felt like sinking into a cloud. I let out a breath and stared at the ceiling for a beat, trying not to overthink everything.

Eventually, I turned onto my side, pulled the covers up to my chin, and let myself disappear into the quiet.

Beep. Beep. Beep. Beep. Beep.

I groaned and shoved the pillow over my head, though it barely muffled the noise. "Turn it off."

"Sorry," Trent grumbled, fumbling for his phone and finally silencing the alarm.

"Why the hell did you set an alarm?" I grabbed my

phone off the nightstand and checked the time. "At seven in the morning on a weekend?"

"I wanted to make sure we had enough time to explore the town," he said, rubbing his eyes.

I sat up, blinking away sleep. No point pretending I'd go back to bed. Might as well hunt down some caffeine.

Trent tossed back the comforter and swung his legs over the side. "There are a few local shops within walking distance that we could check out. Wedding's at five, so we've got time."

"Sure," I replied. "But I need coffee to be awake this early."

Thirty minutes later, with caffeine in hand, we walked the streets of Mount Leston that reminded me of Woodstone. Local shops lined the sidewalks, each one promising something different. I couldn't resist slipping into a few—losing myself for a while in a tiny art gallery and a clothing boutique. Trent stayed close, letting me wander without a word, but never too far.

Eventually, we slipped into a bookstore tucked away on a quiet corner—one of those places that looked like it hadn't changed in decades, with wooden shelves leaning under the weight of countless used books. Behind the counter, an elderly man with wire-rimmed glasses greeted us like old friends, making the place feel less like a store and more like a secret hideout.

I wandered through the aisles until a romance novel caught my eye—the kind with a title promising a happily-ever-after. I flipped it open and was hooked by the first page. Nearby, Trent sank into a worn armchair with a thick history book.

The tension between us, tight earlier, began to ease.

At some point, I moved to sit on the window bench, and

Trent settled beside me. Our shoulders brushed briefly—an accidental touch that sparked a small jolt, but neither of us pulled away. I shifted and leaned against his shoulder as the afternoon light spilled in.

After a few hours, he peeked over the top of his book and caught me staring. His mouth curved into a half-smile. "Find anything good?"

"Just a little love story," I said, grinning. "What about you? Brushing up on your history?"

"Always," he winked. "Wouldn't want you to think I'm all charm and no brains."

"Oh, shut up, you big flirt." I smacked him playfully with my book, which earned us a glance from the store owner.

Trent raised an eyebrow. "Don't get us kicked out before I can buy you that book."

"You're relentless," I muttered, feeling a smile tug at my lips.

He chuckled softly and returned to his reading.

When I finally looked up, the afternoon sun was dipping low, turning the shelves golden. Trent kept his word and bought the book for me. My cheeks flushed as I tucked it under my arm.

I stepped out of the bathroom just as Trent slipped on his dress shoes. He paused, eyes scanning me from head to toe before dragging a hand down his face like he was trying to steady himself.

"Wow, Dotty," he said, voice rougher than usual, throat tight. "You look amazing."

"Thanks."

And what did I do? I did a fake, stupid little curtsy. Because you know, I panicked and thought that was a fantastic idea.

Trent chuckled. I kept my smile light, but my cheeks were already burning.

"Who knew you could clean up, too?" I said.

There was something unspoken in the way he stood— something that shrank the space between us.

Trent was every girl's nightmare and dream rolled into one stupidly handsome man. Effortless hair, sharp stubble, and a suit that fit like it was tailored just for him—broad shoulders, strong frame. His green eyes flickered with amusement.

"Let's get you downstairs. I want to introduce you to some of the guys before the ceremony." He motioned toward the door, hand sliding lightly to the small of my back.

The elevator was tiny—every damn sound and thought amplified. I forced myself against the opposite wall, focusing on the quiet sound of the elevator, and doing my best to push away the thought of what Trent might look like out of that perfectly tailored suit.

The soft ding snapped me back. I stepped out first, needing space before I did something dumb.

Inside, the ceremony room was warm, soft. Fairy lights twinkled from the ceiling, candles flickered everywhere. I looked up at the exposed beams—rustic and elegant. The kind of space I'd dream of designing.

"Wow. It's really beautiful," I said, gesturing around.

Trent looked over at me. "It really is." My heart skipped in my chest, and I glanced down at my hands, unable to keep his gaze.

He handed me a glass of champagne and grabbed one

for himself. I nodded, trying to steady my breath, then turned to my right.

And to my fucking surprise, there was the last person on planet Earth I wanted to see.

Jared. My ex.

The one who cheated on me. Not once, not twice, but enough times to make it a habit.

We'd kept things fairly casual when we dated—busy lives, and little expectations. But exclusive was exclusive. And I wasn't the kind of person to share, at least not knowingly.

Trent caught the change in my expression. "What's wrong?"

I closed my eyes, took a breath, then nodded toward Jared. "Well, that guy over there? That's my ex."

"The one with the ugly ass suit?" he asked.

"Yup, that's the one."

His jaw clenched. "Didn't part on good terms, huh?"

"Nope." I laughed bitterly. "He cheated on me. Repeatedly."

And, of course, because the universe hated me, Jared started to walk right toward us.

Trent leaned in. His breath was warm against my ear. "Play along." His fingers found my waist, pulling me closer.

Heat bloomed inside me, dizzying in the best and worst way.

"Dotty. Good to see you. Here for the wedding?" Jared's smile was too practiced, too casual.

Ugh, fucking asshole.

"Yup, we are." I forced a smile, spinning my glass between my fingers.

Trent extended his hand to him. "Trent Akers. Good friend of the groom, and Dotty's boyfriend."

I chose that exact moment to take a sip of my drink, and almost choked. I barely stopped myself from spitting it all over Jared. Not that he wouldn't have deserved it.

I cleared my throat, catching my breath as I glanced up at Trent, who shot me a wink, his dimple making an appearance.

I hated that charming, stupid wink. And that fucking dimple.

"Oh, I didn't know you were dating again." Jared looked me over like he was trying to find a crack in the armor.

Fuck him.

"Yup." I pulled Trent into an awkward side hug that looked anything but convincing.

I didn't know why Jared even cared about me. He clearly never did before. It had been over a year since we broke up, and I could guarantee he had entertained plenty of women since then.

Trent spun me to face him. "Took me long enough to convince her to go out with me, but eventually, she gave in." His tone was so possessive that it probably would have sent me into a spiral.

Well, if I wasn't already in one.

He grabbed my chin, lifting it so I had no choice but to look directly at him. All my brain cells ceased to exist as his eyes met mine.

I turned my head, but Trent held my chin steady. I forced a weak smile toward Jared, attempting to mask the butterflies fluttering in my chest. Jared just scowled at us both.

"Yeah… Trent here is quite the charmer."

His grip tightened just enough to steal my breath.

He turned my jaw back toward him.

"I just can't resist her," he murmured, his voice low enough that Jared might not even catch it—though the words were clearly meant for him.

Yeah, he was significantly better at acting like this was real than I was.

Jared cleared his throat. "Daisy's my cousin. Small world, huh? Mark's a good guy."

"Small world, indeed. Probably wouldn't mind it being a bit bigger tonight though." Trent's smile was dismissive.

His eyes drifted to where my dress strap had slipped. His fingers brushed the bare skin between my shoulder and the strap, easing it back up like he'd done it a hundred times before.

Yeah. I was dead.

Goner. Deceased. Goodbye, Dotty James—killed by fake flirting and a six-four cowboy who was too damn charming.

Jared cleared his throat again. "Well, I'll let you two get back to… whatever you're doing. Good to see you, Dotty. Nice to meet you, Trent."

Trent nodded as he walked off.

Classical music drifted through the room, soft and steady beneath the low hum of conversation. Wedding guests lingered in clusters, champagne flutes in hand.

Trent and I got pulled into it quickly—half hugs, handshakes, too many people who clearly knew him. I knew he had a life outside of Woodstone Falls, I just hadn't realized how much of one.

I was still chewing on that thought when two guys made their way over like they owned the place.

"Akers, there you are! And you…" He eyed me up and down. "You must be the lovely Dotty James." The man's skin was warm against mine, his voice smooth and full of charm. "Daniel Creasy. Very nice to finally meet you."

Before I could respond, the guy next to him shoved his shoulder. "Stop charming her," he muttered, flipping his long blonde hair out of his face as he reached for my hand. "Nicholas Roberts. Call me Nick." He brought my fingers to his lips. "I see Trent wasn't lying about you after all."

Trent scowled. "Thank you for making this incredibly normal."

"Nice to meet you both," I said, raising an eyebrow but offering a polite smile.

"You two done fawning over her yet?" Trent's jaw ticked.

I nudged him. "Relax, cowboy. They're just being friendly."

"Yeah, cowboy," Nick echoed, smirking.

Trent rolled his eyes. "Guess I don't have to introduce these punks since they already did the honors. You'll meet Mark after the ceremony."

I smiled up at him, and for a second too long, neither of us looked away. Someone cleared their throat.

"Let's go chat, gentlemen," I said quickly, turning to Daniel and Nick. "I want to hear all the embarrassing stories you've got on this guy."

"Oh, we've got stories," Nick said, stepping toward me —until Trent casually blocked him with one arm and rested his other hand on the small of my back.

The wedding planner passed by, letting us know the ceremony was about to begin. We found our seats. Daisy walked down the aisle, radiant in her gown, and Mark's expression as he saw her was priceless. I didn't know either of them, but I had to blink a few times not to shed a tear.

Trent leaned over, his breath warm against my ear. "Is tough little ol' Dotty James getting teary-eyed over strangers tying the knot?"

"Asshole," I muttered, shoving his shoulder.

He laughed softly. "Didn't know you had it in you."

I scowled at him. He had seen me cry plenty of times in my life. Even though it didn't happen often in front of people, I wasn't immune to tears.

"You're cute when you're angry."

"Trenton!" I scolded him.

"Told you," he said with a smug grin, as if I had proved his point.

I glared at him again.

"Stop. You'll turn me on."

After the ceremony, we filtered back into the reception area. Trent handed me another glass of champagne, and I was starting to feel it. I'd forgotten how fast the bubbles always hit me.

Mark and Daisy made their way to us, stopping to greet guests along the way. Trent's whole face lit up at the sight of his friend.

"Akers! Man, thanks for coming," Mark said, pulling him into one of those half-hug, half-handshake things guys always did. Then he turned to me. "And you must be Dotty James."

I gave him a once-over. "Do you guys have a newsletter or something? Everyone here knows who I am."

Mark laughed. "Only good things, promise."

"Daisy, you look gorgeous," Trent said, hugging her.

"Thank you," she said, beaming. "So nice to meet you, Dotty."

"You too. The ceremony was stunning. And your dress is everything," I said.

"Thank you, that's sweet of you," she said, before getting swept off by another guest.

Trent and Mark caught up for a bit, their voices fading into the background as I let myself take it all in.

The music. The laughter. The clinking of glasses and heels on hardwood.

Trent fit here. Effortlessly.

It hit me in slow, overlapping waves—watching him laugh with people I'd never met, people who'd lived whole chapters of his life I didn't get to read. He had a history with these people. Inside jokes. Shared stories. I had... a front-row seat to all the years I missed.

Trent was my best friend for most of my childhood. And then he left. For ten years. And somehow, I'd let myself forget what that felt like. All the hurt from back then —I shoved it down. Let it sit under the surface, disguised as annoyance and cheap resentment. I never stopped to think about how it got there.

Not really.

Until now.

The laughter around me got louder, blurrier, more distant. I took another sip of champagne, even though it wasn't helping.

Normally, I could wall off the hurt and bury it under sarcasm and distance. But this man—this stupid, charming, frustrating man—was the one person who always found the cracks.

Trent looked over at me mid-laugh, and his smile faltered. His brow pulled together just slightly, and I could tell—he saw it. The shift in me.

I turned away, pretending to adjust the strap of my dress.

I remembered the day he left like it had happened last week—the silence afterward, the phone that didn't ring, the way it felt like someone had yanked a thread from the center of me. He had a whole new life. A new version of himself.

And I'd been nowhere in it.

Now he was standing here, in a perfectly fitted suit, drinking champagne and telling stories like we'd never missed a beat. Except we had.

And no matter how many times he smiled at me like nothing had changed… something *had*.

Because the truth was, I didn't know how to reconcile the man beside me with the boy who left. And I wasn't sure which version of him I missed more.

TWENTY

Trent - Ten Years Ago

GHOST TOWN - BENSON BOONE

SERGEANT DAVIDSON HANDED ME A PACKET OF PAPERS. "You're all set, recruit. Bus leaves at oh-seven-hundred sharp tomorrow. Here's your paperwork. Good luck."

"Thank you, sir." My phone buzzed in my pocket. I pulled it out, and Dotty's name lit the screen.

"Hey," I answered.

"Hey," she said. "There's a bonfire tonight at the Reynolds place. Want to come? It might be the last fun thing I get to do before college."

My throat went tight. Last fun thing for *her*. And she didn't even know I was leaving in the morning.

I cleared my throat. "Don't you think it's kind of close to your house? Won't your dad know?"

"It's a mile down the road, Trent. I'm eighteen. I don't care if he knows I'm at a bonfire." She paused. "A bunch of people are camping out. I've got blankets in the truck."

She had no idea how easy it was for me to say yes to her.

"Okay. Let's do it."

Probably not smart to party the night before boot camp. But I'd do anything she asked me to.

She took her time getting ready, and I didn't mind. We loaded the truck with snacks and beer, and drove off just as the sun disappeared behind the hills. By the time we pulled up, the fire was the only thing lighting the field.

Dotty stood near the flames, her cheeks flushed, hair pulled back, singing along, very off-key, to a slow country song playing from someone's truck speaker. The fire lit up her face, and for a second, I let myself believe none of this had to end.

"Dance with me," she said, pulling me up before I could argue.

"Yes, ma'am." Her soft blue eyes made it hard to say anything else.

She rested her cheek against my shoulder, still singing. Not a care in the world.

And I hated myself for knowing I couldn't give her everything she deserved. Not right now. Not with everything breaking loose inside me. She deserved someone steady. Someone with a plan. And I was... not that.

I held her tighter, clinging to this one moment I knew would end far too soon.

The night went on, and I kept looking over at her, trying to memorize the way she smiled when she thought no one was watching. I should've told her. I should've said something. But every time I opened my mouth, fear clamped it shut.

What if she asked me to stay? What if she didn't?

She turned to me, eyes bright from the fire. "Trent."

God. Just hearing her say my name knocked the wind out of me every damn time.

"Yeah?"

"Kiss me."

I blinked. "What?"

She was already backpedaling. "Forget it. I didn't mean —It's probably just the alcoh—"

I kissed her before she could finish the sentence.

She tasted like strawberries and beer. I didn't even like strawberries, but in that moment, I'd have lived on them forever if it meant I got to kiss her again.

I didn't go slow. Couldn't. And she didn't ask me to.

She leaned into it like she'd been waiting, like this wasn't some drunken mistake but something we both knew had been coming for far too long. Her hands gripped the front of my shirt, tugging me closer, and I swear I forgot how to breathe. I angled my head and kissed her harder, deeper—like I was trying to memorize the feel of her, the way she sighed into my mouth, how her body pressed up against mine without hesitation.

Everything. I wanted to memorize fucking everything with her.

My fingers threaded into her hair, and she shivered, her mouth parting slightly, giving me more. It was messy and hungry and way too honest. And still not enough.

God, it would never be enough.

By the time we pulled apart, her lips were kiss-swollen, and her cheeks flushed.

I didn't want to let go either. But I would.

Because I had to.

She hid her face in her hands, giggling.

"I've wanted to do that all summer," she said, peeking up at me. "Figured if you didn't make a move before I left, I'd do it myself."

"Just in time," I said. It came out heavier than I meant.

So I kissed her again.

This time, slower. Deeper. She gasped a little, and I didn't think I'd ever forget that sound.

I'd spent every day since my dad got sick waiting for the other shoe to drop. Then it did. And I was still stuck, no plan, no path, just a mess of guilt and grief and confusion I didn't know how to carry. The James family had taken me in, given me everything. But that wasn't enough. I needed to grow the hell up. Figure out who I was outside of her, outside of that house, outside of this town.

I pulled back.

"This is complicated," I said.

Her smile faltered. "It's only complicated if you make it complicated."

She looked down, quiet for a second. "Just... let me have tonight, okay? Let me pretend I'm the kind of girl who does something reckless like kiss her best friend. Just for tonight. Tomorrow, we go back to normal."

I dragged a hand down my face. "One night."

She nodded, but I don't think either of us really believed it.

The rest of the night played out like a dream I wasn't ready to wake up from. But I knew what was coming. Knew the goodbye I wasn't brave enough to say out loud.

Because while she was thinking about one night, I was already counting down the next eight years.

A few hours later, my alarm jolted me awake, and I was grateful it didn't wake Dotty next to me. I had only an hour before I had to be at the bus station, and waking her up to explain that I was leaving for the army felt too cruel after last night.

After signing on the dotted line, I waited for the right moment to tell her, but chickened out every time I had the chance.

I pulled out a piece of paper and a pen from her truck, writing her a note, explaining that I was leaving, hoping it wouldn't backfire.

Sunshine,

I didn't know how to tell you this, so I didn't, and I will probably hate myself forever because of that.

By the time you read this, I'll likely be on a bus headed across the country to join the army. I've signed for eight years. I wish I could explain what led me to this decision, but honestly, I'm not entirely sure myself. Something inside me changed after my dad passed away. Dealing with his loss has weighed on me more than I've let on, and I can't stay in this town right now.

You and Dorian are off, getting ready to fulfill your dreams, and I'm just here. I need something. Something for me. I'm not sure if the army is the answer to everything, but it seems like a start.

I hope you understand, but just know, if you don't, I get it. I'd be pissed at me, too.

You deserve the world, and I know you will accomplish everything you want to and more.

I think it's time for you to go chase your dreams in Seattle, and it's time for me to figure out what mine are.

Love,

Trenton

Leaving the note next to her, I kissed her forehead and walked over to my truck, where Henry and Chris approached me.

"You're up early. Is today the day?" Henry asked.

While Henry and I were pretty good friends, I hadn't intended to tell anyone, especially since no one else had known, but Henry had spotted me walking out of the army recruiting office one day, so I confided in him that I was enlisting but asked him to keep it quiet.

"Yeah, I leave in an hour," I sighed.

He nodded toward Dotty. "Does she know?"

"She will when she wakes up." I didn't even have the balls to tell her to her face, so the least I could do was admit that to Henry.

"It's probably best that way," Henry said, probably in an effort to comfort me.

"She's special, that one," Chris said.

I gave her one last look and forced a smile. Then I turned, heart aching as I walked away.

"Good luck, man. I'll keep you in my thoughts," Henry said, patting me on the shoulder.

"Thanks, guys. See y'all around."

TWENTY-ONE

Dotty

FATHERED INDIANS - TYLER CHILDERS

THAT DAY, TEN YEARS AGO, PLAYED ON REPEAT IN MY MIND—every word, every moment echoing in the space between us. The man standing here didn't feel like the one who'd left that note. But he was.

The boy who took me for ice cream when I found out I didn't get into my dream college was the same one who shut down, answering with grunts and nods for days.

The friend who stayed late after work to help me fix up a cabin because he knew it mattered to me was the same one who ignored me for weeks in his own house.

And this man—chatting easily with friends he made while we were apart—was the one who left me a damn note after letting me pity-kiss him.

I still couldn't wrap my head around how he'd built a life outside Woodstone Falls. But being here now, all of it finally clicked into place.

Maybe some things don't change—no matter how much time has passed.

I took another sip of my champagne, the bubbles tickling my nose as I listened in to the conversation happening next to me.

Trent patted Mark on the shoulder. "How's civilian life treating you? It's been, what, six months since you left the military?"

Mark grinned. "It's great. I forgot what it's like to actually have a life outside of the military. Daisy and I are settling in here, but I'll need to visit Woodstone Falls soon to check it out."

"It'd be great to have you. Woodstone's always been home, and I'd love to show it to you sometime."

I chuckled bitterly. "Well, let's be honest. It wasn't always your home. You did leave, without even saying anything at that." The words slipped out of my mouth, fueled by the alcohol coursing through my veins.

"Dotty," Trent snapped, his eyes narrowing.

Mark laughed, glancing over at me. "I knew I liked her." He winked. "I'll let you two work things out. Catch you later." He gave a nod and walked off.

Before I knew what was happening, Trent had his hand around my forearm, pulling me into the hallway.

"What the hell are you doing?" I hissed.

"What the hell are *you* doing? You think you can have a few glasses of champagne and say whatever the hell you want?" He let out a breath, seemingly regaining his composure. "You were the one who said we should leave the past in the past. Mark already knows everything about you anyway. He knows I'm the asshole in this situation."

"I'll have you know, I've only had two glasses." I took that opportunity to chug the last of my second glass. "That counts as a couple, not a few." I poked him in the chest.

"What the hell's gotten into you?" He glanced around before opening a door and pulling me inside.

Of course, it was a fucking closet. A dark, tiny closet, complete with a mop bucket that was taking up half of the small space, forcing me closer to him.

I glanced around before turning back to him, raising a brow.

"Why are we in here?" I asked.

"I'm not having this conversation where anyone is going to overhear," he said.

"I don't know why I even agreed to come here," I said, trying to brush past him, but he stopped me. "Ugh, I don't even know who you are anymore. You have this entire life." I gestured all around me. "This entire group of friends you built while you were gone." My voice threatened to crack.

"Dotty…"

"No. Don't Dotty me. This is all a reminder that I wasn't included in that. I really don't need to see how you spent the last decade building an entire life that I wasn't a part of." My eyes burned, the sting of tears hitting before I could stop them.

Something in his demeanor softened. "Dot…" He reached for me, pulling me into his embrace. I fought him, but he remained steady, as he always had been growing up. After a moment, I gave up and settled into his arms.

"I know a lot has happened between us," he said, his breath warm against my head as he held me close. "I know we don't know each other the way we used to, but I want to. And I think we're on the right track," he said.

I nodded my agreement as my face buried deeper into his chest.

"I think so too," I said softly.

"I missed you every damn day for the last ten years. Please don't make me keep missing you."

"I don't know. I don't know if I can do this or if I can even be your friend, Trent."

He pulled back, gently lifting my chin. His green eyes held mine. "Then don't."

I could barely make out his features in the dim light as he reached up, gently tucking a stray strand of hair behind my ear. He inched his face forward, so slowly it felt like I was sinking beneath the surface.

"Trent." My breath hitched, and I dropped my eyes to the floor, unable to hold his gaze.

He pressed a finger to my lips, silencing me. When I looked up, his gaze was already there—fixed on my mouth, leaving it burning from a single glance.

His thumb brushed along my jaw, and the world faded around us. Just him and me, suspended in some breathless in-between. He dragged his bottom lip through his teeth, and it sent a shiver down my spine. A slow-burning fire roared to life deep inside me, consuming every doubt, as he gazed down at me with eyes full of hunger and something even deeper—something that set my heart racing.

"Don't," he whispered, his voice a low, fragile thread as his fingers continued their gentle path along my jaw, leaving goosebumps in their wake. "Don't think, Dotty."

I didn't know how to *not* think—especially around him. All he made me do was *think*, causing my head to spin in a million directions at once, all the damn time.

He leaned in, and his breath was warm against my lips. My heart hammered in my chest, breath catching as I fought to steady myself.

His eyes stayed locked on mine—steady and patient— with a weight that made my knees go weak.

He was waiting. Giving me the choice to close the gap or let it remain.

I was torn between the storm in my head and the fire in my veins. Every nerve in my body screamed for release, for the sweet surrender of his touch.

"Fuck it," he growled as he closed the distance.

And suddenly, he was there—his lips soft and tentative, waiting to see what I'd do. My brain shut off completely the moment I tasted him. It was achingly familiar, yet entirely new. And that was the final straw that made me lose control. I allowed myself to give in for once—to give into him.

It was so painfully real that it felt as if my entire universe had finally aligned—a decade of tension *finally* releasing.

It felt like every moment in our lives had led us here, to this closet, to this exact second with his lips on mine. When his tongue parted my lips, I couldn't help but let out a soft whimper, overwhelmed by it all.

He pulled away, breathless, resting his forehead on mine. "Dotty." I heard the slight hesitation in his voice.

"Don't," I said, echoing his words from earlier. "No thinking right now." I let myself get lost in him again.

His taste drove me higher as his tongue teased my mouth, and my lips parted on instinct. He let out a guttural groan that sent a pulse straight to my core.

He laced his hand in my hair at the nape of my neck, pulling my head down to deepen the kiss. Using his free hand to grab my ass, he picked me up so my legs wrapped around his waist. Suddenly, my back was against the wall.

I pulled away, needing a moment to catch my breath. He stared down at me and rubbed his thumb along my bottom lip.

"I spent the last ten years trying to remember the taste of your lips," he murmured, his voice low and husky. "But this... fuck, this was better than anything I ever dared to dream of."

I rested my forehead on his. "We should get back out there," I said, still breathless.

"Yeah, probably," he said before stealing another kiss from the corner of my mouth. He set me down and turned toward the door.

He turned back around and looked at me.

"What?" I asked.

His response was one more kiss. "To hold me over," he said, guiding me out of the closet.

What the fuck just happened?

I heard Trent apologizing to someone as he walked out of the closet. I glanced up, catching Jared's sharp eyes narrowing as he stood just outside the closet door.

"Oh, hi, Dotty. Trent. Is this the restroom?" he asked.

"No, it's a closet," Trent smirked like he owned the place—the biggest, most satisfied smirk I'd seen all night. "Restroom's down that way." He gave me a quick glance, then pointed with a playful flick of his finger.

Jared's jaw tightened, but Trent didn't give him a chance. He grabbed my hand and started pulling me away.

I elbowed him, half-laughing, half-exasperated.

He just shrugged, that cocky grin refusing to fade. "What? Gotta have some fun messing with him."

TWENTY-TWO

Trent

STARGAZING · MYLES SMITH

THE SHOWER BEAT DOWN ON MY BACK AS I RAN A HAND OVER my face, trying to get my shit together.

Shit, I kissed Dotty.

But she kissed me back.

I'd known I wanted her. That wasn't news. But tasting her? Feeling her lips on mine, her little sighs and whimpers —yeah, that wrecked me. It cracked something open I couldn't patch back up.

Every second we'd spent apart suddenly felt worth it, if only because it led to that moment. One I could play on loop in my head for the rest of my damn life.

And then… we went right back to pretending it didn't happen.

When we got back to the room, I told her I needed a shower—probably a little too casually, like I wasn't coming apart inside. She just nodded and flopped onto the bed, like it was nothing.

Dotty had always been better at pretending than I was. She spent the night tossing out sarcastic little jabs, telling old stories that had my friends howling, and laughed like her lips weren't still swollen from mine. I couldn't stop looking at her. Couldn't believe she was still breathing the same air as me and acting like we were fine. Like I was fine.

The water started to chill, and I let it. Maybe it would cool off the heat still simmering in my chest.

That kiss was burned into me now. Permanent. A core memory I couldn't forget if I tried.

Not that I wanted to.

That fucking kiss.

I shut my eyes and let the memory take me under—her lips on mine, soft but sure, like she'd finally stopped running from us. Like she wanted it just as bad as I did. Her hands gripping me, her warmth seeping into my skin. The taste of her, the way she melted into me.

For the first time in years, the chaos in my mind had quieted. No noise. No what-ifs. Just her.

And it had me craving more—more of her, more of that moment, more of *everything*.

I braced one hand on the shower wall, the water still pounding over me as I wrapped the other around my dick. My grip tightened as I pictured her exactly how I wanted her. On top of me, riding my face, panting my name. Her thighs shaking under my palms. Her mouth wrapped around me, lips wet and swollen, eyes locked on mine.

Fuck.

She wanted it, too—I knew she did—but she was too scared to ask. Too scared to want me out loud.

And maybe she didn't trust it yet, didn't trust me. But if she let me in, if she gave me the chance—I'd give her everything. I'd worship every inch of her, tear down every wall until she forgot what it meant to be hurt by me.

My release built fast, my mind spinning with the memory of her soft gasps against my mouth. Her skin under my hands. Her whisper of my name was like a damn prayer.

Dotty.

I came, biting my lip to keep quiet, knowing she was just on the other side of the wall. It wasn't the first time I'd gotten off thinking about her, but it *was* the first time in years. Ever since I left her that note, I'd forced myself not to go there. Not even in my head.

I leaned against the tile, chest heaving as the water went ice cold.

My pulse finally slowed, but the ache in my chest didn't. I wasn't sure where her head was at or how she'd act when I walked out there. Probably weird. Probably like it didn't mean what it meant.

Still, I wouldn't change it.

If that kiss was all she ever gave me, I'd hold onto it for the rest of my life—and it'd still be the best damn thing that ever happened to me.

Dotty wasn't the type to make things easy. She didn't hand out trust, didn't soften just because someone asked nicely. You had to earn your way in.

Most people never got close. They saw the sharp edges, the quick comebacks, and figured that was all there was. But if you were paying attention, you'd catch it—loyalty that ran deep, wit that could level a damn room, and a quiet strength that made you want to lean in without even realizing it.

She didn't need anyone. Never had. Still, I found myself hoping she'd choose me anyway.

And if she ever let me back in—really let me in—I wouldn't waste a second of it. I'd hold on like hell.

Despite all the uncertainty, one thing remained abundantly clear—I was so fucking in love with her.

Turning off the shower, I stood in the cold air for a moment before grabbing my towel. After getting dressed, making sure I had a shirt on to cover my tattoo, I took a deep breath.

I let all my emotions go crazy for a few final moments before shutting them down and walking out of the bathroom as if I had my shit together.

I didn't.

Dotty tried to be subtle when she spotted me, but I caught her eyeing me up and down.

"Hey," I said, trying to read her.

She blushed, cheeks blooming a pretty pink. "Hi." She bit her lip, and it took every ounce of willpower not to walk up to her and kiss her breathless again right there.

"I had a great time. Thanks for coming with me," I said.

"It was a beautiful wedding. Daisy was stunning." She smiled.

"Yeah. Mark's been head over heels for her since they were eighteen."

"Oh, I didn't know they'd been together that long."

"Yup. High school sweethearts."

"Oh, wow." She smiled again, then a beat of silence passed before she cleared her throat. "So… about earlier…" Her gaze dropped.

"Oh, you mean the kiss?" I cut in. No point pretending we weren't both thinking about it.

"Yeah… that."

I scratched the back of my neck and sighed.

"I don't regret it." She finally met my eyes, and suddenly my breath was short and fast. "But I don't know if I'm ready for this. There's so much history, Trent. I know we said we'd start fresh, and I'm trying. But it's hard to forget everything that happened. Can we just be friends—for now?"

For now. *For now.* I could work with that.

"So, does that mean I'm officially upgraded from acquaintance to friend?" I grinned.

She giggled. "Yeah, I guess so."

"I'll take it."

I'd take whatever she'd throw my way, even if friends were all I got. I knew there'd be fallout from that kiss—it was inevitable—but this wasn't a hard no. For now felt like maybe not right now. Maybe soon. And that was enough to hold on to. At least, I hoped it was.

I opened my arms, and she crossed the room, stepping right into me. I pressed a kiss to the top of her head, letting her warmth soak in, feeling the light she brought into my world.

We stood like that for a moment—wrapped in silence—until I finally spoke.

"Remember the last summer before… before everything happened? When we just enjoyed time together? We watched too many movies, went to more bonfires than I can count, drank cheap beer, and didn't have a care in the world."

She nodded, pulling back to look up at me. Her blue eyes were soft and hazy as she yawned. "Yeah. Why?"

"Maybe we can find that again. Or work toward it—just, you know, the almost-thirty-year-old version. I don't think I can pull off getting drunk all the time anymore. Maybe movie nights and hanging out, like old times."

"I'd like that." Her smile hit me like a punch to the gut. "Me too."

She yawned again. "But hey, it's late. Maybe we should call it a night so we can drive back home tomorrow."

"Yeah. Probably a good idea."

A faint knock at the door pulled me from my restless thoughts. I hadn't slept a wink. I'd just been lying there, mind racing, every breath reminding me Dotty was just a few feet away.

She shifted under the covers, a soft groan slipping out. "Who the hell's knocking at one in the morning?" She glanced at her phone, then back at me.

"Good question," I muttered, pushing myself up and stalking across the room to the door.

What I saw when I looked through the peephole made my blood run cold. I stayed there a moment longer than I wanted, my fingers tightening on the doorknob.

Turning back, I forced my face into something neutral, but the fire clawing inside me was hard to hide.

"Lilies," I spat, dragging a hand down my face as the weight settled hard.

"Well, that's just fucking perfect. What's the note say?" she asked.

I cracked the door open and glanced down the empty hallway. Whoever left the flowers was already gone. I crouched to grab the note from the floor.

It doesn't matter how far you go. I will always find you.

I pinched the bridge of my nose. Dotty stepped closer and plucked the note from my hand.

Her face went pale. Without saying a word, I pulled her

close. She hesitated for a beat, stiff as a board, then melted into me. I wrapped my arms around her, tracing slow, steady circles on her back, trying to ease the tension out of her.

"Let's go back to bed," I muttered. "I'll call Colt in the morning, and we'll figure this out."

"Will we, though? This all seems never-ending."

"Nothing will happen to you. I'll make sure of it."

She let out a shaky exhale, her body easing just a fraction against mine. This guy was escalating, pushing harder than ever before. Hardly anyone knew we were here this weekend—yet somehow, he'd found us. And he made damn sure Dotty knew it, too.

Her hands trembled against my chest, and I could almost hear the thoughts spinning through her mind.

"How about a movie?" I offered. "Might be hard to sleep, but maybe watching something will help."

She pulled back just enough to meet my eyes and nodded. "Yeah, that sounds good."

Dotty eased onto her bed, and I grabbed the remote, sliding in beside her.

"What do you think you're doing?" she asked, shooting me a pointed look.

I smirked, letting my voice drop low. "Come on, Dotty. You really think I'm going to sit all the way over there? I want to be close. So quit overthinking it and just let me."

She rolled her eyes, but this tiny spark of amusement was hiding in them. "Fine."

"What did I say about rolling your eyes?"

She lobbed a pillow at me. I caught it, savoring the rare moment of ease between us.

I turned back to the TV, scrolling through the options. "How about this one?" I asked, sneaking a glance at her.

She scoffed. "Why would I watch a movie when I missed the first thirty minutes? That's the whole setup!"

"I just fill in the blanks," I shrugged, laughing.

"Yeah, no thanks."

Finally settling on something new, we slipped into a comfortable silence. The screen's glow cast flickering shadows, but my eyes were anywhere but on the movie.

Every time I stole a glance at her, she caught me—then offered a quick, almost shy smile before looking back at the screen.

Good thing I'd seen this movie before, because I couldn't follow the plot to save my life. My attention was stuck on the few inches between us—her hand just inches from mine—and the ache to close the distance.

A few hours later, sunlight streamed through the windows, warming the room as I instinctively pulled the body next to me closer. Dotty let out a soft, sleepy moan in response.

Shit.

We'd fallen asleep in her bed. Together.

My whole plan to play it cool, to win her over gradually, was long fucking gone. But I couldn't bring myself to move. Her body, warm and soft against mine, was too addictive. Our legs were tangled, her back pressed snugly to my chest. I let myself indulge, nuzzling her neck and inhaling her scent. It was grounding and intoxicating all at once.

I was so fucking gone for her.

I mean, who the fuck casually sniffs their childhood best friend's neck? Apparently, me.

Dotty squirmed, sending a jolt straight to my dick. She

nuzzled into me for a moment, but then I could tell the exact moment she fully regained consciousness. She stilled and went to pull away.

Nope. Not on my watch.

I caught her waist, gentle but firm, and dragged her right back.

"Stay. Just for a minute," I whispered against her hair.

She hesitated, then melted back in like maybe she didn't mind as much as she tried to pretend. The tightness in her eased, and I let my fingers draw slow circles on her waist like it was the only thing that mattered.

"How did you sleep?" she asked, her voice soft in the quiet morning.

I wanted to see her face, lose myself in those sleepy blue eyes. So I nudged her to turn.

When she did, it knocked the wind right out of me. Seeing her like this—rumpled hair, flushed cheeks, and hazy eyes—was nothing short of pure fucking perfection. I'd seen Dotty half-asleep a hundred times, but this? This was something else. She was here, in my arms, close enough to touch, close enough to kiss.

"I know you said friends..." I started, my voice betraying just how badly I wanted her.

"Trent." Her tone was warning-level firm, but her eyes —God, her eyes—told a different story. Soft. Hesitant. Curious.

I couldn't help myself.

I leaned in anyway. "Just one more," I murmured. "Let me get it out of my system. After today, I swear I'll behave."

It was a lie, and we both knew it.

Her lips quirked into a teasing smile. "Do your worst, cowboy."

The haze of sleep must've knocked her judgment sideways, and yeah—I absolutely planned to take full advantage.

Her blue eyes met mine before fluttering shut. Then she kissed me, and just like that, I lost myself in her once again.

Our last kiss had been frenzied, a chaotic rush of passion and pent-up tension, but this kiss was different. It was slower. We weren't rushing it, and I savored every second.

Her hands slid up to my jaw. I tangled my fingers in her hair, pulling her closer until a raw moan broke from me.

She whimpered softly in response, and that sound—God, that fucking sound—shattered what little control I had left. My grip on her waist tightened as if I could somehow fuse us together.

Her leg slid over my hip, and the faintest brush of her body against mine had me spiraling all over again. The little sounds she made drove me to the brink of madness, but then, before I was ready, she pulled away and rested her head against mine.

I immediately felt the loss of her like a physical ache.

"Fuck, Dotty, the noises you make," I rasped, my voice rough and uneven. "They drive me crazy. *You* drive me crazy."

She smiled, let out a breath, and pulled back. I watched it happen—the shift. That damn mask slid right back into place, and just like that, she was composed, cool, like nothing had happened.

"There's your last kiss, cowboy," she said, like it was a fucking business transaction. "Now get up. We've got a Sunday dinner to make it home for."

With a smug little smile, she climbed out of bed and

walked away—her tiny sleep shorts doing unspeakable things to my brain.

"Stop checking me out!" she called over her shoulder.

"Never."

She flipped me off without looking back and disappeared into the bathroom. I couldn't stop the stupid grin that spread across my face. I was absolutely and totally fucking hopeless when it came to her, and I didn't even care.

TWENTY-THREE

Dotty

A BAR SONG (TIPSY) - SHABOOZEY

THE MORNING AFTER THE WEDDING, I WOKE UP DETERMINED TO act like nothing had happened.

Except, something did happen.

The kiss had been an explosion, and I was already feeling the aftermath of it. I tried to bury it all way deep down. It was easier to convince myself that what had happened between us was nothing but a fleeting lapse in judgment or simply a figment of my imagination.

But standing there in the quiet of the hotel room, I knew better.

It felt right, but everything in my head screamed that it was wrong.

Our lives were too different, our circumstances too complex, centered around completely different places—his in Woodstone and mine in Seattle.

I wasn't cut out for Woodstone. Not the way Trent needed. He deserved a perfect wife—someone willing to stay home, raise his two-point-five kids, and help manage the ranch. White picket fence and all.

But that wasn't me.

My world was in Seattle. I had aspirations, plans, and a future. While I thought about having kids someday, I wasn't ready to be barefoot and pregnant, running around in a milkmaid dress for the rest of my life.

But damn, when I thought about what we could be—what we almost were—it felt like I was standing on the edge of a cliff.

I knew he would try to convince me that we could figure this out and make it work. And that scared me because a part of me wanted to believe him.

Because this wasn't just some guy. This was Trent.

My childhood best friend.

The boy who saw me through things I never let anyone else witness.

The man I spent years pretending to hate because it was easier than admitting how much I felt the opposite.

We had history—real, messy, complicated, and full of feelings. Letting him in meant reopening old wounds and exposing myself to the possibility of new ones.

And after losing my mom, I learned how easily love could slip through your fingers, and how quickly everything could change. I had been a child then, but that grief had shaped me into someone who guarded her heart—someone who couldn't afford to trust in fairy tales or fleeting moments.

So I'd built a life that was safe—one I could control.

Every moment we shared was a reminder of what could never be.

So, I steeled myself, determined to keep my heart locked away and my focus on the life I had to return to in Seattle.

When breakfast arrived, I acted like everything was

normal, but when Trent's gaze lingered on me from across the small table, I knew I was in trouble.

"What?" I asked.

"What do you mean, what?" He chuckled.

"Why are you looking at me like that?" My brows furrowed.

"Like what?" His smile grew, and I knew he was fucking with me.

"Like you're about to say something either really profound or really dumb."

He let out a laugh, leaning back in his chair. "Probably both."

I groaned as my fingers rubbed my forehead. "That checks out."

He licked his lips, then looked me up and down before finally meeting my gaze. "You've changed, that's all. But also… You haven't."

"That's helpful," I scoffed, "Thanks for clearing that up."

"I mean it," he said, his voice softer now. "It's like… you're still you. The same stubborn, sharp-mouthed, secretly-sappy girl who used to make me sit through whatever cheesy drama you were obsessed with, then deny you cried at the ending."

"I stand by that choice," I muttered.

He grinned. "I know you do, but now there's this whole other side of you. You've seen things. Built something. You walk different. Talk different. It's like I'm getting to know you all over again, and I'm not gonna lie—I like it."

I looked down at my hands, trying not to let the smile take over my face. "Yeah… I've been thinking about that too. Yesterday, it hit me. There's this entire part of your life I missed. At first, I was pissed about it."

He raised an eyebrow. "You? Pissed? Can't imagine."

I shot him a look. "But now I think… I'm kind of okay with it. Because the version of you sitting in front of me? You're different, but you're still the guy who used to sneak candy into my locker and pretend it wasn't from him."

I meant every word, because even though I knew nothing could ever happen between us, Trent had been my friend for most of my life before I left for Seattle.

He laughed. "I was so smooth."

"Sure." I shook my head.

We were quiet for a beat. Then he reached across the table and let his knuckles graze mine. A touch so casual it shouldn't have felt like anything. But it did.

Warm. Familiar. Dangerous.

I let myself feel it—for a second. Just one.

Then, I pulled back as my phone buzzed.

I glanced at the screen, and immediately my hand started shaking. My breath caught as I read the text.

Trent sat up straighter. "What is it?"

I stood abruptly, pacing without meaning to.

"Hey." His voice sharpened. "What happened?"

I held out the phone, unable to speak. Just handed it to him and watched his face as he read.

UNKNOWN NUMBER

I hope you liked the flowers.

"Fuck." He pinched the bridge of his nose. "I'll text Colt, let him know what's going on. He already knows about last night."

"Last night?" I asked, too quickly.

"The flowers, Dotty. Not the kiss." He stood up, rubbing the back of his neck.

"Oh." I let out a breath I hadn't realized I was holding. "Yeah, *that*."

With a sigh, he opened his arms—wordless and patient.

I had no fight left in me, so I allowed him to wrap himself around me like he could shield me from everything.

"We'll figure this out," he murmured, pressing a hand to the back of my head. "Just promise me you'll be careful."

"I have been," I said quietly. "You know I have."

"I know." He kissed the top of my head and held me tighter. "I just—God, Dot. I hate the idea of something happening to you."

We stood there for a moment. No movement, no words. Just the comfort of knowing someone still wanted to protect me.

Eventually, I pulled back and looked up at him, pushing everything else down.

"We should get on the road. I told Gracie I'd stop by if we got back in time. She wants her hair braided for school."

"Yeah. Okay," he said, exhaling slowly.

I reached for my bag, but he beat me to it, fingers brushing mine as he grabbed it first.

Then he tipped his head toward the door. "After you."

And just like that, we walked out and headed home.

Trent's truck rocked over the uneven eastern Oregon roads, the steady hum of the engine usually something I found calming. Not today. My thoughts were moving too fast, chasing themselves in circles.

I was ready to shift my focus back where it belonged—

on my career, the promotion I'd been working toward, the life I'd built in Seattle. Clean lines. Clear priorities.

I needed to do better than vague promises about boundaries. What we'd said back at the hotel wasn't going to cut it. If I didn't draw the line now, I'd keep letting things bleed where they shouldn't.

Especially with Dorian waiting at the other end of this drive. He'd clock me in half a second.

I sat up a little straighter, tried to summon some version of confidence that didn't feel paper-thin. Cleared my throat.

I picked at a thread on my jeans. "I meant what I said. I don't regret it. Any of it."

"I didn't think you did."

"But…" I glanced over at him, then back out the window. "It can't happen again."

His hands stayed steady on the wheel, but his jaw tightened.

"My life's in Seattle. Yours is here. That hasn't changed," I went on. "And we just started figuring things out again. I don't want to mess that up. I can't afford to."

There was a beat of quiet before he spoke. "You think this messes it up?"

"I think it could."

He nodded once, like it hurt. "Okay."

"I'm not trying to push you away," I said quickly. "I just —I have to be realistic. We both do."

"Yeah," he said. His voice was low. "I get it. Doesn't mean it's easy."

"I know."

He was quiet for a moment. Then, "Whatever you need from me, Dot. I'm here."

I didn't have a response for that. Just leaned my head against the window and watched the trees blur past.

We arrived back in Woodstone, and Trent quickly took off to work on the ranch, claiming he had some work to catch up on. I retreated to my room and sat down at my desk.

I was glad to have a little space—my head was a mess. I grabbed my phone and opened Noah's contact, thumb hovering over the call button.

Then I chickened out and sent a text instead.

ME

I did a thing

NOAH

What kind of thing?

Well, I kinda kissed the cowboy

No freaking way

Yeah… twice actually

My phone buzzed. I pinched the bridge of my nose, already bracing myself, and answered Noah's video call.

I groaned the second her face appeared.

"Hello to you, too, my love," she said, not missing a beat. "Now, please tell me what the hell happened?"

So I did. Everything. The whole damn weekend, start to finish. No skipped details, no holding back.

When I finally stopped to breathe, she blinked once and said, "I'm sorry, Dotty, but I'm still not seeing the problem."

"Noah," I groaned, dragging out her name. "The problem is that this guy broke my heart, left town, and never spoke to me again. And now we're back in each other's lives like nothing happened."

She waited. I turned away from the screen.

"And I'm leaving soon," I added. "My job's in Seattle. You're in Seattle. I can't let history repeat itself." I blew out a frustrated breath. "What planet is in retrograde? This is too many feelings for one person."

"Mercury," she said flatly.

I looked back at her. She raised a brow.

"What?" I asked.

"Do you realize you just figured out the answer to your own problem?" she said.

"How is Mercury the answer to my problem?"

"Not Mercury," she said, scrunching her nose. "You. A few months ago, you kept saying your life was in Seattle. Just now, you said your *job* is in Seattle. And *I'm* in Seattle. Not your life."

I frowned. "That's what I meant."

"No, it's not. If I wasn't there, and neither was your job, would you still want to go back?"

I opened my mouth. Closed it.

"Mhm. That's what I thought." She grinned. "I love you. You're my favorite human on the planet, but you can't let me be the reason you don't go after what you actually want."

My throat tightened.

"I know your job matters. I know you love what you do, but you can't let it dictate everything. Woodstone's small, sure, but I guarantee there's something there for you. Maybe not the exact same role, maybe not with the same title. But something."

I looked up at her. Her warm brown skin glowed in the light, and her eyes were soft, steady.

And yeah—my own eyes welled up, because everything she was saying cut straight through me.

I'd always insisted I had to get back to Seattle. That it was the goal, the plan, the non-negotiable. But she wasn't wrong. The longer I stayed in Woodstone, the more it felt like something I didn't want to lose.

"I just don't think I could ever really stay," I said finally. "Not for good. I can't throw away my whole career."

"I'm not saying you should," she said. "But don't lie to yourself and say it's just about work or me. I've watched you come alive the past couple of months. You've stopped performing for everyone. You're finally letting yourself be. And yeah, I want you to ride off into the sunset with the hot cowboy, but it's not just about him. It's the town. Your family. The quiet. The way you breathe when you're there."

I closed my eyes and let her words sink in.

"Sit with that for a bit," she added gently.

I groaned again. "Yeah, yeah. I will."

TWENTY-FOUR

Dotty

LIFT ME UP - RIHANNA

OVER THE NEXT FEW WEEKS, I BURIED MYSELF IN WORK. TOOK on extra projects. Said yes to every meeting, every spreadsheet, every coworker spiraling over their own to-do list. I told myself I was just being helpful. A team player.

But really, I needed the noise. The chaos. The excuse not to think too hard or feel too much—or spend any unnecessary time around Trent.

Between work and the cabin, I stretched myself thin, and it worked. For the most part, I managed to avoid him completely. We stuck to casual hellos, the occasional exchange about groceries or cabin repairs. Nothing that lasted long enough to mean anything.

And even though he was giving me space, he wasn't exactly subtle.

He still remembered how I liked my coffee and left a cup waiting for me on the counter, still hot. When he made dinner, he always made enough for two and left mine out with a note. *In case you're hungry.* He'd fill up my water bottle every morning before leaving for the ranch, always with seven ice cubes—no more, no less. Exactly the way I liked it.

He never said a word about any of it. He just did it, like maybe if he showed me enough small kindnesses, I'd forget why I was keeping him at arm's length.

And the worst part? It almost worked.

Each one of those little gestures chipped away at my resolve. No grand declarations, no pressure—just quiet, consistent care, and I hated how much it got to me.

The longer it went on, the harder it got to tell the difference between protecting myself and just being scared.

I stepped inside the ranch house and felt that familiar nostalgic sense of home. My dad rounded the corner from the kitchen, a smile breaking across his face.

"Hey, Dotty. Good to see you."

"Hey, Dad." I hugged him, the weight of the past few months settling just a little. We moved into the kitchen and sat at the dining table.

I'd been seeing Dad more than usual lately, but the guilt still lingered—knowing it wasn't nearly enough. We'd always been close. I guess I was a daddy's girl by default, the way he stepped up after Mom was gone. I could always rely on him to be there. We kept in touch every day in the family group chat, and I called him every weekend, no matter what, when I was away.

"How's work?" he asked, pouring himself some coffee.

"Busy. Good busy, mostly. I'm more productive working from home—less distractions, fewer interruptions. I do miss the office sometimes, but the flexibility here is nice."

He nodded, a soft smile tugging at his lips. "Good. Glad

it's working out. How are you really doing? You seem lighter these past couple of months."

Being back in Woodstone had this strange peace I didn't expect, even with someone quietly watching my every move. But it also cracked open old wounds I'd spent years shoving down.

I sighed, annoyed that both Dad and Noah had said the same thing about me earlier. "It's good. I love it here," I hesitated. "But I'm going back soon. Though I do want to visit more than once a decade. It's just... complicated."

He gave me a look full of understanding. "Life's funny like that. Throws curveballs when you don't see them coming. But I'm glad you're home, even if just for a little while."

I leaned forward, resting my elbows on the table. "I'm stuck in limbo, Dad. Torn between two worlds, and I love both." My fingers fiddled with my necklace chain, tracing the links. "I love my job, but I'm not ready to give it up. I love Seattle, but honestly... I think it's only ever felt like home because of my job... and Noah."

He sighed and rubbed his eyes. "You know, kid..." He met my eyes. "When your mom died, everything changed in an instant. I'd done the one thing that seems to be everyone's purpose in life—I found *her*. I found the person I was meant to be with. And that's why even after nearly twenty years, I have never wanted anyone else." He took off his glasses and massaged the bridge of his nose. "But after she passed, I wanted to run. I felt like I had to escape this town because your mom—she was everywhere."

I reached across the table and grabbed his hand, squeezing gently.

"Dad, you don't have to..."

He gave me a weak smile before continuing. "She was

in the bathroom, getting ready for the day. She was in the kitchen, making us dinner. She was in the post office, running errands. She was on the ranch, lending a hand when we needed it. She was everywhere I looked."

A tear slipped down my cheek before I could stop it.

"But I couldn't run," he said softly. "Because I had the four of you. Without you guys, I might've run from the grief altogether." He squeezed my hand. "Dotty, I don't know why you ran, and I don't need to. But something made you leave. Maybe it was Mom, maybe something else entirely. Or maybe it was everything."

I couldn't hold his gaze and looked away.

"But staying here—rebuilding this life without her, finding a new normal with you and your brothers—saved me. I learned to make new memories in the spaces she left behind. And even though she'll always be in the deepest part of my heart, so is this town." He looked at me, steady. "Wherever your place is—Woodstone, Seattle, or somewhere else—you need to find it. The place that makes you whole, the people that make you whole. You have to let go of what you think you're supposed to do, maybe what you want to do, and accept what's right. For you."

Talking to Dad was always easy. He listened without judgment and knew when to offer advice or just a quiet ear.

But this—him opening up, trying to relate, trying to make me feel less alone—it hit harder than I expected. He wasn't just talking. He was reaching for me.

I didn't have words, so I just nodded and stood to pull him into a tight hug.

He held me close. "You'll figure it out, sweet girl. You've got time. And I'm always here."

"Thanks, Dad," I whispered. "For everything."

He kissed the top of my head. Then, like it was nothing, he said, "Any update on the case?"

I pulled back, wiping away tears. "Not really. I asked Colt to keep the details from me. Trying not to let it stress me out. No major leads. Just waiting."

"Nothing new since Mount Leston?"

"Nothing. It's been weirdly quiet."

"That's a good thing, right?" His smile was hopeful.

I gave a small, unsure nod. "Yeah. I guess."

We spent the next few hours catching up, the warmth of my childhood wrapping around me.

But when I left, I knew I couldn't avoid it any longer—the place I'd been putting off since coming back to Woodstone.

The next morning, I drove the winding back roads, Woodstone Falls blurring past my windows in streaks of green and gray. The early morning mist clung to the trees, and I felt a knot tighten in my stomach. I slowed down, turning onto the path that led to the secluded spot where I had spent hours growing up.

When the turnoff came into view, I eased onto the gravel path, tires crunching as I followed the curve toward the place I hadn't let myself think about in years.

I parked and stepped out. The air was colder here—quiet in a way that felt intentional. The only sound was the crunch of gravel under my boots.

The headstone came into view. I slowed as I reached it, the familiar name cutting straight through me.

Darlene Mae James.

"Hi, Mom," I whispered, voice cracking on the words. "It's been a while. Ten years, actually."

I knelt slowly, fingers brushing across the cool stone. The wind rustled through the trees like a sigh. I blinked back my tears already welling up.

"I don't even know where to start," I said, closing my eyes. "If you were here, you'd know exactly what to say. You always had this way of loving people that made everything feel less heavy." I paused, the memories of her were just out of reach—all blurry edges where sharp detail used to live.

"I'm lost, Mom. I'm so lost." My voice broke, but I fought back the tears. "I worked my ass off to build a life I'm proud of. I love what I do. I love Seattle. But being back here... it's different. I love it here, too. And it's not just nostalgia or convenience—it feels like me here. Like I remember who I am again."

I glanced up at the sky, where clouds moved slowly by. "I love being near the boys. I love that when I get coffee, they already know my order and never ask my name. I love that the beach and the mountains are both just a short drive away, and that I can get lost in the woods in ten minutes flat."

My throat tightened. "And Gracie... God, Mom, you'd love her. She's got your laugh, I swear. She looks just like you. You'd be obsessed with her. It kills me that you'll never meet her."

I moved to sit cross-legged. Cold damp soaked through my jeans, but I didn't care.

"Dad thinks I left to run away from you. Maybe he's right. Maybe I needed distance to figure out who I was without the loss of you. I think I thought it'd be easier... but it never really was. Remember when I used to come to you with all my problems, and you'd know exactly what to say? I need that now more than ever."

I reached into my bag and pulled out my notebook—pages of half-formed thoughts, lists, messy dreams.

"You'd laugh at me. I made a pros and cons list, trying to logic my way through it all, like that would help." I shook my head with a sad smile. "But no matter how I spin it, nothing feels clear. I don't want to give up what I've built in Seattle, but I can't imagine walking away from what I've found here either. How do I find the balance? How do I honor both parts of my life without sacrificing one for the other?"

The silence that followed felt profound, almost comforting. I felt a gentle breeze caress my cheek.

"And don't even get me started on Trent," I said with a shaky laugh. "That man... he's patient and kind and shows up in ways I didn't think people still did. And it scares the hell out of me. I'm terrified of what it could mean if I let myself fall for him. What if I get hurt again? What if it's too much, too soon, too real?"

I looked down at the headstone, biting back another sob. "I wish you could just tell me what to do. I'd even settle for one of those weird metaphors you used to throw at me that didn't make sense until five years later."

I stayed there for a long time—talking, crying, falling quiet. Letting the silence answer in the only way it could.

Eventually, I stood, feeling a strange sense of peace wash over me, though uncertainty remained. I pressed my fingers to my lips and then to the headstone. "Thanks, Mom. I promise I won't let another ten years go by without visiting you."

With one last look, I turned and walked back toward the

car. The path ahead was still foggy, but for the first time in a long while, I felt like I might actually be able to walk it.

TWENTY-FIVE

Dotty

PINK SKIES - ZACH BRYAN

AFTER LEAVING THE CEMETERY, I NEEDED SOMETHING—anything—to pull me out of my head. So, I threw myself into work on the cabin. The scent of sawdust clung to my clothes, and the steady rhythm of hammers and drills dulled the ache in my chest. By the time the sun dipped below the trees, exhaustion had settled deep in my bones. I needed a hot shower, clean sheets, and maybe five minutes without moving.

When I stepped through the front door, Trent was already there, sitting casually on the edge of the couch like he belonged in the center of my storm.

"Hey, stranger," he said.

"Hi," I replied, tugging off my jacket.

"You done avoiding me yet?" His eyes danced, but there was a bite of honesty beneath the teasing.

"I'm not avoiding you." My voice betrayed me, rising just enough to give myself away.

He gave me a look. "Mhm. And I like mint chocolate chip ice cream."

"I knew you didn't like it." I narrowed my eyes at him.

"You got me. How about a movie?" he asked, patting the seat next to him.

I hesitated, torn between the comfort of Trent's company and the safety of my room. I cleared my throat, deciding his charm would not win me over tonight.

"I have a Zoom meeting early tomorrow. I should get some sleep," I said, already halfway toward retreat.

"Alright, alright—no movie," he said, raising his hands in mock surrender. "But come sit. Ten minutes. Talk to me. Pretend you're not ignoring me for just that long."

I turned back toward him. Our eyes met for what felt like the first time in weeks, and his green irises softened me. "Ten minutes," he pleaded.

"Ten minutes," I echoed.

His smile bloomed instantly—dimples and all. I made a point to sit on the far end of the couch, ignoring the gravitational pull between us.

"So, how's work?" he asked, stretching his arm across the back of the couch like he wasn't inching closer with every word.

"Busy. Meetings. Emails. The usual." I kept it vague, unwilling to give too much away.

He studied me like he could see the answers I wasn't saying. "You okay?" He shifted, scooting toward me, his full attention locked onto me. His hand settled lightly on my knee, and I didn't pull away.

"I'm fine," I said because it was easier than admitting the truth.

"You don't have to talk," he said gently. "But I'm here. You know that, right? I'm always here, Dotty."

My throat tightened. Something in his voice undid me.

"I went to see my mom today," I said quietly. "First time since I was nineteen."

His fingers stilled beneath mine.

"I've been back in town for two months and hadn't gone until now. I don't know why I waited so long."

"Grief isn't one-size-fits-all," he murmured. "Colt probably hasn't been back since the funeral. Dorian goes every week. You don't love her any less just because it took you longer." He exhaled, his grip firm but steady. "She'd be so damn proud of you, Dotty. I know I am."

At some point, mine had slid over his, like muscle memory.

My chest tightened, the words settling deep, and when I looked up, his gaze was already on me.

"Thanks," I muttered.

He reached up slowly, brushing a stray strand of hair behind my ear. His fingertips grazed my cheek, and the air between us shifted. My breath caught.

Then—too soon—he pulled back.

I stared at the empty space where his hand had been, trying to gather myself.

"I should sleep," I said, my voice thin. "Early call tomorrow."

"Tomorrow's Halloween," he said, as if he hadn't noticed the emotional whiplash we were both in. "I'm staying in. Gonna pass out candy to the neighborhood kids. Want to do movie night then? No tricks, I swear."

I looked at him. He was smiling, but not with the usual confidence. This one held hope. Hesitation.

"Yeah," I said, almost surprising myself. "Okay."

His eyes lit up. "Yeah?"

"Don't make me change my mind."

I stood slowly, pulse thudding in my ears, and made my way toward the bedroom door.

"Good night, Trent."

"Good night, Dotty."

I didn't turn around. If I had, I wasn't sure what I would've done.

The sun dipped lower in the sky, casting a golden glow over the neighborhood as the first trick-or-treaters began to appear out the window. I knew it wouldn't be long before they started knocking on the door.

Growing up, Halloween had never been my favorite holiday. Despite my sweet tooth, I never cared much for trick-or-treating. Not having many friends outside of my brothers and Trent, combined with the anxiety of running into classmates, made it easier to stay home. Most years, I'd sit on the porch with my dad, passing out candy and watching the other kids race from house to house.

As an adult, my feelings hadn't changed much. Halloween was just another night. Back in Seattle, Noah and I would put on a horror movie and hope for trick-or-treaters, though we rarely got any. Living in a Seattle apartment didn't exactly scream festive neighborhood.

But here in Woodstone Falls, things were different. The crisp autumn air smelled like fallen leaves and candy, and the distant sound of children's excitement filled the street. For the first time in years, Halloween actually felt like something again.

Trent stepped out of his room, and I nearly choked on my own saliva.

"What?" he said with a smug grin, motioning down his body. "Don't like my costume?"

I averted my gaze fast, doing my best not to stare at the

skintight superhero spandex that left *nothing* to the imagination.

"I didn't take you for the kind of adult who still dresses up," I said, sinking into the couch. My joggers and worn graphic tee weren't exactly festive in comparison.

"Gracie always stops by. One year, I wasn't wearing a costume, and she told me I lost uncle points. Haven't made that mistake again."

"Makes sense. She's got everyone wrapped around her finger," I said, laughing.

The doorbell rang, and Trent grabbed the candy bowl, tossing a handful into each tiny pumpkin-shaped bucket. Once the first round of kids left, he sat next to me on the couch and started a classic Halloween movie—though we didn't get far. Every few minutes, the doorbell chimed again. We took turns manning the door, trading off like clockwork. By the time we were four bowls deep, another ding echoed through the house, and Trent stood up with a smile.

"I got this one." He rounded the couch, and I tried—really tried—not to stare at how stupidly good that costume looked on him.

From where I sat, I could still see the porch. A little girl dressed as a princess stood there, grinning up at Trent.

"Thank you, mister! Oh, and here—someone back there asked me to give you this."

Trent froze.

"What is it?" I asked, already sitting up.

He turned, his jaw tight. "A note."

Dread unfurled in my chest. I was on my feet before he could move. I snatched the paper from his hands.

Trent blinked, startled—then bolted after the girl.

"Wait!" he called out.

My heart thudded as I unfolded the note, stomach dropping fast.

I have to tread carefully now, but just because my messages have become scarce doesn't mean I have stopped thinking about you. Every moment I'm consumed with thoughts of us together. Soon, very soon, our worlds will collide, and everything will be as it should. Just you and me, forever.

The words blurred as my stomach twisted violently. I barely made it to the bathroom before I was on my knees, heaving into the toilet.

I didn't know how long I was there puking up my guts when Trent crouched beside me. He gently pulled my hair aside, and his hand rubbed slow, steady circles on my back.

"Sorry," I muttered, swiping at my mouth with the back of my hand.

"No need to apologize. Wouldn't be the first time I've seen you lose your cookies." His voice was light, but I could sense the tension in his body.

"I called Colt," he added. "He's on his way. Dorian's still out with Gracie, but said he'll be home soon."

I nodded. "Did you find out anything from the girl?"

"Yeah. Talked to her mom too. She didn't know what was going on. The girl said some guy in a mask gave her the note and told her to bring it here, then ring the bell."

I swallowed hard. "Trent…" My voice cracked. "This is not good."

"I know, sunshine."

Trent pressed a kiss to the top of my head.

I wanted to let it soothe me, but the moment it landed, a slow burn of frustration lit beneath my skin. Just when I'd started to feel safe again—just when the air had stopped tasting like fear—I was right back to watching shadows and second-guessing every knock at the door.

He helped me up, pulled me into his arms, and for once, I didn't resist. I ignored every alarm in my head, every warning that whispered too close. Right now, I didn't care. I just needed to feel something solid. I needed to feel him.

We stayed like that until his phone buzzed.

He rose, offering me a hand. "You good? Colt's here."

I nodded, voice still stuck somewhere behind my ribs. "Yeah. I'm good now."

He made sure I was steady before leading me out of the bathroom.

Colt stood just beyond the doorway, arms open like he'd been waiting. "Love you, Dotty."

I stepped into his hug and let the steadiness of it ground me. "Love you, too."

He pulled back, taking the note from Trent. His fingers pinched the bridge of his nose as he read it, and he started to pace toward the living room.

"I've been pushing for extra man-hours on your case. This," he said, lifting the paper, "might finally get us some."

The doorbell rang again. I seized the distraction like a lifeline and slipped away.

I opened the door to find Gracie beaming up at me.

"Auntie!" Gracie squealed, launching herself into my arms. Her princess costume crinkled as she hugged me tight.

"Hey, sweet girl! I missed you, too." I wrapped her up,

her arms tight around my neck. "And don't you look absolutely royal?"

Dorian gave me a long look. "Let's leave this outside for the night." He grabbed the candy bowl from my hands. "It's slowing down anyway."

"But what about me?" Gracie asked, spinning toward him. "Don't I get some candy?"

Dorian grinned and angled the bowl toward her. "How could I forget? Pick two. No trading later."

She gasped as if he'd given her keys to a kingdom, carefully selecting her prizes before skipping inside.

I lingered on the porch for a moment, watching her disappear into the glow of the living room. The moon hung high, pale and full, casting shadows that felt longer than usual.

"Hey, Gracie," I called gently. "Why don't you go say hi to your uncles? Maybe put on something for us to watch?"

"TV this late?" she gasped, spinning mid-stride. "Halloween really is the best holiday!"

She bolted toward the kitchen, blonde curls bouncing.

Trent and Colt barely had time to register her before she wrapped them both in quick hugs and darted off again, already flipping through channels.

Colt raised an eyebrow. "Well. That was fast."

Dorian chuckled. "Told her she could watch TV after she said hi. Guess she figured the quicker the better."

"Must be the sugar," Colt muttered with a smirk. Then his tone shifted. "So, how bad is it?"

Dorian glanced at me before unfolding the note. His jaw clenched as he read. "I don't even know what to say to this." His eyes flicked up. "What the hell's wrong with this guy?"

Colt rubbed at the back of his neck. "No leads. We've hit

nothing but dead ends, but I'm still pushing. We'll get something soon."

"Let's hope that's not too late," Dorian muttered.

Their voices faded to background noise. All I could hear was the echo of those words—the ones scrawled in crooked handwriting.

No matter how badly I wanted to feel safe again—wanted to believe it was behind me—I knew the truth now.

He wasn't finished.

And I was terrified he never would be.

The weeks passed in a blur. Work piled up. I dodged Trent whenever I could, and the cabin renovations kept dragging on. Mornings meant staring at spreadsheets and emails. Evenings meant sawdust in my hair and wood stain under my nails. The days bled into each other, as the bright colors of fall faded into the dull gray of early winter.

Thanksgiving was coming up fast. It would be my first real holiday in Woodstone with my family in years. The thought of sitting around the table with Dad, my brothers, and Gracie felt really good.

Still, there was that knot in the back of my mind. The damn stalker that refused to go away. It hung over everything, making it hard to relax, no matter how much I tried. I wanted the holiday to feel safe. To feel normal.

But it didn't.

The cabin was also tough. Every spare minute went toward fixing it up—installing fixtures, sanding floors, staining wood. When Colt and Dorian couldn't make it out, Trent stepped in. Having an extra set of hands helped, even if we mostly worked separately. The place was starting to look like a home, but my savings were shrinking fast.

And for some ungodly reason, I thought sanding and staining the floors would be easy. It wasn't. The sander I rented was supposed to suck up the dust, but instead it kicked up a cloud that covered me head to toe by day two. A pain in the ass, honestly.

Trent came through and finished the sanding while I was at work one day. No clue how he did it, but I didn't ask.

Between the long workdays and late nights at the cabin, I was drained, but seeing family regularly made it worth it. My manager hinted a promotion was finally in reach, and I was relieved remote work hadn't killed those chances.

Glancing at the clock, I realized it was already past five and decided to clock out for the weekend. Trent knocked on my door as I closed my laptop.

"Come in," I said, turning away from the desk he'd built for me.

He filled the doorway, arms propped up like he owned the place. My chest tightened for no good reason, except maybe because I was still trying to erase what his lips felt like.

"Hey, Dorian and I are heading to the bar. You in?" His smile was easy, with those damn dimples showing.

I sighed. "You know what? Yeah. I could use a drink after this week."

"Get ready. Dorian's the DD tonight." He winked.

I don't know why that little, dumb gesture hit me so hard. One flick of an eyelid, and suddenly my heart was doing something it shouldn't, something it couldn't.

Outlaw's parking lot was packed tight under the Friday night glow, so we ended up squeezing in along the roadside behind a long line of cars. Music spilled out from inside, loud enough to pull a crowd.

Dorian swung open the doors, and Trent slid a hand to the small of my back, steering me inside. The band was better than I expected for a small-town gig, which only made the place feel more alive.

It was so jammed we had to shove our way to the bar, and I almost lost Dorian and Trent in the crowd. When Trent noticed I was falling behind, he grabbed my hand, and guided me through. Once we finally reached the bar, Dorian started ordering drinks and nodded at Trent.

With a casual charm, Trent flipped his hat backward and leaned in close to whisper in my ear, "Tequila soda, right?" His voice was low and rough, and his calloused hand, squeezing mine, sent a jolt straight down my spine.

I looked up at him through half-lowered lashes and muttered, "Yes, please." I bit my lip before I could say something dumb, like how ridiculously good he looked with that hat flipped backward.

TWENTY-SIX

Trent

FAST CAR · LUKE COMBS

I LEANED OVER THE BAR, SHOUTING OUR DRINK ORDERS TO THE bartender over the music. The moment I glanced back, I caught Dotty watching me, her eyes lingering longer than she typically let them.

She was making it really fucking hard to respect her boundaries. I'd given her space the past month, kept my hands to myself, because being close to her was like standing next to an open flame—sooner or later, I was going to lean in too far.

I glanced down at her, and yup, definitely leaned in too far. My self-control already hated me.

I dipped my head close to hers, my lips just brushing the shell of her ear. "Stop biting that lip."

She froze, just a fraction of a second, enough to tell me she heard me. Enough to tell me she knew exactly what she was doing.

She bumped her shoulder into mine, a smirk tugging at her mouth. "Or what?" she said in a playful tone, but there was bite under it. "Like you'd actually do something with Dorian right there?"

My gaze flicked to him, who was laughing at something someone was saying, with not a clue in the world that his sister was testing me like this. *Pushing me.*

I let my lips ghost her ear again. "It's cute you think I give a damn what your brother thinks."

Her breath caught—barely, but I felt it. Saw it in the way her eyes locked on mine before she looked down, tracing her necklace chain.

The bartender slid our drinks to us. She took a sip and nearly choked, setting hers down hard.

"Shit, you okay?"

She waved me off. "Yeah. Just… really strong," she said, coughing.

I grinned. "Aw, you poor thing."

"Fuck off." She shoved my chest, not even trying to make it convincing.

So I swiped her drink.

Her eyes narrowed. "Trent," she warned.

I took a slow sip, watching her the whole time. Let the burn slide down my throat without a flinch. Without blinking. Just staring at her like I had all the time in the world.

Then I saw it—a faint smudge of lip gloss on the rim. A perfect little imprint of her pretty lips.

Before my brain could remind me why that was a bad idea, my tongue was there, dragging over the spot. I didn't break eye contact. It was sweet, tempting, and exactly what I shouldn't want. But I did. A low sound worked its way out of my chest before I could stop it.

And fuck, I wanted to kiss her.

Her mouth opened—a sharp little inhale. Then she licked her lips, as Dorian turned his attention our way.

I leaned in, my voice low. "Hmm," I hummed. "Now I

know exactly how you'd taste if I kissed you again," I said turning away.

I spotted a table opening up, and snagged it before anyone else could. Dotty slid in across from me, and Dorian dropped down beside me.

The band cranked out familiar covers, couples singing along. The air was warm, the kind of crowded that pressed you into people whether you wanted it or not.

I looked to Dorian. "How's work been? Haven't seen much of you lately."

"Busy, as usual," he said, rolling his shoulders. "Gracie's Christmas break is coming up, so I'm cutting back to spend time with her."

"That's good. She'll love that," I said.

Dotty tucked a strand of hair behind her ear, looking at him. "When I'm not working, I can help watch her. My office slows down for the holidays."

"Thanks, Dotty. That'd be great."

Out of the corner of my eye, I caught someone approaching from the left.

"Anyone sitting here?" Austin gestured to the empty spot beside Dotty.

"Yes," I said, at the same time Dotty said, "No, go ahead."

This fucking guy.

"It's good to see you again, Dotty." He greeted her first, then nodded to me and Dorian.

Again.

This mother fucker was trying to make a move on my girl. Except she wasn't my girl. She made that pretty damn clear.

But still, fuck this guy.

"It's nice to see you too." She gave him a flirty smile

that had my blood boiling, even though I had no ground to be upset.

I knew he'd done her cabin inspection, but I didn't realize they were on smiling terms.

They started talking. I tried to ignore it. Really fucking tried. But every laugh she gave him, every lean toward him, was a slow twist of the knife right in the chest.

Dorian must've sensed the shift in my mood because he stood, patting my shoulder. "Yeah, I'm gonna go grab us another round." Then he walked off, leaving me alone with them.

They kept talking, and Dotty had that little tilt to her head like she was actually interested.

When Austin leaned in a little too close to say something in her ear, I caught the moment her energy changed. She pulled back slightly and stopped matching his flirting. Still, they went back and forth until she shook her head and leaned in just enough to tell him something.

I pretended not to watch, even though my eyes were locked on them.

He gave her a tight smile, his jaw tense and eyes harder than before. Then he stood. "See you around," he said, stalking off.

"What was that about?" I asked.

She exhaled, reaching for her drink. "He asked me out. I said no." She arched a brow. "Don't get your panties in a bunch, cowboy."

"He seemed pissed."

She scoffed. "I can handle myself."

Yeah, I knew she could. Still didn't stop the knot in my chest. I wanted her to be mine. Wanted every guy in this place to know it. Hell, I wanted everyone in the world to know it.

I wanted *her* to know it.

My jaw tensed, and I tried not to take it out on her, knowing it wasn't her fault she was every man's walking wet dream.

Dorian returned with our drinks, and the music filled the bar. Dotty seemed to relax, swaying to the music.

A familiar song started to play, and I found myself singing along. Dorian shot me an amused look, and I shrugged.

"What? I like this song."

Dotty, still moving to the beat, joined in, singing the lyrics under her breath. Our eyes met across the table. Her lips curved into something playful.

And then, still singing, she started dancing.

I didn't even hesitate. Pushing back from my chair, I walked over and held out a hand in question.

She peered up at me through her lashes, then to Dorian.

"Go," he said. "I'm going to go say hi to some guys at the bar. Go have fun, if you even know how."

Dotty slipped her hand into mine, and something in my chest cracked wide open.

No thinking, no second-guessing—just this desperate need to be closer. I wove us through the crowd toward the dance floor, her grip steady in mine, like she'd been waiting ten years to hold my hand again and wasn't about to waste a second of it.

The moment I turned to face her, she went all in—pointing right at me, belting the chorus, hips rolling like we weren't smack in the middle of Outlaws with half the damn town watching. It seemed like she was performing just for me, the way she used to in her bedroom with the door locked and the music turned low so her dad wouldn't hear.

And damn, I was gone. Completely gone. Not just grinning—drowning in the sight of her, the way she pulled me into her orbit like gravity had been broken all these years and was finally working again.

Everything else dissolved. No voices, no music pounding from the speakers, no decade of silence stretching between us. Just her—laughing like we'd never missed a beat, teasing me with that look that seemed like she remembered exactly how my hands felt on her skin.

Her hair caught the bar lights, copper and gold tangled together like a sunset I'd been chasing in every other woman's face since she left. A few strands broke loose, brushing her cheeks, and my fingers ached—actually fucking ached—with how badly I wanted to reach out and tuck them back, to find an excuse to touch her that wouldn't give away how completely she still owned me.

Those freckles she probably figured nobody noticed were still there, faded from winter but stubborn as hell, scattered across her nose like a map I'd memorized in another life. I wanted to trace every single one with my mouth until she made that little sound she had made when I kissed her.

It hit me like a physical blow—this wasn't just wanting her body back in my bed, though God knows I did. This was the terrible, beautiful realization that I'd never stopped loving every contradiction she carried. The sharp, unflinching side that could stare down anyone who crossed her. The vulnerable one she thought she'd buried so deep no one would ever find it again. The woman standing here with me right now, laughing like the last ten years were just a bad dream we'd finally woken up from.

I was ruined. Had been since the day she left, and seeing her now, I knew I'd spend the rest of my life trying to earn my way back into her story.

The song ended, and the band jumped right into another popular cover. Dotty laughed, her smile lighting up the dimly lit room, but I couldn't look away. I was done keeping my distance.

"Let's go sit back down. I need another drink," she said.

Before she could take another step, Austin's laugh cut through the noise right next to us—loud, confident, the kind of laugh that said he owned every room he walked into. He was leaning against the bar, talking to some redhead, but his eyes kept drifting back to Dotty. Watching her like he was cataloging every move she made, every smile she gave me.

The way he looked at her, like he had every right to keep looking, made something dark and possessive tear through my chest.

I caught Dotty's wrist and spun her back to face me, my grip tighter than it needed to be. "Not yet."

She blinked, startled by the sudden intensity in my voice, and I could see her trying to read what had just shifted between us. But all I could think about was Austin's hands on her. Austin driving her home. Austin knowing things about who she'd become while I'd been stuck frozen in the memory of who we used to be.

It was completely irrational—they barely knew each other from what I knew, but logic wasn't exactly running the show when it came to Dotty.

Part of me—the part that had been starving for her for ten years—wanted to show her exactly who she belonged to. Not Austin with his easy charm and his clean slate. Not anyone else who thought they could just walk into her life and claim space there. Me. It had always been me.

But that wasn't who I was supposed to be. She asked for

space. Not the kind of man who marked his territory like some animal.

Still, seeing her with him tonight, watching her laugh at his jokes while I'd been reduced to memories and for nows—it stole my breath and left me raw.

I could see the confusion flickering in her eyes as I pulled her toward the small, hidden office I knew was tucked away in the back. Small-town connections—like knowing the owner since high school—came in handy when jealousy made you desperate for somewhere private.

The door clicked shut behind us, muffling the bar noise to a distant hum. In the sudden quiet, I could hear my own ragged breathing.

Dotty turned to face me, eyebrows raised. "What is it with you and these cryptic doors that lead to tiny spaces? What's wrong?"

I dragged a hand through my hair, every word I wanted to say tangled up somewhere between anger and desperation.

"Wait…" Her voice dropped, understanding creeping across her face. "You're jealous, aren't you?"

I closed the distance between us. She was close enough that I could see the flecks of gold in her blue eyes, close enough that her breath ghosted across my skin.

"Yeah," I said, my voice rougher than I intended. "I am. I'm fucking jealous anyone else thinks they even have a chance with you." I swallowed.

Her eyes softened as she looked at me.

And that was it. Every wall I'd built, every reason I'd given myself to stay away—gone. I reached for her face, thumb tracing the curve of her cheek like I was trying to memorize the moment before everything changed.

"Tell me I can kiss you," I said, my forehead resting on hers.

"Yes," she whispered.

And I fucking snapped.

I couldn't resist any longer. I pulled her to me, sealing my mouth over hers.

The taste of her was like coming home and falling apart all at once. Ten years of missing her, of wondering what if, of pretending I'd moved on—I poured all of it into that kiss. She pulled me closer, and I was done for.

I kissed her like I was trying to make up for every kiss I'd missed, every night I'd dreamed about this moment.

The force of it stole the breath from my lungs. She pushed me back against the door, her fingers twisting in my shirt like it was the only thing keeping her anchored to earth. When she made that soft sound against my lips—half sigh, half surrender—I swear to God I saw stars. If I ever made it to heaven, that sound would be waiting for me at the gates.

I spun us around, pressing her back against the door, and she met me with equal desperation. Her hands were everywhere—my chest, my shoulders, threading through my hair and pulling me deeper into her. When she wrapped her legs around my waist, fitting against me like she was made for this, for me, I nearly lost what was left of my mind.

"Fuck, Dotty," I breathed against her lips.

"Shut up, and kiss me, cowboy," she breathed.

"Yes, ma'am," I murmured against her lips before trailing kisses down the column of her throat. When I found her pulse point, she let out a soft whimper that sent my heart racing. It felt like I had just ran a damn marathon.

Dotty was rocking herself on me, and I nearly came in

my pants like a fucking teenager. When she pulled back, I was grateful for the reprieve even as I mourned the loss of contact. My mind was spinning with a thousand different thoughts, all centering on one desperate hope—that she wouldn't stop this.

"I need you," she whispered.

Those three words shattered me.

"Tell me I can touch you," I said, my voice barely recognizable. "Please."

She pressed her forehead to mine, her breath warm against my skin. "Yes. *Please.*"

The corners of my mouth lifted. "Mm, I like it when you beg."

I turned her gently, lifting her onto the small desk. My hands found her hips, positioning her exactly where I needed her to be. Standing between her parted legs, the air between us practically crackled with electricity. The only light in the room streamed in from the bar around the doorframe, casting a soft glow that outlined her features. It highlighted the delicate color creeping across her face.

"You look so pretty when you blush for me." My thumb rubbed her cheek, slowing down the moment to savor every second.

She hummed softly, leaning into my touch. I let my other hand drift lower, pressing against her through the denim. Her sharp intake of breath was like a match to kindling, and I captured the sound with another kiss. She was sweet and spicy and all the things I dreamed about for ten fucking years.

"More," she whispered, pressing her mouth to mine.

I kept our lips connected as I worked her jeans open, my hand slipping beneath the fabric. I wanted to savor this, to give her back every moment of torment she'd unknowingly put me through. I traced my tongue up her throat. When I slipped a finger inside her, she gasped so prettily I nearly forgot my own name.

"All this for me, baby?" I asked, marveling at how ready she was for me.

She looked up at me through her lashes and nodded. I began to move, finding a rhythm that had her breathing in short, sharp gasps. When I curled my finger, she let out a sound that went straight to my soul.

"Again," she commanded softly.

I repeated the motion that drew another beautiful moan from her lips. "That's my good fucking girl."

I worked her steadily, watching every expression cross her face, cataloging each breathy sound she made. The noise from the bar faded to nothing as I focused entirely on her. My free hand came up to rest gently at the base of her throat.

I could feel her body beginning to tighten around my fingers, could see the telltale signs of her approaching her release.

"Eyes on me," I said, my voice rough.

"Yes, cowboy." Her eyes snapped open to give me a playful eye roll that somehow made this moment even more perfect.

"What did I tell you about rolling your eyes?" I withdrew my hand completely.

"What the hell?" she protested, pushing against my chest.

Instead of answering, I brought my fingers to my lips, tasting her slowly. The sound I made was involuntary—she was everything I'd imagined and more. Ten years of wondering, and now I knew.

"Going to behave for me now?" I asked.

"Probably not," she said with a breathless laugh, "but maybe I'll wait until after you finish what you started."

I slipped two fingers back inside her, and the curse she breathed made me grin.

"Oh fuck," she moaned.

She was so responsive, so perfect, rocking against my hand like she was made for this moment. I could feel her climbing higher, could see the way her breathing changed, the way her body wanted more.

"That's it, baby. Take what you need," I urged her. "Come for me."

When she came, the sound she made rewrote something fundamental in my brain. I kissed her through it, swallowing every beautiful noise as she trembled against me.

For a moment after, she stayed pressed against me, her forehead resting on my shoulder as her breathing slowly evened out. My hand moved to her back, tracing gentle circles as she came down from her high. This was the part I'd never let myself imagine—the quiet after, when she was soft and pliant in my arms. And it was just as good as the rest of it.

"God," she whispered against my neck, and I felt her lips brush my skin as she spoke. The word was barely audible, more breath than voice.

"I know," I murmured back, pressing a kiss to her temple. I wanted to tell her how incredible she was, how this felt like everything I'd been missing for ten years, but something in the way she'd gone still warned me to tread carefully.

That's when I felt it—the subtle shift. Her muscles tensing slightly, her breathing becoming more deliberate. She lifted her head from my shoulder, and when her eyes met mine, they were different. The hazy, satisfied look was replaced by something guarded, almost panicked.

"Oh," she said softly, as if she'd just remembered where we were, who we were. Her hands moved to my chest, not pushing me away, but creating the smallest amount of distance. "Oh, God."

I watched it happen in real time—saw the exact moment reality crashed back in and her walls started rebuilding themselves, brick by brick. Her breathing changed, became more controlled, and she pulled back both physically and emotionally.

"We should... we should go back out there," she said, not quite meeting my eyes.

"Dotty..." The word escaped as barely a whisper, my hand reaching through the charged air between us. "Wait."

Her eyes found mine for a heartbeat—wild, conflicted—before darting away. "Dorian will wonder where I am," she said, her fingers trembling as she worked the buttons of her jeans.

I opened my mouth to speak, to say something that might keep her here, but she was already moving. She slipped toward the door, pausing only to smooth her hair with shaking hands.

The soft click of the latch was deafening in the sudden silence. I stood frozen in the aftermath, still feeling the warmth of her skin, the echo of her breath against my neck.

The air hung heavy between us as we stepped into my house after Dorian dropped us off.

"Are you ready to stop ignoring me now?" I asked.

"I'm not ignoring you." She kicked off her shoes by the front door, avoiding my eyes.

"Yeah, I've heard that before."

I moved to the kitchen, filling two glasses with water and adding seven ice cubes to hers.

"Stop bullshitting me, Dotty."

"What do you want me to say, Trent?" She sank into a chair at the dining table, accepting the glass I offered. Her elbows found the table's surface as she cradled her head.

"The truth. What's going on in that head of yours?"

"I don't know." She ran a hand through her hair, frustration bleeding into her voice. "I show up in town, and you either ignore me or act like nothing ever happened between us ten years ago. Then I get sick, and you take care of me. You always feed me or leave me coffee. You take me Scoops, and then almost kiss me on the porch."

"Dot…"

She stood abruptly, the chair scraping against the floor. "You go from being grumpy to completely avoiding me, to acting like everything's fine, like we're just back to normal. Then, back again. You kissed me at the wedding, and I was sure I'd never feel anything like *that* again, not in this lifetime. But then today?" She stopped mid-step, her breath hitching. "Today completely shattered that theory." Her voice cracked as she turned to face me fully. "And now you want answers from *me*? You think I have them all figured out? Well, I don't. I don't *know* what the hell is going on in my head right now."

I scrubbed a hand through my hair, pulling at the strands like I could physically extract the right words. The anger that had been simmering beneath my skin all day threatened to boil over—not at her, never at her, but at myself.

"I didn't know how to act around you when you came back, and it turned into an everyday battle in my head," I admitted.

"What do you mean?" she asked, her voice soft and tentative, like she wasn't sure she wanted to hear the answer.

"I mean, you drive me crazy in a way no one else could ever even come close to doing. I accepted a long fucking time ago that you were the love of my life, while simultaneously being the one that got away. You got here, and I constantly battled with the need to find an excuse to see you, so I could get my temporary fix, and wanting to never lay eyes on you again, so I didn't have to suffer another day that you weren't *mine*."

I exhaled sharply, stepping closer to her.

Dotty didn't say anything, just watched me, her gaze full of questions I wasn't sure I had the answers to. I took a deep breath and continued, my words coming out in a rush, almost like I couldn't hold them back anymore.

"I knew I could never have you back, but you've been the only one I've ever wanted. I was completely numb the day I left you that note—I knew I'd destroyed everything. I was nineteen and stupid, enlisting without even having the guts to say goodbye to your face."

My hands clenched, a mixture of desire and pain making my chest ache. I had no idea if she could feel it too, the pull between us that was both beautiful and tormenting.

"And I was willing to live with those consequences. You know, it's manageable when you aren't here to do that. I may have had to will you away in my head every goddamn day, but it was doable." I turned around, facing the kitchen sink, and rested both of my hands on the edge of the counter, looking out the window. I let out a breath.

"Then you come marching back into town, and it's unbearable, Dotty. It's truly fucking *unbearable*. It's unbearable to see you, to see this amazing life you've built for yourself, knowing that *I'm* the reason I'm not a part of it now."

When I finally turned back around, she had moved closer, standing just a few feet away. Her face was unreadable, giving me no clue what was going through her mind.

"I… I don't understand," she whispered.

"Let me make it perfectly clear then." I closed the remaining distance between us until she had to tilt her head back to meet my gaze. "I've been in love with you for my entire life. You coming back to Woodstone has been my undoing. Watching you go on a date with Henry, someone who I genuinely think is a stand-up guy, made me want to rip my fucking hair out. He doesn't deserve you. Hell, I don't know if I do either."

She placed her palm flat against my chest, right over my racing heart. "You love me?"

I reached toward her face but stopped myself, my hand hovering inches from her cheek. I closed my eyes, exhaling slowly. "I always have. Never stopped."

When I opened my eyes again, hers were blazing with an intensity that took my breath away.

Within a heartbeat, her demeanor shifted from stillness to pure fury. She took a step back and pointed at me. "But you left. You left Woodstone. You left *me*." The first of her tears fell, my heart plummeting with it. "We spent years tiptoeing around the fact we liked each other, and then I decided one night, *fuck it, Dotty. You never do shit for yourself. Just make the first fucking move.* And not only did you kiss me back—you pretended everything was fine." She pinched the bridge of her nose, shoulders shaking. "Then I woke up to a fucking letter saying you'd left. Not just left— you'd enlisted for eight years. How can you possibly say you've always loved me? You *left* me."

I fought to keep my voice steady. "You're right. I left, and for that, I am sorry. I know it's not an excuse, but I was a terrified kid drowning in grief. Dorian left, my dad died, you were getting ready to move to Seattle—nothing was the same. I had no direction, no idea what to do with my life." I stepped forward, reaching for her chin to lift it until she met my eyes. "I did leave. But don't think for a second I don't wish I'd done it differently. Because it cost me you."

Tears streamed down her face. I wiped them away, cupping her cheek.

"You know why I never made a move?" I asked. "Because I convinced myself I didn't deserve you. Hell, if I wasn't enough for my mom to stick around, how could I possibly be enough for you? So when you kissed me that night before I left for boot camp, I didn't say a damn thing. I wasn't going to ask for more than you were willing to give. If I couldn't have you forever, I'd take whatever pieces of you I could get, even if it was just that one night."

"For someone so smart, you're pretty fucking stupid sometimes."

"Can't argue with that." I let out a bitter laugh. "When I left, I tried convincing myself it wasn't a big deal to skip town without telling anyone. Told myself no one gave a shit about me anyway. By the time I realized how fucking stupid I was, I was too scared to call and apologize. Dorian warned me not to—said you were hurt, that you needed space. I wanted to do right by you for once and respect that."

"I was heartbroken, Trent." Her voice broken, then hardened again. "I left and never came back because I was too scared to show my face here. This town…" She gestured around us, her voice breaking. "It only represented pain. My mom died here. You left me here. I had no one, no friends. Nothing good ever came from this place for so long, so I made it easier on myself to stay away."

Her words came out razor-sharp, filled with years of resentment. "Besides, you don't want me anyway. You deserve more—more than a fucked-up girl with attachment issues who will never settle down. I'll never be that wife who stays home and helps you run the ranch. That's not who I am."

"Is that what you think I want?"

"It's what you need, Trent. Not me. That will never be me."

I reached up, tucking a strand of hair behind her ear, then rested my forehead against hers. "Have you asked me what I want? Not what you think I need, but what I actually want?" I whispered.

She didn't reply.

"Dotty, I'm sorry for everything I did. I'm so fucking sorry—for how I handled it, for not telling you about enlisting, for leaving you a goddamn letter. I hate myself for that, but I'm not sorry that I'm so fucking in love with you that I've been half a man for the last decade without you. Can't you see, I don't want anyone but *you*."

All at once, her lips crashed into mine. It took me a second to register what was happening before my hand found the back of her head, pulling her deeper into the kiss.

After a moment, I pulled back. "What are you doing?"

"Kissing you, cowboy. Shut up."

TWENTY-SEVEN

Dotty

LAST NIGHT · MORGAN WALLEN

"Kissing you, cowboy. Shut up."

That was all he needed to give in completely.

Fighting the urge to kiss him was a losing battle, and the need to feel his rough hands gripping me overwhelmed everything else.

Trent was in love with me. My best friend—the one I grew up with, who patched my scraped knees, who stayed up until the sun rose to talk to me, who always made me brave—was in love with *me*.

His mouth was hot and dangerously addictive. The stubble on his chin scratched lightly against my skin, and suddenly I wondered how it would feel elsewhere. I whimpered as his tongue stroked mine again.

"I need you," he said. I wasn't sure if I had ever seen this side of him, but I wouldn't mind getting to know it better, especially if he kept talking like that.

I pressed up on my tiptoes, craving another kiss.

"Fuck, how is it that just your touch gets me hard?" he growled, hoisting me over his shoulder and striding into the living room.

I slapped his ass and he laughed, the sound warm and reckless. When he finally set me down, I glanced up at him.

"Please tell me I can have you," he breathed. His voice was low and husky, and the hair on the back of my neck stood on end.

"I already said yes." He cut me off with a kiss.

His hand cupped my jaw, tongue slipping between my lips. He tasted of mint and something unmistakably him. I could drown in this.

He grabbed my ass with both hands and lifted me again. My legs instinctively curled around his waist as he peeled off his shirt with one hand.

I froze, eyes locking on the tattoo etched across his chest.

"That is…" My voice faltered as I lowered myself until my feet touched the ground.

"A sun," he finished quietly. My fingers traced the simple ink, and I peered up, speechless. He blushed, and there was something about seeing a six-foot-four cowboy, who exuded sex appeal, blushing that just did it for me.

He exhaled slowly, eyes closing briefly before meeting mine again. "After we lost Steven, Mark and I got matching tattoos. Steven teased us for being too scared to get ink, so this was our roundabout way to honor him and hold onto what matters. Mark's got a daisy, for obvious reasons."

"But… a sun? Why?"

He exhaled slowly, his eyes squeezing shut for a moment before they opened again, locking with mine. "When I was out there—lost in the desert's hell, surrounded by chaos—I couldn't make sense of anything. But thinking of you… how you were out there living, fulfilling all your dreams—that kept me from losing myself. You kept me going, Dotty. Even in silence, your strength and your light were my anchor. You made it all bearable."

I responded by stealing his mouth again, desperate to be closer. I needed him to keep going. To keep *me* sane.

Kissing Trent felt like standing at the edge of a mountain—knowing the fall would change everything. My stomach twisted with fear, but my body moved on its own, taking the leap. I was terrified, but the pull was stronger than anything else.

He pulled back, eyes searching mine, thumb brushing my cheek gently. I leaned into the warmth, needing it to hold me steady.

"I need you," I said, echoing his earlier words. I pulled him back to me, my hand finding the button of his jeans.

His green eyes scanned me like he was memorizing every inch. "So impatient," he teased, a slow, knowing smirk curling his lips. "You sure about this?"

"If I have to say it again, I'm going to fucking scream. *Yes*."

He lowered his forehead to mine, letting out a slow breath. "I just need to know you're sure."

Then, like a promise, he sat me down on the couch and sank to his knees.

"I need to taste you," he murmured, peering up at me.

His eyes flicked up to mine, searching, waiting for the answer he already hoped for. I nodded, biting my bottom lip.

Slowly, he slid my jeans down my legs. Then my underwear followed, and my heart pounded in my chest. My nerves tangled with anticipation, twisting into a raw ache that throbbed beneath my skin as I sank back onto the couch.

Despite the storm inside me, all I could focus on was the

feel of his hands mapping every inch of me like he was memorizing how I trembled under his touch.

His fingers curled around the backs of my thighs, steady and possessive, lifting me just enough to shift me to the edge of the couch.

When his fingers slipped inside me, a low, guttural groan slipped past his lips. It sent a shiver racing down my spine, setting fire as he began to move, slow and purposeful.

"Still this wet for me, sunshine?" His voice dropped.

I smiled, biting my bottom lip. "Fuck, Trent."

His fingers stayed deep, his tongue dragging over me before sucking hard enough to pull a sound from my throat. He licked again, sending waves of sensation crashing through me. I couldn't stop the moans or the way my hips moved, chasing the high he was giving me. His hand tightened on my hip, fingers pumping, thumb circling in perfect rhythm.

"More. I need more, Trent," I gasped, desperate and dizzy.

He pulled back just enough to meet my eyes, fingers still curled inside me.

"I like the sound of my name on your lips."

He slid his fingers in again, and I lost myself, clutching his hair. His free hand found my breast, pinching and rolling my nipple until sparks exploded through me.

"So fucking responsive," he murmured, voice low and rough, and it sent chills racing down my spine.

His mouth came back down, licking, sucking, coaxing every last bit from me. My hips rocked, desperate.

Then he pulled away, breath ragged. "That's it, Dotty. Take what you need."

His voice was a command, and I obeyed, grinding

against his mouth until I shattered. My orgasm hit hard, stealing my breath as I cried out, my thighs trembling around his head. He kept going, licking me through it until I was shaking. The aftershocks rippled through me.

When I finally caught my breath, I looked down to find him wearing a smug little smile. And even though I'd just come on his tongue, the way he was looking at me—like I was the only thing that mattered—had me wanting more.

"That's my girl. You look so fucking pretty when you come for me." He climbed up beside me and kissed me. I tasted myself on his tongue and didn't give a damn. I reached for him, hand sliding under his jeans. His groan was raw and deep.

"Trent," I breathed. "Please. Fuck me before I lose my mind."

He smirked. "Damn, Dotty. Who knew you had such a mouth on you?"

"Says the dirty-talking cowboy." I winked, sliding his jeans and boxers down.

His length sprang free, and I swallowed hard, taking him in.

"It'll fit, baby. Don't worry. We'll take it slow."

My mouth went dry, but he was already leaning over to grab a condom from his wallet. I stole it from him, ripping it open before rolling it.

In one quick motion, he flipped me, so I was straddling him. "Ride me, sunshine. Take my cock and put it where it fucking belongs."

I captured his lips with mine, kissing him with desperate hunger until my lungs burned for air. When I finally pulled back, breathless and dizzy, I positioned myself above him and slowly sank down.

A whimper tore from my throat as my body stretched to

accommodate him—the sensation I'd been both craving and fearing. But the initial discomfort melted away within moments, transforming into something deeper, more consuming. That delicious burn spread through me like wildfire.

Trent's hands found my face, his thumbs brushing against my cheeks as he swallowed each breathy gasp that escaped me. His eyes never left mine, dark with desire and something softer—something that made my heart race even faster than his touch.

"You're absolutely killing me, sunshine," he breathed against my lips, his voice rough with need.

The feeling of being so completely full, so perfectly connected—it was overwhelming. We found our rhythm together, each movement building something electric between us. I could feel his restraint beginning to fracture with every thrust, every breathless moment.

"You were made for me, Dotty," he groaned, his voice breaking slightly. "Look at how well you take me."

My fingers tangled in his hair, pulling him against my chest with desperate need. He captured my nipple with his mouth, sucking with an intensity that made my back arch, then pulled back to lock eyes with mine—those green depths holding something that made my soul ache.

As I lowered myself down again, he wrapped his strong arms around me.

"That's it, baby. Just like that."

His hands found my shoulders, pressing me down into him. The sensation sent shockwaves through me as he filled me even deeper, and I watched the last threads of his control finally snap.

"I need you to come for me," he whispered urgently, his breath hot against my ear. "Let me feel you fall apart."

His thumb found my clit, circling with practiced preci-sion, and I fell apart again—trembling, burning, crying out his name as waves of pleasure crashed over me.

The sound he made—low, raw, completely undone—was something I wanted to carry with me forever. A thou-sand times wouldn't be enough.

He cupped my face with both hands, pulling me down for a kiss. "You are so damn beautiful," he murmured against my lips.

His arms encircled me completely then, our bodies pressed together with nothing between us but shared breath and thundering heartbeats.

And that's when it hit me—the terrifying, wonderful truth that changed everything.

I was so screwed.

So entirely, utterly, completely screwed.

Because I was in love with Trenton Akers.

TWENTY-EIGHT

Trent

US. (FEAT. TAYLOR SWIFT) - GRACIE ABRAMS

DAWN CREPT THROUGH THE CURTAINS. DOTTY'S BODY CURVED against mine, her back to my chest, and I pulled her closer without thinking. I inhaled the scent of her neck, groaning at just how perfect she was.

She stirred, turning in my arms with a sleepy sound that went straight through me. "Morning," she said, voice rough.

I kissed her instead of answering. I needed to taste her again. She melted into me for a heartbeat before pulling back.

"We need to talk." The words came out reluctantly.

"Later," I said, already moving to get up. "Let me get you fed—"

Her hand shot out, fingers wrapping around my wrist. "No. Talk first, then breakfast. Otherwise, I'll avoid it for another ten years, and then I'll hate you again. And I *really* don't want to hate you again."

Something in her voice stopped me cold. I settled back down, watching her face.

"Okay," I said, bracing myself. "Let's hear it."

She sat up, gathering the sheet around herself. "I don't know how to do this." The admission came out quietly. "Whatever this is."

My throat went dry.

"I want it," she said quickly. "I want *you*, but…" Her fingers found that necklace of hers, worrying the charm. "I just… need a second to figure out the next step. Please."

The silence stretched. I reached for her face, thumb brushing her cheek. She leaned into the touch like she couldn't help herself.

"I'm not going anywhere, Dotty."

"But I am. I have to go back to Seattle." Her eyes closed. "That's the problem."

"Then we figure it out."

She looked at me as if I'd offered her something impossible. "Can we... keep this quiet? Just for now?"

The question landed like a punch, but I nodded. "Whatever you need."

I kissed her again, softer this time. I tried to pour everything I couldn't say into it—that I'd wait, that I'd fight for this, that losing her again wasn't an option.

When we broke apart, she was breathing hard.

"Breakfast," I said against her lips. "And then we plan Thanksgiving. Like normal people."

Her laugh was shaky. "Normal. Right."

A few days passed in a haze of stolen moments. Whenever we were alone, I couldn't keep my hands off her. Weeks ago, I'd convinced myself one taste would be enough—that I could scratch this itch and walk away clean. What a joke that turned out to be.

One taste had ruined me.

Now I craved her like an addiction. That moment in Mount Leston played on repeat in my head for weeks, tormenting me with phantom touches and half-remembered sighs. And fuck, now that I knew the sound she made when she came apart—that sweet, breathless gasp—I'd never get enough.

She was everything. The way she smelled like vanilla and something uniquely her. How she threw her head back when she laughed, even if it wasn't nearly often enough. The fierce way she loved her family. How she threw herself into her work like it mattered. How she'd roll her eyes at me but couldn't quite hide her smile.

She was pure sunshine, and I was already burning up.

I found her curled on my couch after another long day at the ranch, completely absorbed in some book with cartoon characters on the cover.

"What's got your attention today?" I asked, taking off my boots.

She glanced up, her eyes soft. "Romance novel. Got a problem with that?"

"Not at all." I grabbed it from her hands. "But now I'm curious what makes you tick."

I flipped through random pages, not really reading, just enjoying the way she watched me.

"Hey!" She lunged forward, trying to snatch it out of my hands. "Give that back!"

The movement brought her tumbling across my lap, and I wasn't about to waste the opportunity. My arm circled her waist, pulling her down until our mouths met. She melted against me for one perfect moment before pushing back with mock indignation.

"Oh no, you don't. No distracting me when I need to

talk to you." But even as she said it, her fingers lingered against my chest. "It's nothing bad, just... work wants me in Seattle next Monday. They said I could video call, but they were pretty clear it would go better face-to-face." Her teeth caught her lower lip. "I'd be gone maybe a week."

The words hit like ice water, but I kept my voice steady. "No problem. I'll be right here when you get back."

Before she could spiral into overthinking, I kissed her again.

She groaned against my mouth. "Also, I haven't touched the cabin all week. I really need to wrap things up soon, before…" The sentence hung unfinished between us. "Before I head back after New Year's."

Yeah, that's when reality crashed down hard.

We both knew she was going back soon. We'd just been dancing around it, pretending we couldn't see the calendar pages turning.

"I know you're leaving." I traced my lips along her jaw, soft kisses that felt like promises I wasn't sure I could keep. "I don't know what you're thinking, but I'm willing to figure out how to make this work."

Her breath caught. "I know."

Then she was pulling her shirt over her head, pushing me back against the cushions. I was spent and breathless, when her name spilled from my lips like a prayer, I wondered if wanting something this much could possibly end well.

We were huddled around the ranch house table, drowning in board game carnage. Sawyer, home for Thanksgiving break, was destroying all of us. The cocky little shit was loving every minute of it. Gracie held onto second place like a champ, while I was getting my ass handed to me in spectacular fashion. Dotty sat somewhere in the middle, jaw tight. She hated losing more than anyone I knew.

A timer went off in the kitchen. "Turkey's done. Need a hand over here," David called out.

Colt scraped his chair back. "Yeah, I got you."

Dotty caught my eye and motioned her head toward the back hallway.

"Alright, I'm tapping out before this gets any more embarrassing," I said, gesturing at my pathetic score.

"It's okay, Uncle Trent. Sometimes we win, and sometimes we lose," Gracie said sagely.

Dorian chuckled, ruffling her hair. "Brutal honesty. I like it."

"Thanks, G." I smirked before slipping away.

I found Dotty already waiting by the back door. The hallway was tucked away from everything—just a bathroom, some family photos, and enough privacy to get into trouble.

"Hey—"

She cut me off, fisting my shirt and pulling me down to her. Her mouth found mine, all heat and need, like she'd been thinking about this for hours. Maybe she had. I buried my hand in her hair, and she made this little sound that went straight to my dick.

"Needy much?" I murmured against her lips. "Considering I had you bent over my kitchen counter this morning."

Someone cleared their throat.

Dotty jerked back so hard she smacked the wall, rattling every picture frame in the hallway.

Dorian leaned against the doorframe, arms crossed, trying not to laugh. "Don't mind me. Just need to piss."

"Oh my God." Dotty covered her face with both hands.

"Didn't see anything," Dorian said, walking past us. "Definitely didn't hear anything about kitchen counters."

Her phone buzzed. Then again. She looked down and went rigid.

"Shit. Noah's been calling." Three missed calls lit up her screen.

Dorian sobered instantly, lingering instead of heading into the bathroom.

Dotty answered as another call came in. "Noah? Are you okay?"

I couldn't make out Noah's voice, but whatever she was saying made Dotty's face go white.

"Okay. What do you need? What can I do?" she asked, then paused. "I'll be there as soon as I can. I'll book the next flight. We'll figure this out."

She hung up and sagged against the wall.

"What happened?" Dorian's voice was sharp, clipped.

"I guess the FBI showed up at the apartment looking for Noah's boyfriend. She's freaking out. She has no idea what he's mixed up in, and they're treating her like she might know something." Dotty ran both hands through her hair. "She's terrified. I have to go back to Seattle. Now."

Dorian pulled out his phone without hesitation. "There's a flight in two hours. It's an hour's drive to the airport. Go back to Trent's and pack."

"I have a meeting the following Monday anyway. I'll probably just stay through then."

Something cold settled in my chest. A week could turn into two. Two could turn into permanent.

I pulled my keys out of my pocket. "Go pack. I'll drive you to the airport."

"No."

That single word landed like a punch.

"Dotty, you can't drive when you're this rattled," Dorian said.

She shook her head. "I need to think. Process this. The drive will help."

What she meant was she needed space—from me, from us, from whatever this was turning into—and to face the end that distance would inevitably bring.

"You sure?" I asked, even though I knew the answer.

She nodded. "I'll be fine. I'll text you when I get there."

I needed time to convince her it would be okay, to show her that whatever came next, while terrifying, would be worth it.

I needed more time.

But pushing now would only make her run faster.

"Twenty minutes," Dorian said. "That's all you have if you want to make that flight."

"I'll be quick," she hesitated, then stepped toward me.

Dorian and I exchanged a glance. He nodded.

"Fine," I said. "But you text me when you get there, when you land—everything. We'll pick up the truck later."

"Fine." She echoed the word, softer this time. "I'll be back in ten to say bye."

I pulled her into me, and she gave me a look.

"He already saw us," I said.

I kissed her, probably longer than I should have, with her brother standing right there. She melted into it for a second before pulling back.

"Go," I said. "Take care of Noah. We'll figure out the rest later."

She nodded and disappeared down the hall.

Dorian waited until her footsteps faded. "So."

"I'm not asking for your permission to be with her."

"Chill, I already told you that you don't need it." He clapped my shoulder. "But I'll still kick your ass if you hurt her."

"I have a feeling it won't be me doing the hurting," I said quietly.

He frowned. "What's that supposed to mean?"

"I'm in love with her, man. Have been for years, and she's about to run."

"I knew you were close, but I didn't expect you to be in love—at least not yet."

"Let's be real. Was I ever not in love with her?"

Dorian studied me, then sighed. "Where's her head at?"

"She wants to keep this quiet. Says she needs time to figure things out." I leaned against the wall. "But now she's leaving early, and I've got a bad feeling that distance is going to make it real easy for her to convince herself this was a mistake."

"She's scared. Always has been. She thinks she's not worthy of love. She keeps almost everyone at arm's length, even me lately." He rubbed his forehead. "Losing Mom, growing up without a lot of friends, you leaving—it all shaped her. Made her shut people out."

"I know."

"I see how she looks at you. How she's always looked at you." He studied my face. "Don't let her run, Trent. If you love her, fight for her."

"I will."

This time, I meant it.

TWENTY-NINE

Dotty

THE 1 - TAYLOR SWIFT

Running on autopilot, I walked through Trent's front door, the weight of the situation pressing down on me. I quickly pulled out my phone and called Noah. She picked up on the first ring.

"Hey," she said.

"Hey, so Dorian booked me a flight that leaves in less than two hours. I should be there before nine. I'll take a taxi to the apartment," I said, my voice betraying a slight panic despite my best efforts to stay composed.

"No, I'll come pick you up," she replied, her tone equally strained.

"Okay, but what exactly happened?" I asked. The details she gave me earlier were rushed and frantic, a scattered mess that was hard to piece together.

"I don't even know… But it's bad. John is being investigated. He left for his work trip the other day, and I haven't heard from him since. This morning, the FBI showed up to question me."

"What did they ask you?" I asked, my mind racing with possibilities.

"If I knew where he's been. I don't even know what he's being investigated for. They wouldn't tell me anything."

"I'll talk to Colt. He might not have much sway, but it's worth a shot," I offered, hoping to provide some comfort.

"Thanks, Dotty. I hate that you're coming back under these circumstances, but I'm really glad you'll be here," she said, a hint of relief in her voice.

"Me too. I'll send you my flight details, but I need to finish packing. See you soon. Love you."

"Love you too." I hung up and immediately texted Colt, asking him to look into anything he could about Noah's boyfriend.

Frantically, I packed my things, debating whether to leave one of my suitcases behind—an unspoken excuse to come back. In the end, I couldn't bring myself to do it. I packed everything, erasing any trace that I had ever been in Trent's guest room.

With my meeting coming up and Noah needing me, I had no idea when I'd return. Maybe that was the point. Maybe I was running—not just from Seattle, but from Trent, from what we were becoming. The fear of letting him in fully had me gripping the edges of my suitcase so tightly my knuckles ached.

I shut the door, then drove back to the ranch house. Rain streaked down the windshield, blurring my view of the road, the dreary weather a perfect mirror of the storm brewing inside me.

The fragile bubble Trent and I had built over the past few days shattered the moment Noah called, forcing me to face everything head-on. We'd both been avoiding the inevitable, clinging to ignorance for as long as we could, but reality wasn't willing to wait any longer.

As the ranch house came into view, I spotted Dorian,

Trent, and Colt standing on the porch, talking despite the cold and rain. Dorian's face was tight as I pulled up.

"Why do you all look like that?" I asked, my pulse quickening.

Dorian ran a hand through his hair. "Colt." He nodded toward my brother.

Colt's voice was unusually gentle. "Have you heard of the Marketplace Murderer? The guy that's been all over the news lately."

A chill ran down my spine. "The guy who finds girls online, meets them to buy something, then kills them?"

"Yeah," Colt confirmed.

I frowned. "Okay… Did they finally catch him?"

Dorian shifted uncomfortably, glancing at Trent and Colt before answering. "Well… kind of."

The three of them exchanged looks, and unease curled in my stomach. "Can someone tell me what the hell is going on?" I demanded.

Trent exhaled slowly. "They think that's Noah's boyfriend."

His green eyes were dim under the gray sky as the blood drained from my face, and my skin turned clammy. "What? No way. I know the guy. He doesn't seem capable of something like that."

Colt's expression hardened. "He must have known the FBI was onto him. He disappeared a few days ago, and no one knows where he is."

My head spun. "There's no way. Does Noah know?"

"No, *I'm* not even supposed to know this," Colt admitted, pushing his long, dark hair from his face.

I pressed my fingers to my temples. "What the actual hell is going on lately?"

Trent pulled me into a hug, his body pouring life back

into me when I felt so drained. Colt shot Dorian a glance, raising his eyebrows. Dorian shook his head in response.

"Don't let Noah go anywhere alone," Dorian said.

Trent checked his watch and let out a breath. "You need to get to the airport, or you'll miss your flight."

"Let me say bye to Dad, Gracie, and Sawyer first."

Inside, they were sitting at the dining table, mid-conversation.

"I have to head out," I said, walking over. "But I wanted to say goodbye."

Dad stood and pulled me into a hug, pressing a kiss to the top of my head. "There's a container of food on the counter. Take it and eat on the way. I love you, Dotty. Please be careful."

"I always am, Dad. Love you."

A small body latched onto my leg. "But Aunt Dotty..." Gracie's bottom lip wobbled. "I'm not ready for you to go bye-bye."

I bent down, meeting her at eye level. "Me either, Gracie girl, but I promise I'll see you soon." I squeezed her tightly, swallowing the lump in my throat.

Sawyer approached as I stood, Gracie still clinging to me. "Love you, sis. Be safe."

"Love you too," I murmured, my voice thick with emotion.

Dorian opened the front door. "Dotty, you need to go."

With one last glance, I stepped onto the porch.

Colt pulled me into a hug. "Love you." His voice was softer than usual, his walls momentarily down.

"Love you too. I'll see you soon." My words wavered.

Dorian hugged me next. "Please let me know how it goes... and how Noah is."

Trent shot Dorian a quick look, and something passed

between them—an unspoken understanding, but I caught it. *I won't ask about him, you if you don't ask about me.*

I nodded. "I'll be back this time."

Trent's hand found the small of my back, fingers splayed wide, guiding me to the truck with a touch that felt like both protection and possession. He reached for the door handle, pulled it open with a sharp metallic groan, but his body remained close to mine, blocking my path.

When he turned me toward him, his movements were slow.

His eyes found mine in the fading light, and the intensity there stole my breath. Ten years of silence lived in that gaze. I could see him wrestling with words that had been buried too long, his jaw working like he was chewing on confessions.

"I—" The words cracked in his throat.

"Don't." My whisper was barely audible, because if he said it now, if he finally gave voice to what had been burning between us all this time, I'd shatter. Or worse—I'd never be able to walk away.

His thumb brushed across my cheek, and I hadn't even realized I was crying. The touch was feather-light, reverent, like I might disappear if he pressed too hard.

Neither of us wanted this to be goodbye. But goodbye was written in the space between us, in the way he held me like something slipping through his fingers.

So I kissed him.

I crashed against him like a wave breaking on shore, desperate and inevitable. I kissed him like I was drowning and he was air, like I'd been holding my breath for ten years and this was my first chance to breathe. I kissed him like we were nineteen again, when the future felt infinite and love felt like enough to conquer everything.

I kissed him with a decade of suppressed longing, with the ache of every glance we'd stolen and every touch we'd denied ourselves. With the terror that this might be all we'd ever have—this stolen moment in a parking lot, surrounded by the ghosts of who we used to be.

My hands found his chest, felt his heart hammering against my palms. His arms circled me, pulling me against him like he could press me into his bones, make me part of him forever.

I kissed him like I loved him.

Because I did. Because I'd never stopped. Because even if tomorrow we'd pretend this never happened, even if we'd spend another decade dancing around each other—right now, in this one moment, we were finally telling the truth.

He pulled back, resting his forehead on mine. "Text me when you get there and keep me updated on what's going on," he said, trying to mask the cracks in his voice.

"I will," I replied, reaching up on my toes to give him one last kiss. I hopped in the truck, the engine roaring to life. I knew if I didn't leave at that exact moment, I might never want to.

THIRTY

Dotty

THE NIGHT WE MET - LORD HURON

THE DRIVE TO THE AIRPORT WAS EXACTLY WHAT I NEEDED—quiet.

After that night at the bar with Trent, I needed a moment to bring myself back to reality—back to Seattle.

Silence settled around me like a soft exhale, steadying the storm in my head and pulling my attention toward Noah. That's what mattered. Not the chaos twisting inside.

As I drove, I occasionally glanced in my rearview mirror, noticing a dark SUV that seemed to be keeping pace with me. I dismissed the feeling, chalking it up to my overactive imagination. It was likely just someone else from Woodstone or a neighboring town heading to the airport, given that there was only one road out.

Just a coincidence.

The Shadow Ridge airport came into view—the hum of travelers, the flash of planes taxiing. I found a spot in long-term parking, shut off the engine, and pulled out my phone, sending a quick text to everyone letting them know I made it.

As I went to step out of the truck, I noticed the dark

SUV from earlier pulling into the spot next to mine. Its heavily tinted windows obscured any view of who was inside. I hesitated, but dismissed it as paranoia.

I grabbed my bag from the backseat and slung it over my shoulder, locking the truck behind me. As I started walking toward the bed of the truck to grab my suitcases, I felt a slight prickling at the back of my neck, an uneasy feeling that I tried to ignore.

My focus was on getting through security and catching my flight.

Suddenly, the SUV's door slammed shut, and footsteps hurried toward me from behind. Before I could react, a strong hand seized my arm, yanking me back. I tried to scream, but a rough hand covered my mouth, stifling my cries.

My breath caught in my throat as my hands clawed at his grip. I twisted my body and lashed out with my foot, striking at nothing but air. I twisted again, muscles burning, but his hold didn't loosen. Cold fingers clenched harder, dragging me step by step toward the waiting car.

My phone slipped from my grip and hit the pavement with a sharp crack.

Then, the backseat swallowed me whole, the door slamming shut and plunging me into darkness. My heart hammered loud enough to drown out everything else.

I needed to think. To find a way out.

A voice broke through the silence—cold, sharp.

"And here I was thinking I wouldn't see you today."

I froze. The voice was familiar, but it felt like a nightmare just out of reach.

I looked up and caught the barrel of a gun aimed at my head. Behind a black ski mask, only cold eyes stared back.

"What... what do you want?" I asked, my voice steady though inside I was trembling, just waiting to break.

"I want you, Dotty. I need you. It's time we were together."

That voice crawled under my skin.

He had found me.

"You haven't been alone in months, and now you think you can run from Woodstone? Sorry, but I can't let you disappear again. Not for ten more years."

My mind scrambled to place him. The fear was sharper now, the space shrinking around me.

I frantically tugged at the handle, my heart pounding in my chest as I realized my escape route was sealed off.

"Who are you?" I whispered, buying time, hunting for a way out.

He laughed—a low, cruel sound that filled the car.

"Oh, Dotty. Don't pretend you forgot me. I've been watching. Waiting for the right moment."

My heart pounded louder in my ears as my hands trembled. Before I could respond, a sharp blow struck my temple. Pain exploded, and everything faded into darkness.

THIRTY-ONE

Trent

HOLD ON - CHORD OVERSTREET

DORIAN, COLT, SAWYER, AND I SAT AROUND THE TABLE. DAVID had already called it a night, and Gracie was curled up asleep on the couch. Dorian was my closest friend, and Colt and Sawyer felt like the older brothers I never asked for but somehow needed. Still, even with them here, something felt off.

My chest felt tight, like it wouldn't stretch all the way. My mind kept circling back to Dotty.

Her leaving felt all too familiar, except this time, she was the one who was leaving, not me.

A cold weight settled in my gut, twisting tighter with every second. Then Dorian's phone rang, breaking the silence.

His brow creased. "Hey, Noah. What's up?"

He stood, listening. Then, he put it on speaker so we could all hear.

"What do you mean she's not there?" His voice was tense

Noah's voice came through, frantic. "She texted me her flight details. It landed over an hour ago. I was waiting for her, but she hasn't shown up. Her calls go straight to voice-mail. I don't know what to do, Dorian. I'm ready to get in my car and drive to Woodstone. Am I overreacting?"

An icy fear gripped my chest, tightening with each passing second. I stood and started pacing the room, my mind racing through worst-case scenarios.

What happened? Was she okay? Did her phone die? Did she get on the flight? Did *he* take her?

Colt was already on his phone, calling someone.

"Looks like we're heading to the airport," Sawyer said, slipping upstairs to grab his stuff.

Colt pulled the phone from his ear and said, "Calling my guy in Seattle now," before disappearing into the other room.

Dorian sighed, voice low but steady. "I don't think you're overreacting," he said into the phone. "But stay where you are. Let's figure this out first. Call me if anything feels off. Go home, don't open the door for anyone except Dotty. I'll check with the airline, find out if she boarded. I'll let you know as soon as I hear."

"Okay, thank you." Her voice cracked.

"It will be okay," he said before ending the call.

I swallowed hard. "Let's go. Now."

Sawyer came down with a duffel bag. "No time to waste. I talked to Dad—he's watching Gracie."

Dorian crouched to scoop Gracie off the couch. "Let me get her to bed first."

My hands shook, vision blurry. The only thing I could focus on was the terrifying thought that someone had taken Dotty.

My Dotty.

The love of my life. Missing.

I couldn't think straight.

"I'm driving," Dorian said, voice hard as steel as he climbed back down the stairs.

I didn't hesitate. I just grabbed my shit and hopped in the car.

I couldn't lose her. Not again.

Not like this.

As we sped down the highway, my thoughts kept returning to her last words to me. I clung to them, hoping against hope that we'd find her safe. That we'd bring her home.

The car was filled with a tense silence, the kind that felt suffocating. Dorian's grip on the steering wheel was white-knuckled, his jaw clenched so tight I thought his teeth might crack. Colt kept checking his phone, waiting for an update from his contact. Sawyer sat stiffly in the back, his fists pressed against his knees, his eyes dark with something unspoken.

We were running out of time.

We had to find her.

And when we did—whoever took her wouldn't live to regret it.

Dorian confirmed that Dotty never boarded. We raced to the airport, cutting the hour-long drive in half. Colt stayed on the phone with the police the entire way.

Dawn was breaking, but it felt wrong—too bright for what was happening. Dotty had been missing for hours now. The longer we drove, the heavier the silence in the car became. I kept telling myself there had to be some reasonable explanation for why she never made it on the plane. Maybe she'd gotten sick, or there was a problem with her ticket, or she'd changed her mind about the trip. But even as I ran through the possibilities, I knew none of them made sense.

We pulled into the airport parking garage, and I was out before the car had fully stopped. My legs felt unsteady, but I needed to move.

"Slow down," Dorian called, catching up to me.

I spun around. "There's no fucking time to slow down! Dotty's been missing for hours. There's some psycho who's been stalking her, and you want me to slow down?"

My voice grew louder, echoing off the concrete walls. I knew I was losing it, knew Dorian didn't deserve to be on the receiving end of my panic, but I couldn't stop myself.

Dorian's expression softened. "You're right. I'm sorry. Let's find her."

Sawyer caught up to us. "Colt's coordinating with the police. They're pulling security footage."

Colt joined us, sliding his phone into his pocket. His hair was tied back, and there were dark circles under his eyes. "Her phone last pinged somewhere in this garage. We need to split up and check every level."

The next twenty minutes felt endless. The parking garage smelled like exhaust and concrete, and every footstep echoed too damn loud. We combed through rows of cars, calling Dotty's name even though we all knew she wouldn't answer. My throat started to hurt from all the yelling, but I couldn't stop.

"Over here!" Sawyer's voice carried across the level above us.

We all ran toward the sound. Sawyer was standing next to a familiar pickup truck—the one Dotty had borrowed from him.

"That's it," I said, but my relief was short-lived.

Something caught the light under the truck. I crouched down and felt my stomach drop. Dotty's phone was there with the screen cracked. When I stood up and looked in the truck bed, her suitcase was still there, too.

"Don't touch anything else," Colt warned, already pulling out his phone again. "I need someone at the airport now." He paused. "I know, but this is my sister, Lilah. If I hadn't taken this into my own hands, we wouldn't have even found this." His jaw clenched. "Fine. How long?"

"What was that about?" Sawyer asked.

He hung up and then turned to us. "Someone is coming, but I'm officially too close to the case to do anything."

The next hour was torture. We sat on a concrete barrier near Dotty's truck, watching airport security tape off the area while we waited for the police to arrive.

Colt made phone call after phone call, trying to get updates and coordinate with different departments. Dorian kept trying to get me to eat something from a vending machine, but the thought of food made me sick. Sawyer paced, checking his watch every few minutes.

I'd been through hard times before. I survived combat deployments where I didn't know if I'd make it home. I watched my dad slowly die of cancer when I was a teenager. The day they told me my best friend had been killed by an IED. But this felt different. Those other times, I'd known what I was fighting against. This was just waiting, helpless, while someone I loved was god knows where.

When the detectives finally showed up, I was ready to climb the walls.

The lead detective was a woman with red hair and sharp green eyes. "Shadow Ridge Police Department. I'm Detective Dodge," she said, shaking hands with each of us.

"This is Detective Carter. Please, call me Lilah," she added, a slight smile tugging at the corner of her lips. "Lord knows your brother refuses, so someone should."

She turned her gaze toward Colt, whose stoic face gave away nothing. "Detective Dodge."

She started asking Colt questions and then grabbed Dotty's phone, placing it in an evidence bag.

I completely zoned out, unsure of how Dorian, Colt, and Sawyer were holding it together while the fear and helplessness was eating me alive.

Lilah nodded toward the truck. "We've processed the scene and pulled some security footage. Why don't we head back to the station so you can take a look?"

The drive to the police station felt like it took forever, even though it was probably only fifteen minutes. Every traffic light, every slow-moving car ahead of us felt like the cruelest form of punishment. Every second that had delayed us was another moment Dotty was at risk.

By the time we arrived, we all rushed out of the car as if it were on fire. My heart pounded with dread.

The police station was exactly what you'd expect—fluorescent lights, beige walls, and the smell of bad coffee. Lilah led us to a small conference room with a table covered in manila folders and a tablet computer.

"This way," she said, pointing down a long hallway.

"Normally, we don't allow family in for an investigation, but today is your lucky day. I know Colt from… the police academy, and I unfortunately owe him a favor, but if anyone asks, this wasn't me," Lilah said, glaring at Colt. "Especially with Chief already on your ass to stay away from this investigation."

"Thank you, ma'am. We appreciate it," Sawyer said, his hand running back and forth through his hair.

"What do we know?" Colt asked, towering over Lilah as his eyes stayed locked on her.

She glared at him. "Before we look at the footage, I need to know more about the situation," she said, settling into a chair across from us. "Colt mentioned on the phone that Dotty has been dealing with a stalker."

I nodded. "For years. It started with flowers and notes, but the notes got more threatening over time, and now she's been getting unknown text messages too."

"Seattle PD has been involved, but they never found much evidence. I've been looking into it in Woodstone, but no dice," Colt added.

"Any suspects?"

"Nothing concrete."

Lilah made some notes, then turned the tablet toward us. "This is from the parking garage security camera. Fair warning—it's not easy to watch."

The footage was grainy and the angle wasn't great, but it was clear enough. At 6:17 p.m., Dotty's truck pulled into a parking space on the third level. For a couple minutes, nothing happened—she just sat in the truck, probably checking her phone or gathering her things. Then, at 6:18, a black SUV pulled into the space directly next to her.

"That's interesting," Colt said, leaning forward.

"What?" I asked.

"The SUV. Look at the plates, the tinted windows. That's either law enforcement or someone trying very hard to look like law enforcement."

Lilah nodded. "We are running the plates right now."

A few minutes later in the video, Dotty finally got out of the truck. She walked around to the back to get her suitcase, and that's when everything went wrong. The SUV's driver door opened, and someone in dark clothing got out.

The person moved quickly, coming up behind Dotty while she was focused on getting her luggage.

What happened next made me want to burn everything to the ground. A person dressed in all black, including a mask, stepped out behind Dotty and overpowered her.

Damn, my girl fought back, but she couldn't take on a grown man when caught off guard. The whole thing was over in less than thirty seconds. The person forced her into the SUV, and by 6:22, they were gone.

"Jesus," Sawyer breathed.

"We tried to trace it on different traffic cams, but lost him. It looks like it was heading north," Lilah said.

"Back toward Woodstone," Dorian said.

"Could be," Lilah said.

I couldn't speak. Seeing it happen, even on a grainy security video, made it real in a way I didn't want to even think about.

Detective Carter came into the room carrying a folder. "We got the registration information back on that SUV."

Lilah opened the folder and read for a moment, her expression growing serious. "The vehicle is registered to Officer Henry Reynolds, Woodstone Falls Police Department."

Colt snatched the papers. "There's no fucking way."

I couldn't think, breathe, or even exist, it seemed.

There was no possible way one of my best friends had taken Dotty. The man who had stalked her for years. I couldn't think beyond the loud, pounding pulse in my head. Each beat was a painful reminder of how much was at stake. I clenched my fists, nails digging into my palms, the physical pain a mere distraction.

Lilah picked up her phone and turned away. "I need everything you can get on Henry Reynolds of Woodstone

Falls. Now." She paused. "I don't care. Put a rush on it." She hung up.

Detective Carter was already on his phone. "I'm calling Woodstone Falls PD now."

The next few minutes were a blur of phone calls and questions.

She took a deep breath, facing us. "Tell me about Henry," she said, her voice all business.

Colt spoke first, meeting her gaze. "I work with him— seems like a stand-up guy. He's a good cop. Trent"—he looked to me—"You know him pretty well."

"Yeah, he's a good friend of mine." I could barely get the words out. "We were friends in school and reconnected after I moved back to Woodstone a couple of years ago. He went on a date with Dotty in October." My voice cracked, and Sawyer grabbed my shoulder.

"You didn't know, man. There's no way you could've known," Sawyer said, trying to comfort me.

I told them everything I could think of about Henry, but even as I was talking, pieces were clicking together in my head. Henry always seemed to know a lot about what was going on in town. He'd ask about Dotty sometimes when we'd grab a beer, casual questions that I'd thought were just friendly interest.

I paced back and forth. I couldn't think through the blood rushing in my ears.

"How well do you know his property?" Lilah asked.

"I've been out there a few times. It's pretty isolated— about ten acres, old farmhouse, couple of old buildings on the property."

An officer entered and set a file down. "This is every- thing I could find on Henry Reynolds. We're still digging, but I'd say this is your guy. I called the flower shops he frequented. I sent over a picture, and the owner said it looked like him. Said he always paid in cash and used a fake name. She never questioned it because he tipped well."

Lilah grabbed her phone. "Hi, I need a warrant. I'm sending over the info now."

"We have to find her. Now," I demanded.

"We're working on it," Detective Carter said, hanging up his phone. "But it's going to take some time."

"How much time until the warrant comes back?" I asked.

"Few hours, maybe more."

"We don't have hours. Every minute we sit here is another minute she's with him."

Lilah glanced at me. "I understand your frustration, but we have to do this right. If we screw this up, anything we find gets thrown out in court. Is that what you want?"

"I want her alive! That's what I fucking want."

"Trent," Colt scolded me. "You will not talk to her like that."

I sat back down, but I wasn't happy about it. None of us were. We were going to have to wait while Dotty was out there somewhere, probably terrified, with someone she'd trusted enough to go on a date with.

The waiting was going to kill me.

I couldn't sit still. I'd pace to the window, then back to my chair, then to the door. My nerves were wound so tight I felt like I might snap.

The clock on the wall ticked loudly in the silence, reminding me how much time was slipping away. Funny how I'd never noticed that sound before, but now it was driving me insane.

Dorian, Colt, and Sawyer sat quietly, handling this better than I was. The weight on my chest kept getting heavier. We'd done everything right, followed protocol, but the waiting was killing me. Not knowing if she was okay. If she was hurt or scared or cold or hungry.

I looked out the window. The sun was moving further up in the sky while the world went about its business, completely unaware of the hell happening inside my head.

The phone finally rang, cutting through the quiet. Lilah answered, listening carefully before nodding.

"We got the warrant," she said.

Twenty minutes later, we pulled up to Henry's ranch as the sun started to set, throwing long shadows across the property. The old farmhouse sat at the end of a gravel drive.

Lilah walked up to the front door and knocked. Henry opened it slowly, confusion written across his face.

"Officer Reynolds, we have a warrant to search your property."

THIRTY-TWO

Dotty

ANGRY - PARAVI

My eyes fluttered open. Pain exploded through my skull —a vicious, pounding rhythm that made even my teeth ache. Every heartbeat sent fresh waves of agony cascading behind my eyes.

The world swam into focus. I took in my unfamiliar surroundings—an old abandoned barn filled with the silhouettes of broken-down trucks, some covered in tarps.

A rope bit deep into my wrists, the sting flaring as my hands were tied to a wooden beam behind my back. A sharp groan escaped me. Movement stirred just beyond my sight, and my body tensed, bracing for whatever was coming.

"Why, hello there," the voice sneered from the shadows. "Nice of you to finally wake up."

Where did I know that voice from?

The man walked up behind me, still out of sight, and rolled a bottle of water next to me.

"Promise, it's not poison," he said.

He circled the post, finally coming into view. My jaw dropped, and I couldn't believe my eyes.

"Chris Reynolds?" Disbelief hollowed out my chest, leaving me gasping.

"Who else were you expecting?" That smile—I'd seen it a thousand times growing up, friendly and warm. Now it twisted his features into something monstrous.

"What... I don't understand?" I stammered, my voice barely above a whisper.

This was Chris. Chris, who was always friendly. Chris, who'd driven me home when my bike chain broke when I was twelve. Chris who—

"What don't you understand, Dotty?" His voice dripped with sarcasm and disgust, making my stomach churn.

"How?"

"You come back for the first time in a decade and think I'm not going to keep an eye on you? I put a tracker on your truck on one of the first nights you were back in Woodstone. You probably don't even remember, considering how much you drank."

He began pacing, hands clasped behind his back.

"You should know, I don't like my woman drunk." He sighed, a look of feigned disappointment crossing his face.

His woman. Ice flooded my veins.

"What the hell are you talking about?" The words exploded from me, anger overriding fear. "Why did you do this?"

"Well, the plan wasn't to take you back here *tonight*," he scoffed. "When I saw you leaving in the middle of Thanksgiving, I knew something was off. Then I watched you speed down the road past my ranch, and it confirmed my suspicions." He laughed, a cold, hollow sound. "I followed you to the airport and could only assume you were going back to Seattle, back to your safe little life. I couldn't allow that, Dotty. Not when I finally have you."

"I've never been yours!" The shout tore from my throat, raw and desperate.

"Oh, but you will be." His eyes narrowed to slits, pupils dilated with sick excitement. "Settle down now, or I'll have to gag you. We're on the edge of my property, but sound carries. My brother might hear."

He slowly walked back and forth in the barn, weaving through the abandoned cars, then turned to glance at me. His eyes were cold and calculating.

A sob escaped from my lips before I could stop it. "Please. Let me go," I pleaded.

Nausea crashed over me in violent waves. I doubled over as much as the ropes allowed and vomited, bile and acid burning my throat. Chris walked back over to me before crouching down. His fingers gripped my chin, forcing me to meet his gaze.

"I can't do that. You are mine. Don't you get it?" he asked. "You are the answer to everything. We are meant to be together."

I let my head hang, still feeling the dizziness of being knocked unconscious earlier. "I don't understand, Chris. You were my friend."

"Friend?" He barked a laugh. "No, that was Henry. Tell me—did you sleep with him on your little date? Did you spread your legs for my brother like some common whore?" He spat on the ground. "How do you think it made me feel when you finally come back to town and agree to go out with *my brother*?"

My vision blurred, consciousness threatening to slip away again. Chris stood and resumed pacing.

"You think you can waltz back here after all these years

and pretend nothing happened? That everything's fine?" His voice dropped to a whisper. "You left as a frightened teenager, Dotty, but you came back looking exactly like *her*."

I couldn't make sense of his words. My head felt so heavy that I could barely stay awake.

"Here's what's going to happen. Tonight, you rest. You recover from our little... misunderstanding. Tomorrow morning, we drive somewhere far from here—somewhere no one knows our faces—and we get married. I don't care where we settle afterward, as long as you're my wife."

My resolve hardened as I glared at him. "I will *never* marry you." I managed to collect enough saliva in my dehydrated mouth to spit at his feet as he stood before me.

"Oh, sweet Dotty. You have no idea what lengths I'll go to for our future." He studied his fingernails with theatrical boredom. "You can fight this all you want, but I always get what I want. If you won't come willingly... well, perhaps I'll pay your family a visit instead."

"Don't you dare touch them," I hissed.

"I obviously got to *you* easily enough. It wouldn't take much to destroy Sawyer's career. A few anonymous complaints about misconduct, some carefully placed rumors. And Colt and Dorian. Well, one phone call to the right people..."

Despite everything, I almost laughed. His plan was so pathetically small, so desperately human.

"You underestimate my family. They will hunt you down like the coward you are." Despite the fear coursing through me, I refused to show any more weakness in front of him.

"You still don't understand, do you?" His voice was low and menacing. "Everything I've done, everything I continue to do, it's all for you."

When I didn't respond, he kneeled down again. His presence was suffocating, his breath hot against my face. He forced my head up from where it hung.

"Pathetic. You are pathetic, just like your mother."

My mother?

My confusion must have been written all over my face.

"Your mother. She begged for her life in those final moments, too, you know."

My brain tried to compute what he was saying, but the ache in my head made it hard to put the pieces together.

"What… what do you mean, my mother?" I asked, my voice hoarse and unsteady.

"Come now, Dotty." His finger tapped against his temple in mock thought. "You're smarter than this. How exactly do you think I know about your mother's last moments?"

The truth hit me like a freight train, stealing my breath and shattering my world into a million razor-sharp pieces.

"You." The word was barely a whisper. "You killed her. You were the one who hit her car."

"Bingo." He stood and moved to one of the covered vehicles, gripping the tarp like a magician about to reveal his greatest trick. "Turns out there's a brain in that pretty head after all."

The tarp fell away, revealing a pickup truck, its front end crushed beyond recognition.

"I was eighteen," he said, voice light as if recounting a fishing trip. "House party, too much beer, thought I could make it home. Woke up in a ditch with your mother's car wrapped around mine." He shrugged. "She was still alive when I got out. Kept begging me to call for help."

My vision went white at the edges.

"But what was I supposed to do? I was drunk, underage. My whole future ahead of me. I wasn't about to throw it all away for some soccer mom." Another shrug, casual as commenting on the weather. "So I drove home. My dad caught me, beat me bloody, but he kept my secret. Been hiding the truck out here ever since."

The truck that killed my mother. Sitting here for twenty years like a trophy.

He killed my mother.

Bile rose in my throat again at his admission.

"My family is not going to stop until they find me." I tried to keep the fight alive and needed to say the words aloud to convince myself they were true.

Enough time had passed that they would know I never showed up in Seattle. They would be looking for me already.

I believed it. I had to.

Chris let out an evil chuckle. "You think they will find you now? Nobody has found this truck in twenty years, sweetheart. What makes you think they'll find you now?"

"Then why?" I screamed, the sound echoing off the barn walls. "Why come after me? Why now?"

His hand rose in warning, and I flinched despite myself. "Ah, ah, Dotty. Watch your tone." He began pacing again, lost in his own twisted narrative. "I've been fascinated by you since that night. The guilt—oh, it ate at me for years. I felt responsible for leaving you motherless. So I started watching you, keeping tabs. When you moved to Seattle..." He clicked his tongue. "Well, that complicated things. Notes were the only way to maintain our connection."

The letters. All those years of fear, of looking over my shoulder, of never feeling safe. All him.

"But then you came back." His voice turned reverent, worshipful. "After all those years, you came back looking exactly like her. Like your mother. It was a sign, don't you see? Fate giving me a chance at redemption."

Exactly like her. The pieces clicked into place with sickening clarity. He wasn't in love with me—he was in love with a ghost, a memory of the woman he'd murdered.

"The only problem was Trent," he continued, spitting the name like a curse. "Your little boyfriend complicated my plans. I thought I'd taken care of that years ago when I made sure he knew you were too good for him. But then you go and sleep with him the moment you're back in town."

Trent. I thought of our time together—how he made me feel safe, seen, and loved. How we'd left things between us. If anyone would fight to find me, it was him. I just hoped he already knew something was wrong.

"I watched your mother die, Dotty, and ever since that night, I was haunted by her memory. I watched you grow up. You are so strong, so resilient. I knew you were my key to redemption. I know marrying you, making you my wife, will be the key to solving all of it."

"You are obsessed with me because of what happened to my mother? Because I look like her?" I yelled, attempting to keep the tremble out of my voice.

"Obsessed, yes," he agreed. "But also in love. You see, Dotty, you are not just the woman I desire. You are the key to my salvation, the one who can make me whole again. You either leave here as my wife or not at all," he said, flashing his gun.

Tears welled in my eyes, threatening to spill over, but I refused to let them.

"You are sick, Chris. We will never be together. *Never.*" I scowled at him. He bent down again, grabbing my chin and lifting it to meet his gaze.

"That's where you're wrong, Dotty," he whispered, his breath hot against my ear. "But we have all the time in the world to work through your... resistance."

Darkness crept in at the edges of my vision, and then there was nothing.

THIRTY-THREE

Dotty

SLOW IT DOWN - BENSON BOONE

EVERYTHING HURT. THAT'S THE FIRST THING I NOTICED AS consciousness crept back in—this bone-deep ache that seemed to radiate from everywhere at once. My pulse hammered so loud I could barely think past it, and fuck, my wrists were on fire. The rope had rubbed them raw, each slight movement sending fresh jolts of pain shooting up my arms as the metallic taste of fear mingled with the blood in my mouth.

"Well, well. Sleeping beauty finally decides to join us." His voice was a chilling blend of mockery and menace. Bile threatened to rise again, but I swallowed it down.

He'd already stolen enough from me. I wasn't about to hand him my dignity too.

Ten years. Ten goddamn years of looking over my shoulder, jumping at every unexpected sound, living like a ghost. He'd ripped away any sense of safety I'd ever had. Worse than that—he'd taken my mom. The one person who was meant to always be there for me. He had stolen my peace, my sense of security, and every ounce of freedom I once had.

But I was still here. Still breathing. And that had to count for something.

His phone rang, shattering the tense silence. He looked at me and pointed, a sinister smile playing on his lips.

He glanced down at his gun tucked into his waistband. "Not a word, got it?" He turned slightly away. "Henry, hey. Yeah, just messing around in the barn. You know how it is." A pause. "Nah, nothing urgent. We'll catch up later."

After he hung up, he moved to what looked like a mini fridge in the corner, pulling out some sad-looking sandwich fixings.

He set a paper plate with a pathetic excuse for a sandwich in front of me, like this was some kind of picnic. My hands were still tied behind my back.

"I'll cut you loose if you behave yourself, just let me eat first."

That smug little smile on his face made me want to spit in his face. I narrowed my eyes at him.

"Watch that attitude." His voice went ice cold.

The slap came fast and hard, snapping my head to the side. Stars exploded behind my eyes, and I felt the warm trickle of blood from my nose. The edges of my vision went fuzzy.

I nodded quickly, biting down on my tongue hard enough to taste blood. I needed to stay awake.

"See? We understand each other." His voice went sickly sweet again. "This is how it's supposed to be. You and me. Everything I've done has been for us." He leaned closer. "You should be thanking me."

I wanted to laugh at the insanity of it, but I didn't have the strength. Instead, I focused on staying awake, staying present. I had people counting on me.

My brothers. Dad. Little Gracie with her gap-toothed grin.

Trent.

The blood from my nose was starting to drip onto my shirt now, and my vision kept going in and out of focus. Chris noticed me wavering and started tapping my cheek, harder with each tap.

"Stay with me, sweetheart. We're just getting started."

I was running on empty, but I held on. I had to.

Because the last thing I'd said to Trent couldn't be good-bye. I wanted to run back to him and tell him that I was scared, but I was willing to be scared with him.

I needed a chance to tell him I was done denying what was always between us and finally let us be happy, free from our past mistakes. I wanted to finally let myself be happy.

Because Trent made me brave.

THIRTY-FOUR

Trent

BRUISES - LEWIS CAPALDI

"WHAT THE HELL ARE YOU TALKING ABOUT?" HENRY demanded. He turned to me, eyes searching for answers, and in that moment, I could have killed him right there for everything he had done.

Lilah stepped forward, her presence commanding despite her small frame. She was fucking scary.

"Officer Reynolds, you need to tell us where Dotty is."

Henry's brow furrowed deeper, disbelief etched on his face. "Again, what the hell are you talking about? Dotty?" His voice wavered.

My patience snapped. Pushing past Lilah, I grabbed Henry's shirt and yanked him close until our faces nearly touched.

"Where. She. Is."

Henry recoiled. "I… I really don't know what you're talking about. I haven't seen her in weeks," he stammered.

Colt cut in, his voice razor-sharp. "Who else has access to your SUV?"

Henry hesitated. "Uh… my brother, I guess. He has a

spare key, but—" His words faltered as realization dawned. "It's here now. Parked outside."

And then it clicked.

It wasn't Henry.

It was *Chris*. The truth slammed into me, knocking the breath from my lungs. A sickening twist of rage and dread coiled in my gut.

Sawyer's voice snapped me back to the urgency of the moment. "It might be here now, but it wasn't last night when Dotty was fucking kidnapped." His friendly demeanor had vanished as he stepped directly behind me, looking down at Henry.

Dotty's face flashed behind my eyelids. Her laugh. The way she'd looked at me before everything went to hell.

I should have known.

"Dotty was taken?" Henry's voice broke on her name.

"Officer Reynolds, tell us where your brother is," Lilah's voice brooked no argument.

"He said he was working on an old truck in the barn."

A cold chill ran down my spine. "We need to find him. Now," I demanded.

We moved in formation across the yard. Once we arrived at the barn, Lilah cleared her throat and whispered,

"I'll go in alone for this. We don't know if he's armed or where his head's at." Her tone was resolute, leaving no room for argument.

"Like fucking hell you are," Colt said, stepping closer, his jaw tight. "You will do *no* such thing. I'm coming with you."

Lilah turned to face him fully, her eyes flashing with warning. "No, you won't. Chief will find out, and you'll lose your badge, *Detective James*."

Colt's nostrils flared, his fists clenching at his sides. "I don't give a damn about my badge if it means keeping you and my sister alive," he shot back.

Lilah held his gaze. "That's not your call to make."

His throat bobbed as he swallowed hard, but after a beat, he exhaled sharply and jerked his chin in a reluctant nod. "Fine," he muttered, his voice rough. "But if you don't call out the second something goes wrong, Lilah, I swear to God—"

"I will," she interrupted, softer this time. "Just trust me."

Colt growled but reluctantly nodded.

I took a step forward, determined to confront Chris, but Lilah's glare stopped me in my tracks.

"You're not going in either," she stated, pointing a warning finger at me.

"Try and fucking stop me."

Colt gave Lilah a pointed look and shrugged. "I'm not holding him back. That's my sister in there."

"Fine," she conceded reluctantly, her gaze narrowing with concern. "But you follow my lead."

The heavy doors of the barn groaned as Lilah shoved them open. The dim overhead light flickered, barely keeping the darkness at bay, casting long, twisting shadows that slithered over the dirt floor.

At the far end, a figure hunched over the hood of a rusted truck. Chris. His posture was eerily calm, methodical even, as if he had all the time in the world.

"Christopher Reynolds," Lilah called, her voice sharp, slicing through the stillness.

He straightened slowly, turning with a smirk that sent ice crawling down my spine. His eyes gleamed with something dark.

"So," he drawled, "You've finally come for her."

"Where's Dotty?" I demanded, my pulse hammering. My hands clenched at my sides, every muscle in my body coiled, ready to snap.

Chris cocked his head, his expression twisting into mockery. "I knew you were stupid, Trent, but are you blind too?"

He nodded toward the corner of the barn, and my stomach dropped.

Dotty.

She was slumped against a support beam, rope cutting into her wrists. Blood had dried beneath her nose, and a bruise bloomed purple across her cheek. Her chest rose and fell in shallow breaths. Rage ignited inside me, a violent inferno clawing at my restraint.

"Might as well wake her up for the show, don't you think?" Chris taunted.

I took a step forward, but he moved first, crossing the space with an eerie casualness before backhanding her across the face.

Her head snapped sideways. A soft moan escaped her lips as her eyes fluttered open, unfocused, searching. When they found mine, something inside me shattered.

"Trent," she whispered, her voice cracked and broken.

Chris chuckled, low and taunting. He reached for his gun, leveling it at her temple.

"Don't," I growled, my voice a threat laced with desperation.

Lilah already had her gun drawn, her aim unwavering. "Put the gun down," she commanded.

"We all know I can't do that," Chris replied, his gaze flicking between us.

Chris's grip on the gun didn't waver. "See, I thought she might be my salvation. Turns out—" he leaned closer to

Dotty, his breath stirring her hair. "If you can't save me, what good are you?"

Something inside me snapped.

I surged forward just as Chris's finger tightened on the trigger.

"This is for trying to take what is mine," Chris declared coldly, his aim shifting away from Dotty, past Lilah, and toward me.

In an instant, everything blurred into motion. The sound of gunfire echoed through the barn. Pain seared through me—sharp and burning.

The impact sent me staggering, my breath escaping in a strangled gasp. The world tilted, my vision tunneling.

As if from a great distance, I heard Dotty scream my name, her voice a lifeline in the chaos. Lilah caught me as I stumbled back.

We hit the ground, my mind fighting against the suffocating weight pressing down on me. My shirt grew wet, warm—blood pooling, spreading.

Chris now loomed over me, his smile widening like he was savoring the moment. "You should've stayed out of this," he sneered. "You should've known better."

His gun swung back toward Dotty.

"No," I gasped, forcing my body to move, but my limbs felt sluggish, heavy.

Behind him, Colt came into view, his expression carved from stone. His voice was quiet, but it cut through the heavy silence like a blade. "No, Chris. This is for trying to take someone who belongs to no one but herself."

Chris's finger curled around the trigger—

Another shot rang out.

Chris's body jerked violently. His face twisted in shock, then pain. He staggered, his gun clattering to the floor, his knees giving out beneath him. The barn went deathly silent, the echoes of gunfire fading into the void.

And then—

Dotty was there, her hands pressing against my chest, trembling. Her face swam in and out of focus, her panicked voice just a distant hum.

"Stay with me, Trent. Please, stay with me."

I tried to tell her I would. Tried to say her name.

But the darkness was already there dragging me down.

THIRTY-FIVE

Dotty

ANOTHER LOVE - TOM ODELL

THE WAITING ROOM SMELLED LIKE DISINFECTANT AND BURNT coffee. Fluorescent lights hummed overhead. I'd been staring at the same water stain on the ceiling tile for what felt like hours, doing anything to avoid looking at my hands. Even scrubbed clean, I could still see Trent's blood under my fingernails.

The cheap hospital chair creaked every time I shifted. My sweater had a loose thread, and I kept winding it around my finger until the tip went numb, then I unwound it, over and over.

Somewhere beyond those double doors, Trent was fighting for his life while I sat here unraveling yarn.

The barn floor. The spreading dark stain. The way his eyes had slipped closed.

"Dotty?"

Noah appeared beside me. She must have broken every speed limit between here and wherever she'd been when she got the call.

She sat beside me, squeezing my hand gently. "Any news?"

I shook my head, my throat burning with the effort to keep it together. "Not yet. They said it could be hours." My voice cracked. I let my head fall against her shoulder.

"The waiting's the worst part. He's strong, Dotty. He's gonna pull through."

God, I wanted to believe her. I *needed* to believe her.

But my mind kept replaying the moment Chris pulled the trigger.

I counted ceiling tiles, then started over. Watched other families cycle through their own private hells. A woman clutched rosary beads. A man paced the length of the room, phone pressed to his ear, explaining the same thing over and over to what sounded like every relative he'd ever had.

Then, finally—*finally*—his doctor walked in.

"Trent Akers' family?"

I was on my feet before he even spoke, my pulse hammering. Noah and my family were right behind me.

"How is he?" Dorian asked, his voice softer than I had ever heard. Noah came up behind him, giving his arm a small squeeze.

"Stable. The surgery went well, but we're not clear yet. Next day or so will tell us more."

I swallowed hard and sighed.

"Can we go in to see him?"

"Yes," the doctor said. "But only one at a time until he wakes up."

"You go, Dotty." Dorian's voice was firm, his gaze steady. "He needs you."

I nodded, unable to speak past the lump in my throat.

The walk down the hallway felt endless, each step echoing in my head. The white tile, the too-clean smell, the quiet beeping of machines behind closed doors—it all blurred together until I stood at the entrance to his room, my fingers curled tightly around the doorframe.

I forced myself to step inside.

Trent looked smaller somehow, dwarfed by the bed and all the machinery. Tubes snaked from his arms. The steady beep of monitors filled the silence where his voice should have been.

I pulled a chair closer and took his hand. Still warm. Still Trent, under all the medical bullshit.

"Keep fighting," I whispered, my voice breaking. A sob rose in my throat. "You can't give up now—not before my mom can prove us wrong."

I found myself matching my breathing to his, like I could will some of my strength into him.

After a while, the silence was too much. So I started talking.

"Remember when we were eight and you fell out of that tree? You were so mad that you couldn't climb for weeks." I traced circles on the back of his hand with my thumb. "Dad said you'd never sit still long enough to heal properly."

The words kept coming. Stories I'd forgotten I remembered. The time he'd taught me to drive stick shift in the Walmart parking lot. How he'd stayed up all night helping me finish my college applications. There was so much history.

Dawn crept across the linoleum floor in pale rectangles. Somewhere down the hall, a coffee machine whirred to life. The hospital was waking up, but this room stayed suspended in its own quiet little bubble.

That's when I felt it—the smallest movement. His fingers, tightening around mine.

My breath caught. "Trent?"

Another squeeze, deliberate this time. Weak but unmistakably there.

I laughed, or maybe sobbed. It was hard to tell the difference anymore. "There you are."

THIRTY-SIX

Trent

YOU'RE STILL THE ONE (ACOUSTIC) - BAILEY
RUSHLOW

THE DAMN BEEPING WOULDN'T SHUT UP. MY HEAD FELT LIKE someone had stuffed it with cotton balls, and everything hurt in that weird, distant way that meant serious drugs were involved.

"Come back to me."

Dotty. She sounded scared, really scared, and that got me moving faster than any amount of willpower.

I cracked my eyes open. Big mistake. The lights were harsh as hell, and everything was blurry and white. But there she was, holding my hand like her life depended on it.

"Sunshine," I mumbled. My throat felt like I'd been gargling gravel.

She burst into tears. "Oh thank God." She squeezed my hand harder.

"Hey, I'm okay." My voice sounded like shit, but at least it worked. "Takes more than some asshole with a gun to get rid of me."

She laughed through her tears, which was exactly what I was going for.

"Do you have any idea how scared I was?" she asked, but she was smiling now.

"Probably about as scared as I was when he took you."

Her face crumpled a little at that, and I immediately regretted bringing it up. Before I could apologize, she was reaching for something on the bedside table.

"The nurse said you'd be thirsty. Your throat's going to hurt for a while because of the breathing tube." She held up a cup with a straw. "Slow sips."

The water tasted like heaven, even though swallowing felt like swallowing razor blades. Worth it.

A doctor walked in—older woman, no-nonsense vibe, the kind who'd probably seen everything twice. "Mr. Akers. I'm Dr. Cunningham. I'm glad to see you're awake. How are you feeling?"

"Could be worse." I tried to sit up a little and immediately regretted it. "What's the damage?"

"You were shot in the chest. The bullet damaged your right lung and just nicked the edge of your heart, which caused your lung to collapse and some bleeding around your heart. We had to go in and patch you up, get that lung re-inflated."

"But I'm going to live?"

She nodded with a smile. "You're going to live. Might take a while to get back to a hundred percent, but you'll get there." She typed something on her tablet. "Your girlfriend here hasn't left your side, by the way. We practically had to force-feed her."

I looked at Dotty. She was blushing, probably at being called my girlfriend, but she didn't correct the doctor.

"Speaking of family," Dr. Cunningham continued, "there's a small army in the waiting room. I can let a few of them back, but let's keep it to three at a time so you don't get overwhelmed."

After she left, Dotty and I just looked at each other for a minute. There was so much to say, but also nothing that needed saying. She was here. I was alive.

"Is he really gone?" I asked quietly.

She nodded. "Chris is dead."

The relief hit me like a wave. "Good. That bastard got what he deserved."

"Trent…"

"What? He kidnapped you. He shot me. I'm not going to pretend to be sad about it."

She didn't argue with that. Smart woman.

"Come here," I said, patting the bed beside me.

"You're hurt. I can't."

"I'll be worse if you're not next to me in ten seconds."

She rolled her eyes but carefully climbed onto the bed, curling up against my good side. Having her close felt better than anything the doctors could give me.

"I was so fucking scared," she whispered into my shoulder.

"Language, sunshine," I teased, and she pinched my arm. "Ow. I'm wounded, remember?"

"You're an idiot is what you are. Running toward gunfire like some kind of damn hero."

"Worked, didn't it?"

She was quiet for a long moment. "Yeah," she said finally. "It worked."

I squeezed her hand. "I'm surprised you're not in a hospital bed too. Did you get checked out?"

"Yeah, I'm fine. Just a concussion." She gave me a pointed look. "Don't worry about me."

I let out a rough, humorless laugh. "I'll always worry

about you, Dotty. You were fucking kidnapped. I thought I lost you forever." My voice wavered.

Her fingers tightened around mine. "Hey," she murmured, tipping her head up to meet my gaze. "I'm right here."

She smiled, but I saw the sadness lingering beneath it.

And I swore I'd do everything in my power to never see that fear in her eyes again.

I kissed the top of her head, breathing in the faint scent of her shampoo, cut through by that strange sterile note every hospital seemed to have. Her hair was warm against my lips.

"You okay?"

"No." Her voice trembled, barely audible. She drew in a sharp breath, like she was trying to gather every scrap of courage left in her. "I'm scared, Trent."

"Dotty…" I said quietly, brushing my thumb over her hand. "We don't have to talk about this right now."

"We do. I need to say this." She let out a breath. "I'm scared, mindblowingly, insanely scared. But I refuse to pretend I'm not in love with you for another second."

The damn heart rate monitor gave me away by beeping a little faster, but before I could respond, she kept going.

Her chin wobbled as tears slid down her cheeks. "I don't know what this means—your life in Woodstone, mine in Seattle, but for the first time in my life, I don't care. I've spent years letting fear make my choices for me, keeping myself in a safe little box where nothing could hurt me. And then you—"

Her voice caught. She exhaled a shaky breath that seemed to rattle through her whole body.

"It's okay. Take your time."

She closed her eyes and exhaled. "Then you walked

your stupid way back into my life like you never left, and suddenly, I felt everything again. You wrecked me in the best and worst ways. You made me feel things I swore I'd buried, things I didn't think I'd ever be capable of feeling." A broken laugh slipped through her sobs. "You ruined my perfectly numb, comfortable life. I might never forgive you because you made me love you when I thought I couldn't love anyone. I love you so much it terrifies me."

Her eyes lifted to mine then—wet, fierce, and completely unguarded. "I'm so stupidly in love with you, Trent."

My heart slammed against my ribs.

"Well," I said, my voice rough, "that's good because I'm so stupidly in love with you, Dotty. There was always something about you—something I could never shake, even when we were just kids tearing up your dad's ranch, when love was simple and life didn't feel so damn complicated." I tightened my grip on her hand, grounding myself. "Your light, your fire... you pulled me in from the start. Even with all the years between us, even with everything that's happened, I never stopped loving you. I couldn't if I tried. For as long as I can remember, my heart has been yours, Dotty. It's always been you. It always will be."

Lifting her hand to my lips, I pressed a kiss to her knuckles, letting it linger. "I fucking love you, and I will never apologize for that."

Her face crumpled, and fresh tears spilled over. She let out a soft, shaky laugh, blinking up at me. "I love you too, cowboy."

I pulled her close, kissing her softly, unable to hide my smile, knowing I would hopefully be stealing her kisses for years to come.

I was almost convinced her kisses alone could heal me.

Each touch of her lips seemed to infuse me with warmth and strength, mending the fractures I thought would never heal. Her mouth was everything I needed and more. Her lips were soft whispers gently caressing my skin.

"Say it again," I whispered between kisses.

"I love you," she echoed, and despite the bullet hole in my chest, I felt like a million bucks.

"I need to go let everyone know. I know they are anxious to see you," she said.

I groaned. "But I don't want you to leave."

"I'll be right back. Don't be clingy." She winked before striding out of the room.

A few minutes later, there was a knock on the door, and Dotty entered with Henry.

"Hey," I greeted.

"Hey, Trent." Henry peered down at his feet. "This is a little awkward…" He cleared his throat. "But I wanted you to hear it from me. I had no idea about the stuff Chris was involved in." He glanced up, his eyes red. "If I had known, I would've stopped it. I'm so sorry, man. I never thought he could do something like this."

"Hey, it's not your fault. Chris was sick. You did every-thing you could. Please don't blame yourself."

He paused, taking a breath. "Thanks, man. That means a lot." He rubbed his brow. "I wanted to apologize. I know you probably want to see everyone else, so I'll leave you be. Let's grab a beer once you're feeling up to it."

"Definitely. I'd like that."

I didn't hold anything against Henry. We'd been friends a long time, and even if we weren't as close as I was with Dorian, he'd always shown up when I needed him. Having a shit brother didn't change that.

Dotty glanced at me. "The guys wanted Henry to speak

with you first. I'll wait in the waiting room and send them in. Then, I'll come back with my dad," she said.

"Okay, but I'm going to need one more kiss."

She shot me a playful look as she crossed to the bed, leaning down until her lips met mine. The kiss was soft—enough to stir something in me, but not nearly enough to satisfy.

"No, sir," she said with a grin. "You need to rest."

"Can't a guy make out with his girlfriend after a near-death experience?" I asked, tilting my head toward her.

"Girlfriend, huh?" Her eyes widened, but she didn't back away.

"Did I stutter?"

"No," she said, smirking, "but you know your voice does sound a little funny."

"I'd prefer wife," I said, my lips tugging into a half-smile, "but I don't care as long as you're mine."

"Let's start with girlfriend." She gave me one last smile, her gaze lingering just long enough to make my chest ache, before turning and walking out the door.

A moment later, Dorian, Sawyer, and Colt walked in.

"Hey, guys," I rasped, my throat already feeling the strain.

Dorian's expression broke into a warm smile. "Good to see you awake, brother."

Colt gave me a slow once-over and cleared his throat. "You look like shit."

I huffed a laugh, which sent a sharp ache through my ribs.

"At least you'll have a nice scar to show off to all the ladies," Sawyer said, grinning.

"There's only going to be one girl for me now," I said without thinking.

Dorian grinned, and Colt's eyes narrowed, and then he smirked. Sawyer, on the other hand, looked like he'd just been dropped into the middle of a conversation without instructions. His gaze bounced between us.

Finally, Dorian put him out of his misery. "Dotty."

Sawyer blinked. "Dotty? Our sister Dotty?"

"Yes, you dumbass," Colt said, shoving his shoulder.

Sawyer's eyebrows shot up. "Oh, shit. Okay. Actually… yeah. Makes perfect sense when you think about it."

"It does, doesn't it?" I said, the truth of it settling warm in my chest.

Sawyer grinned. "Well, guess getting shot brings everything out in the open."

"Sure does," I said, and for once, nobody felt the need to argue.

THIRTY-SEVEN

Dotty

REWRITE THE STARS - MICHAEL GEROW

"You were right, Mom," I murmured, a soft laugh escaping me.

The cold winter air wrapped around me as I knelt before my mother's grave.

"We're barely even official, but I already see you were right all along. Funny how life circles back, isn't it?" I traced the engraved letters of her name with trembling fingers.

Childhood memories flooded my mind, faint echoes of laughter and advice, of moments when my mother's quiet wisdom had guided me. She had always seen something between Trent and me that we hadn't understood—a connection that transcended friendship, a bond that apparently even time and distance couldn't sever.

I guess mothers really did know everything.

"We thought you were crazy then, but now... now, I wonder if you saw things more clearly than we ever did."

The graveyard seemed to hold its breath as I spoke, the stark beauty of winter adding to the solitude. Snowflakes began to drift lazily from the gray sky, adding a soft layer of white to the earth around me.

"I miss you. God, I miss you." The words caught in my throat. "I wish you were here to see this come to fruition, just as you said it would." Tears threatened to spill over, and I didn't blink them back, finally allowing my grief to overwhelm me.

"I may never understand why you were taken from us, and why I never got to know you beyond me being a ten-year-old little girl," I confessed, my tears falling to the cold ground. "I'll spend the rest of my life wishing I had the opportunity to get to know you more. But while I only knew you for a short period of your life, I know that you will know me at every stage of my own."

Lost in my thoughts—in the quiet of the cemetery—I didn't hear him approach until his presence was beside me. His hand found mine, warm and steady.

"She'd be so proud of you, Dotty," Trent's voice broke the silence.

I leaned my head on his shoulder, letting myself feel everything I had suppressed for two decades. I pulled back to look at him.

"She's proud of you too," I said softly. "She loved you as her own, Trent. I don't remember much from before she passed, but I know she loved you. Always."

Trent's smile was small, almost bittersweet, but it was enough. He pulled me in closer, wrapping me in the warmth of his embrace, and for the first time in a long time, I didn't feel so alone.

A Few Weeks Later...

"Congratulations, Dotty. You'll start your new position at the beginning of the new year. Use the next few weeks to wrap up any current projects, and we'll transition you to the new team that you'll be supervising."

"Thank you. For everything," I replied, my voice filled with gratitude.

"No need to thank me. You earned this. I'll miss having you on my team, but I know you'll do great things in your new role."

"Thank you. Take care."

As soon as I hung up the phone, I let out an excited squeal. Noah walked in from the other room, peaking her head into my bedroom.

"Uh, you good?"

"I got it! I got the promotion!" I exclaimed, barely able to contain my excitement. Noah rushed in, jumping up and down before pulling me into a hug.

"Oh my God! Congrats! I knew you could do it. You deserve this."

Tears of joy filled my eyes. "Thank you." I glanced around my room, now filled with packed boxes.

Had I started packing before I even got the promotion? Yes. Did I have a good gut feeling, and packing was my way of manifesting it into reality? Also, yes.

A few weeks after Trent was released from the hospital, my manager had let me know that the promotion I wanted was open. The best part? It was fully remote, with only quarterly meetings in Seattle required.

So, I was moving to Woodstone Falls. I was done letting life pass me by, content with the comfort of routine. Somewhere along the line, Woodstone had become my home again.

I was ready to be happy, to be near my dad, my brothers, my niece, and Trent.

"Knock, knock," Trent said, tapping on the doorframe. He looked at Noah's and my tear-streaked faces. "Oh shit. What happened?"

I laughed through my tears. "I got it."

"You got it?" he asked, pushing through the doorframe.

"I got it!" He barreled toward me, sweeping me off my feet, twirling me around.

"I knew you would, sunshine. I told you—they'd be stupid not to see how amazing you are."

Noah made a gagging sound. "Gross, get a room."

"Noah, you're literally in my room."

"That's true. I might just be bitter because you're leaving me," she admitted.

"You know, you could come with me," I pleaded.

It wasn't the first time I had asked, and I knew it wouldn't be the last.

After finding out her boyfriend was a serial killer, I wanted her close, but I understood why she didn't want to uproot her life. But with John still on the run, it all worried me.

"I've got a classroom full of kids depending on me, and I'm not bailing halfway through the year. And I'm definitely not skipping town just because my boyfriend ended up on the FBI's most-wanted list." She tried to make it a joke, but the crack in her voice told the truth.

Knowing she had let someone like John in had really messed with her head. I tried to be there for her in every way I could, but I knew she struggled with it all. Seeing her hurt made me want to fix everything, because if anyone deserved a happy ending, it was her.

"Noah," I scolded.

"I know, sorry. I deflect with humor." She gave a short laugh. "You do too, though…"

I shot her a look that made her grin fade. "If you ever need a safe space—or just a weekend away—I'm here."

Trent cleared his throat. "Dotty's right. Once we finish the cabin and move in, you can use my place anytime. No pressure, but the offer's there."

"Thanks, Trent. Turns out you're not so bad after all," she teased.

"Well, I made him grovel a little," I said, grinning as Trent kissed my cheek.

"Come on—help me carry out the last of my boxes and I'll buy dinner."

"Only if it's pizza."

"Deal."

With boxes in hand, I walked through my apartment door for the last time, feeling a sense of freedom. I was leaving behind a life I thought I wanted and stepping into something so much more.

A life with my family. With the hot cowboy I'd fallen for at nineteen, and again at twenty-nine. A life where I didn't have to choose between love and career, because somehow, I'd been lucky enough to keep both.

A life where all the puzzle pieces finally fell into place. I looked back at the door I had crossed countless times throughout the years.

"You ready?" Trent asked.

"Yeah," I said, meeting his charming smile and taking his outstretched hand.

"Let's go home."

THIRTY-EIGHT

Epilogue - Trent

FIVE YEARS LATER

I PACED BACK AND FORTH IN THE DRIVEWAY, EYES FIXED ON THE cabin. Dotty and I had made this place our home over the last five years, and every corner held a piece of us.

Just north of the cabin, I'd proposed to her four and a half years ago. I wasn't exactly known for patience, and I'd wanted to pop the question the minute I got out of the hospital. But Dotty asked me to wait six months. So I did. Hardest six months of my life, but worth every day.

The front porch we'd fixed up together—that's where Dotty told me she was pregnant. Our bedroom, the one with the paint color we'd debated for weeks, had seen countless late nights watching shows and talking until dawn.

The living room had hosted family dinners, game nights, and holidays. As Dotty's dad, David, got older, it became easier for us to take over Sunday hosting duties. We'd put so much work into this place, and made it perfect for everyone.

"Let's go, Dotty!" I called out as she appeared in the doorway.

"My water broke, Trent. I didn't die," she said, giving me that look I knew well.

"Exactly! Your water broke!" I waved toward the truck. "We need to get you to the clinic."

"I'm not giving birth in the driveway just because I took a minute to braid my hair. Relax. I'm the one in labor here." She made her way down the porch steps, and I rushed over to help.

"Already put towels on the seat and called the clinic. They're expecting us," I said, trying to keep the panic out of my voice. Dotty, meanwhile, looked completely calm.

Once she was settled in the truck, I pulled onto the gravel road, keeping it slow and steady. At least until the next contraction hit—then I couldn't help pressing the gas a little harder.

She breathed through the pain. I kissed her hand as she exhaled. I couldn't imagine what it felt like to have a baby trying to exit your body, but Dotty? She handled it with grace. After a minute, her body relaxed, and she flashed me a tired smile.

"This girl's already causing trouble, just like her father."

"What can I say? Strong genes." I kissed her hand again, grinning despite myself.

We pulled up to the clinic, and Mia was already waiting with a wheelchair.

"I can walk," Dotty said immediately, opening her door.

"You don't have to," Mia replied gently, as Dr. Patterson joined them.

"Thanks, Mia," Dotty said, accepting the help but staying on her feet.

I kept close as we walked in, my hand in hers. My nerves were all over the place, but Dotty's calmness steadied me somehow.

Watching her handle each contraction was incredible. She never complained, never lost her focus. There was quiet determination behind her eyes that made me proud as hell.

A few hours later, I was holding our daughter.

Dotty lay exhausted but glowing, and when she looked at our baby, something in my chest tightened. Hair mussed, no makeup, eyes tired from labor, but there was something about her in that moment that took my breath away.

I watched her gently stroke our daughter's tiny hand, still amazed we'd made it here together.

"You did amazing," I said quietly, emotion thick in my voice. "I'm so proud of you."

Dotty looked up at me with that soft smile, the same love in her eyes that had been growing between us all this time. Everything felt exactly right.

"He's right," Mia said from her computer. "Textbook delivery."

"Thank you," Dotty said softly, never taking her eyes off the baby. "Want to hold her?" she asked me.

"Absolutely." I pulled off my shirt, and Dotty raised an eyebrow. "Skin-to-skin contact. It's good for bonding."

Yeah, I'd bought and read six new dad books cover to cover while Dotty made fun of my *sudden interest in literature*.

She carefully transferred our daughter to my chest, and I settled the blanket around her small body to keep her warm. She was tiny, wrinkled, and perfect. Her little fist wrapped around my pinky like she was already planning to have me wrapped around her finger for the rest of her life.

"I'll give you some privacy," Mia said, stepping out. "Call if you need anything."

Sitting there with our daughter on my chest, Dotty beside me, my heart felt like it might explode. I'd never experienced anything this deep, this complete. Not sure I ever would again—unless Dotty decided she wanted more.

"We need to give her a name," Dotty whispered.

"I think I know the perfect one." I looked down at our daughter, already completely gone.

We'd spent weeks going through names, but seeing her now, I was certain.

"Darlene. Darlene Mae Akers."

Dotty's eyes filled with tears. "Yeah… I think you're right." She reached behind her neck, taking off her necklace and letting Darlene's little grasp take hold of it. "You're definitely too little for this right now." She wiped her tears and let out a breath. "But it was your grandmother's, and then it was mine, and someday, it will be yours."

She looked at me with a smile that nearly stopped my heart.

And damn, I was the luckiest guy alive to have these two beautiful girls in my life.

Looking back on everything Dotty and I had been through—from running around the James family ranch as kids to those ten years apart—it was hard not to see how it all led to this moment. As much as I wished I could have had that extra decade with Dotty, but somehow everything had worked out exactly as it should. Led to her becoming my wife, the mother of my child.

I caught her watching me, biting her lip with that playful look I knew meant trouble.

"You look good like this, cowboy. Shirtless with a newborn—I could get used to the view," she teased.

Yeah… I think I could get used to this, too.

Acknowledgments

First of all, I want to thank me for being me and doing all this hard work.

Okay, but really… This book was born from a love of reading and a dream, but I made that happen.

But who I truly need to thank here is my husband, Mr. Jerr (Jerr daddy? What do you want to be called?) This book would not have happened without you. You were my number one fan from day one, ready to shout from the rooftops, *my wife wrote a book!* before I was even ready to admit to the world that what I was doing was anything more than a hobby. You sacrificed so much for me to be completely delusional and follow this dream of mine. I am forever grateful for the husband and father you are for our family.

To my momma, who, unlike Dotty, I have had the privilege of knowing every single day of my life, thank you. Thank you for always doing what is needed, whether that is helping me flesh out my plot holes until eleven at night or meeting my babies exactly where they are at. You are the best mom and a kickass nana.

To my sisters, Mary and Kate, for being the first ones to read my words and meet these characters that lived only in my head for months. Thank you for believing in me and helping this book become what it truly is.

To Maddi at EJL Editing, girl, this book was a hot mess when it first arrived in your inbox, and you gave me the tools and information I needed to craft it into an actual story. Thank you for being my biggest cheerleader throughout this whole process.

To the team at Books and Moods that killed this cover design, thank you for taking my silly, crazy ideas and turning them into more than I could have ever imagined.

And lastly, but most importantly, *YOU*. My readers, thank you for being here. Whether you received an ARC, randomly found this book on KU, or even if your husband works with mine and bullied you into reading this, thank you for taking a chance on my words. This book has been fueled by Diet Coke and the constant reminders of how many of you wanted to read this story.

So many of you have been hyping me up, rallying behind me, and getting so excited for this book. I hope I delivered.

If not, there is always daddy Dorian…

Content Warnings

- Death of a Parent/Grandparent
- Grief and Loss
- Descriptive open-door sex scenes (chapters 26 & 27)
- Violence on Page
- Captivity/kidnapping
- Gun Violence
- Discussion of a fatal car accident
- Stalking
- Vulgar language